The Parables of Virginia Bean

Books by Kathryn Elizabeth Jones

A River of Stones

Parable Series

> Conquering Your Goliaths: A Parable of the Five Stones
>
> Conquering Your Goliaths: Guidebook
>
> The Feast: A Parable of the Ring
>
> The Gift: A Parable of the Key
>
> The Parables of Virginia Bean

Heaven 24/7

> Living in the Light
>
> with M. Celeste Martin

Marketing Your Book on a Budget

Susan Cramer Mysteries

> Scrambled
>
> Sunny Side-Up
>
> Hard Boiled
>
> Over Easy

Brianne James Mysteries

> Tie Died
>
> Buckled Inn

The Space Adventures of Aaden Prescott

> Light*Shade*
>
> Light*Descending* – Spring 2019
>
> Light*Source* – Fall 2020

The Parables of Virginia Bean

1 – Conquering Your Goliaths:
   A Parable of the Five Stones
2 – The Feast:
   A Parable of the Ring
3 – The Gift:
   A Parable of the Key

KATHRYN ELIZABETH JONES

Idea Creations Press
www.ideacreationspress.com

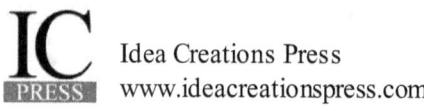 Idea Creations Press
www.ideacreationspress.com

978-1-948804-05-9

Publisher's Catalog-In-Publishing Data

Jones, Kathryn Elizabeth, author
The Parables of Virginia Bean / Kathryn Elizabeth Jones
First trade paperback original edition. | Salt Lake City; Idea Creations Press, 2018.
ISBN 978-1-948804-05-9 | LCCN 2018909405
Inspirational Fiction | Christian-Fiction. | BISAC: FICTION / Christian / Classic & Allegory / Parables

Printed in the U. S. A

Table of Contents

CONQUERING YOUR GOLIATHS

A Parable of the Five Stones

To my readers:

May this book help you in conquering your own Goliaths.

And like David, may you find God.

Foreword

Kathryn Jones is a writer. She is a researcher. She is brilliant. Most of all, she is a light to all those around her and with her creation of "Conquering Your Goliaths" she's given us yet another gift. This gentle story reminds us that we are all in Divine company…especially when we least expect it!

You will also never pick up a stone again without a moment of recognition. The simplest things in our lives are the most profound and this book is a "must-have" on so many levels. It's a simple book. An easy to understand book. A thought-provoking book. It's a book that lifts your spirit and your awareness.

When I first met Kathryn, there was no doubt of her conviction to write. She is a spectacular woman whose talent for helping others through written word is obvious page after page.

Are you listening? That's the beginning of your journey with Kathryn and from there; "Conquering Your

Goliaths" will make you stronger in heart, in the faith that You Are Loved and in your devotion to Spiritual growth.

You will definitely read this book more than once.
Angel Shannon

Life Enrichment Advisor – Tranquility Circle, Inc.

Angel has been in Media, Communications and Promotions for 30+ years. Her primary goals have shifted from marketing to public speaking. Teaching others how to relax in a stressful world is her goal which is why she founded her own company, Tranquility Circle, Inc. She offers solo sessions, workshops and seminars…and is manifesting a women's day retreat.

Contact Angel at:

http://www.tranquilitycircle.com

Prologue

It wasn't fair. In all her travels, and there had been many within the city of Idaho Falls, Idaho, Ms. Virginia Bean had never stopped for much more than a "fair share" moment. It wasn't that silence wasn't a good thing; it's just that silence of any kind wasn't for Ms. Virginia Bean and she could prove it.

Today, as in every day, she'd worked longer than necessary putting on her makeup, and more time than expected cleaning her house and organizing her day so that others would see how good she looked even when she was away. She'd prayed, yes, but it was always one of those quick dose methods, those that kept her in the black with the Lord and out of the red with her own guilty conscience.

She left the house at half past eight, journeyed to her job at the Regal Doughnut Factory and placed her feet smack dab on the spot where she'd stood for ten not so glorious years. She'd tried to make them glorious, of course, and her hands had proved faster and quicker than most; still, after a long day of standing and an even longer evening of cleaning up, she was ready for a vacation.

At least that's what she told herself.

Unfortunately, on this blistery summer day in early August, Ms. Virginia Bean got just what she needed but didn't want.

A firing, of sorts, happened that day; the factory was closing down, or, at least, losing some ground and opening up in New York, far across the country from Ms. Virginia Bean.

The job opportunity, if you could call it that, was no longer a stone's throw away, and Ms. Virginia Bean was determined to find another career to her liking and so she'd gone walking in the hot air to find it. She'd left her two-bedroom home without a formal jacket and had put up her blond hair in a loose bun, an elegant style that made good use of her fragile face. She could already feel the make-up's foundation warming against her fair skin as she walked, fine lines of sweat finding its way from her neck and onto her beautifully constructed green chemise blouse, but she continued forward. It wasn't like her to stop.

At the light she turned right and tried to ignore the bleating of someone's horn. Either it was a male well-wisher or she'd stepped in front of someone's perfectly manicured car. Ms. Virginia Bean liked to think of cars being well manicured, or sloppy, as the case may be, and she was determined that if she could not afford a car of the first variety, she wouldn't drive her car at all. The rest, shall we say, is history.

Today, Ms. Virginia Bean had an interview with a fellow by the name of Frank Spurt; a funny name for a gentleman purporting excellence in his purified drinking water company. Western Falls was the name, after the bit more classic state name and city of "Idaho Falls," and bottled water was Mr. Spurt's game. Ms. Virginia Bean liked water;

she drank it all the time, even when she didn't need to. But drinking water was good for Ms. Virginia's skin and she knew that she'd look that much younger down the road if she continued to drink it by the bucketful's. And so, she did.

Though she'd had no experience in working at a bottled water company, Ms. Virginia Bean knew about standing on her feet for long hours; and about relieving the customer of his/her unwanted burden that would only cause more problems to the manufacturer if she happened to miss the defect. Ms. Virginia Bean had all the knowledge she frankly needed, or so she reasoned. She was positive she'd get the job and that her past experience would glean the trust the boss would need to hire her. With an added boost of courage, Ms. Virginia Bean walked into the glowing building and looked around.

Thank heavens for air conditioning! The place was spotless, sort of like her home, only better. There were glass tables without a mark on them, and shiny floors without a scratch, and alongside the wall, real plants that needed to be watered. What a joy!

She walked up to the front desk, and seeing no one there, rang the silver bell.

No one came.

She rang again. The noise sounded more like a trumpet, but Ms. Virginia Bean tried not to let the strong sound startle her.

Finally, an old gentleman in a flannel shirt and long brown corduroys that reached beyond his shoes opened a door she'd never noticed before. He smiled up at her. "An appointment?" he asked. His voice was like water tumbling from a water fall. It was strange, but Ms. Virginia Bean tried not to stare. Instead she said, "Well, why yes. I have an appointment with Mr. uh, Spurt."

"Yes, yes." The old gent looked down at something on the counter, something she couldn't see because of the glare. "Follow me."

The same door opened. It had no knob, not even a crease was visible to let a person know that the door existed. "Right this way," he continued as Ms. Virginia Bean followed his heavy steps. They were suddenly in a great room without tables or chairs or anything that Ms. Bean would have previously considered an office. The room consisted of floors that glittered and walls that shone surrounded by a myriad of windows that revealed a menagerie of trees. Nothing else.

After some time, another door opened. In it sat a gentleman. This one wore a fisherman's cap and displayed a smile like someone who'd just discovered a secret but wasn't yet ready to let it out.

"Ms. Virginia Bean?" he asked.

She sat, for suddenly she could see a white chair in front of his pure white desk.

"Yes."

"We have been waiting a long time for you," the man said. His voice was different than the first but similar in the way that water was. Instead of a water fall, his voice was more like the sound of water just before it reached the shore. Again, Ms. Virginia Bean tried not to stare. "You're probably wondering why I've invited you here," he said.

Virginia thought she might have blushed, but she couldn't be sure. Her feet were moving on the shiny floor, they were hard to keep still and she forced her hands to sit quietly on her lap. For some reason, this man demanded attention, and not just because he was the boss.

There was a moment or more of silence.

"I'm here for my interview," she said.

"Yes, the interview." He smiled, and she could see love in that smile, if such a thing as love in a smile is really possible. The smile lit up his blue eyes and drifted into her heart. The feeling made her happy and sad at the same time. It was strange and wonderful.

"So, you've come for faith," he said.

Ms. Virginia Bean was momentarily confused. "Faith?" she asked. "I've come for an interview."

"As I said, faith," the old man answered. From some unknown place he handed her a rock. It was white and smooth and she could see tiny silver veins like a hand within it.

"I thought you bottled water here," she said.

"Well, yes," the man answered. "Lots and lots of water but take the stone, it's your first after all, and you'll need it to find that job."

Ms. Virginia Bean didn't know what to say. She'd come to this strange place for an interview and all she'd managed to get was a rock? But she held out her hand and took the rock anyway. It was warm and light in her hand and she felt suddenly younger than her 35 years.

"Now, this stone is special," said Mr. Spurt. "If you listen closely, the stone you hold will tell you what you need to know."

"That's crazy," she said without thinking.

The man smiled, lighting up the room. "Not crazy, special. If you listen, you will not only hear what you need to do, you will begin to have the faith to do it. Listening is the first stone of five from David's bag."

"The first…what?"

She sounded like a broken record, one of those vinyl disks that nobody used anymore to play music. Everything was so high-tech, so other-worldly, so...

"Your mind is racing," said the man. "When you slow it down, you can hear. See this room? Feel how quiet it is?"

Ms. Virginia Bean tried to slow down her feet. She tried to grip the arms of the white chair and suddenly realized there weren't any arms.

The old man laughed. "You don't need to be afraid, Virginia, all you need is a listening ear; a moment that you can hear the voice."

"From the stone?"

The man nodded and stood. Ms. Virginia Bean followed; it was the right thing to do. She held the warm rock in her right hand, and as she did, something happened.

"You are also beloved," a voice said. It came from the stone.

The voice startled her, but only for a moment. Something like light ran up her right arm and entered her heart. When the feeling ended, she was still holding the stone and the man at the desk was gone.

Listening

Ms. Virginia Bean carried the white stone with the silver flecks all the way out the inner doors, past the front desk and beyond the glass doors with the golden handles attached, all the way back to her two-bedroom house. It took her approximately half an hour. She didn't notice the hot air, or the way her hair stuck to her face, or even, the wet mess underneath her armpits. She was only thinking of the stone.

What had just happened?

She sat on her perfectly manicured black leather couch and sighed, but Ms. Virginia Bean didn't grab for the glass of water on the end table; at least not right away. She prayed, and it wasn't one of those prayers she'd offered just that morning. This one took some thought.

"Please, God," she said. "I think I'm going crazy. I have this rock that this old man gave me and I never had my interview and I'm not even sure what happened and…"

The words stopped in her throat as she remembered the old man's council: "If you listen closely, the stone you hold will tell you what you need to know."

Ms. Virginia Bean tried to quiet her thoughts by thinking of the white room with nothing in it but the old man and herself. She thought of the silence and how surprised she'd been when she heard the words, "You are also beloved."

She thought of the stone now as she prayed: "Please help me, God."

And then, Ms. Virginia Bean, listened.

It took some time but Virginia was able to tune out the cars, the noise of children playing outside, even the sound of the water faucet dripping in her only bathroom. She felt peace as she'd never felt it before. After some time, Virginia wasn't sure how long, she decided to walk back to the bottled water company and thank Mr. Spurt, but when she arrived in her old car, the building wasn't there. In its place was a grocery store. Inside it were children and adults and food and counters and shelving with food, and much more confusion than Virginia had anticipated upon her return.

At first Ms. Virginia Bean considered that she'd somehow forgotten the address; that the mere thought of returning to the strange place had made her forget how to arrive there, or that she'd somehow turned down the wrong street. But there it was in incredible black and white, *North Shore, Main* written on the same piece of paper that had gotten her there in the first place. There was no mistaking that she was at the right place, so where was Western Falls?

It didn't occur to Ms. Virginia Bean that if she quieted her mind that perhaps the stone, now safely within her green purse, would speak to her; tell her what to do, but she was so frustrated at the thought of not being able to talk to Mr. Spurt that the idea never occurred to her. Instead, she returned home and took a nap.

Ms. Virginia Bean slept for two hours and upon awakening, forgot about the stone and turned on her favorite movie. She made some snacks and sat in front of the television until 11 p.m. She was depressed about her lack of a job and knew she needed to go hunting for another one but had no desire to make the effort. She didn't pray; she didn't even think about praying.

Sleep finally claimed her about 1 a.m. and Virginia dreamt about the strange man and the strange stone and the strange place she would never see again. The thought of it bothered her more than she figured it should and she reasoned that she must be losing her mind. But in the morning, she went to her purse and the stone was still there, a reminder that she had truly been at Western Falls. So where was the building now?

She prayed again, and the prayer had stopping and starting points all the way through. She asked questions, listened for answers and was about to give up—nothing was speaking from the rock that she could hear, when she heard it:

"Who is David?"

"Who is David?" she asked herself, opening her eyes as if somehow, he would be standing right there before her. "Who is David?"

Well, she knew some David's but the old man had said something about David's bag. She knew few men who carried bags of any kind, though the popularity had increased in recent years. She thought of all the David's she knew but couldn't remember any of them carrying a bag. Mr. Spurt had also said something about faith. What did faith have to do with David and a bag? And then the words she'd heard from the rock returned: "You are also beloved."

Me, *beloved*? Hardly. But when Mr. Spurt said it she'd truly felt something from him; she'd truly believed it was the truth. And now?

If she was beloved, the job would come, well...easy. It would be spelled out in black and white. God himself would help her. She thought about this for a while and then the answer came. It was like a stirring in her heart, a breeze in her ears.

Maybe she didn't know this David, well not exactly. Perhaps she'd only heard about him. Wasn't he a shepherd of some sort in Bible days? Wasn't he the David that defeated Goliath?

The thought of it seemed strange and wonderful at the same time. Could David's bag be the bag he carried the stones in?

Within moments she was searching in the old, dusty Bible she had stored on the top shelf...

[And David] "chose him five smooth stones out of the brook and put them in a shepherd's bag which he had, even in a scrip; and his sling was in his hand: and he drew near the Philistine" (1 Samuel 17:40, KJV).

Ms. Virginia Bean fortunately had some faith inside her because she was suddenly very much...aware.

"Knowledge is not only power," the stone said, "it will lead you to answers."

"What sort of answers?"

The stone was silent. She thought of what it represented and the thoughts of what it meant moved Ms. Virginia Bean to tears. She began to think of new ways that she might search for her job. She decided to make a list, the world "beloved" still trying to make a home within her soul.

One week later she'd found the answer, though she hadn't yet found a job.

Beloved was the meaning of the name, "David" as given to the David who slew Goliath. Not surprisingly, once she had that knowledge, she was able to find the building easily. She knew more of what the first stone meant even before she entered Western Falls and met up with the old man in corduroys.

"So, you've returned," he said first, gazing at the stone she held in her right hand.

"So, I've returned," she answered. "Is Mr. Spurt in?" she asked.

The man laughed. "Actually, I think you'll want to call him, Stream," he said.

"Stream? Why? Am I meeting with someone else?"

The man didn't answer her but opened the door without the knob and led her through the empty room of windows whereupon another door opened. Like before, Mr. Spurt, now Mr. Stream was sitting behind his desk. A chair was waiting for her.

"Well, well, well," the old man said. "I am honored at your return."

"I have come for a bit of knowledge," Ms. Virginia Bean said.

The old man didn't answer her, at least not directly. "Do you mind if I call you daughter?" he asked. "Besides, I think you're in for a spiritual name."

"A spiritual name?"

"Yes. A name fitting your newer and larger thought processes."

"And what thought processes would that be?" she teased.

21

"Why don't you tell me?"

And so, they discussed David. What she knew about him, that is, and what she was doing to learn more. "I have tried prayer," she said, "and reading the good word, but now I have some questions for you."

He sat waiting for her to continue. He wore the same cap and the back window was opened. She could feel a slight caressing breeze.

"Was David really beloved?" she asked first.

"As sure as I'm sitting here," came the reply, followed by one of those captivating smiles that took her in and made her want to stay with him forever.

"Well, what made him beloved? What did he do to get such an honor?"

"Do? Nothing. He's my son."

The man was silent then, and Virginia wondered if he'd suddenly gone to sleep with his eyes open. And then the man, now known as Mr. Stream, continued: "My children always get the benefit of my great love. There is no doubt that I love them. If they come to me, as you have, they will learn that their birthright is at the heart of what they need to be successful."

"Their birthright?"

"Yes. Place your stone on the table."

Virginia reached inside her purse and took out the stone.

"See the silver veins here?" the man said, tracing his wrinkled fingers over the lines. "The veins represent my hand. When my child takes my hand and I walk with him or her throughout their life, they are never alone. Never."

Virginia tried to capture the thoughts of the old man. He seemed to be saying that her birthright entitled her to walk with him—to hear him. He seemed a good enough man and truly seemed to care about her life, so why wouldn't she want him to walk with her?

"I think I understand what you mean," she said, touching the rock lightly with her forefinger.

"Your birthright gives you ample opportunity to set out into the world and to do all that will be required of you. Your birthright is the power and the connection with me that you need to be successful," he said.

"Will I ever make lots of money?" said Virginia, but she had asked the wrong question.

The man frowned. "Perhaps you should think about getting that job first," he said. "What have you done so far?"

Virginia thought. "Well, I've made a list of opportunities, and I have prayed about my job, and I have read scriptures relating to David and Goliath. Did you know Goliath lived in a town named Gath?"

The man nodded. "And do you know what Gath means?" he asked.

"Winepress," Virginia said, feeling smarter than she should have.

"I am glad you came to me this day," he said. "And do you know the significance of the winepress?"

"The winepress?"

"I have another Son who is beloved. You may know him."

Virginia thought of all the David's that hadn't fit into her personal agenda and tried to think of someone she would have in common with Mr. Stream. She couldn't think of anyone but the man in the brown Corduroys.

"Your right of course," said Mr. Stream, seeming to read her thoughts. "My Son has sacrificed for all of my children. He is the winepress, a fine word to study as you make your way to finding that new job."

Virginia smiled. She couldn't help it. And then a thought occurred to her. "You said something about getting me a spiritual name. What is it?"

"Study more about my Son," he said, "and you'll know. In fact, you know already."

If Mr. Stream's Son was the man in the brown corduroys, the answer would be easy. She would just have to ask him on the way out.

"Any more questions?" the man in the fishing cap asked.

Virginia shook her head 'no' and stood, taking the stone in her right hand and placing it inside of her purse. The weight of it was light and the burden easy to carry. She shook Mr. Stream's hand and walked to the door that opened naturally as she came to it. She walked through the empty room of windows and through the second door leading to the main entrance. The man in the brown corduroys stood at the desk waiting for her.

"Did you get all of your questions answered?" he asked as if somehow, he knew that she'd not received the answer to one.

"All but one. What is your name?" she asked. She had meant to ask what her spiritual name was, but something about the unknown man standing before her allowed the question to be asked. Perhaps it was because Virginia knew that her name was connected to his and that knowing his name would be a clue to knowing her own.

This she knew for sure. When the man in the brown corduroys looked at her with that same love that Mr. Stream had, she was assured that the information she was going to receive was correct.

"I am the Son," he said.

On her drive home Virginia thought of her spiritual name in connection with the Son. Somehow, the man in the fisherman's cap had shown her that she was related to them both: The Father and the Son, and so her spiritual name would reflect that.

She thought about David now, and all the time he had for reflection as a shepherd. She studied more about him and more about how sheep were gathered into their stalls at night. The best shepherds never walked behind their sheep but in front them, and the sheep knew their shepherd because they knew his voice and followed him. She learned about wolves, and how they would try to attack the sheep at night when they thought the shepherd was sleeping. She discovered that the entrance to the stall where the sheep were enclosed at night was always protected by a crown of thorns above the entrance that kept them safe until morning.

David must have known the Lord even before he heard his voice. He must have studied about his life and reflected on how his personal life could grow and change with the Lord's help. He'd had many nights under the stars to think about it. And Virginia had many nights in her future to consider who she was.

That her birthright made her a daughter was difficult for her to take in—at least at first—but knowing this helped Virginia to search out her own name and discover its meaning.

"Pure." That's what her name meant, and the last thing on Virginia's mind was that she could represent such a pure word. She was far from pure. She'd made many mistakes in her life and had fallen many times; more times than she could count. If she said the right thing, she was sure to do the wrong thing. If she tried to do what was expected, she always fell short. She was as far from the word, pure, as the letter Z was from A in the alphabet.

How could she be a pure daughter? How could Mr. Stream even suggest that she was a "daughter"? How could she be a daughter that was pure? It just wasn't realistic.

Doubt surrounded Virginia's mind until it was all she could do to stay awake. She watched television, ate snacks, drank plenty of water, and when she retired near 11 p.m., she did so with a lunge and a forgotten prayer. She dreamt of reality as she saw it with mistakes and choices that always made her fall short and look small to herself: she thought of the man behind the white desk frowning at her and not really caring if he did so. She thought about being muddy wet and thinking of herself as something far from the pureness her name suggested.

When she awoke, Virginia had a headache. She forgot about prayer and about the ideas she had circled in the paper and had located on the Internet for a new job; until she found the stone.

It felt smooth and warm in her hand and she walked it to the couch and sat with it for a time, without the television blaring or snacks on the coffee table, or even thoughts of returning to bed and getting a few more hours of shut-eye. She merely held the rock in her right hand and spoke to it about her fears until her fears were calmed and she could hear what it spoke.

"It is time," it said, "for you to return to God."

A shaft of sunlight came through the window at just that moment and Virginia knew that the words were not only real, but true. They rested in her heart and spoke to her about her potential as a pure daughter of the birthright.

She returned to Western Falls and to the reception area where the Son was waiting for her.

"So, you've returned," he said.

"Yes. And I thank you so much for the opportunity."

"How is the job hunting coming?" he asked.

"Very well, thank you. I have four interviews set up this week, and two more next week. I've come to ask Mr. Stream about it; see if he can help me with my worries."

"Well, there is no question that he can," said the Son. "Just go through the door, walk through the room of light, and continue forward as you have done before."

"The room of light, so that's what it's called," said Virginia.

"That's what it's called," repeated the Son, and she walked through the first door. This time Virginia noticed that not only were there multiple windows but she could hear sounds other than cars and people coming from the other side. It was almost as if the wind spoke to her and welcomed her. But Virginia wasn't sure if she should speak back to the wind and so she continued through the second door and to the feet of Mr. Stream whom she now knew as God. But she could not call him God, at least not yet.

"Virginia," he said, rising from his high-backed chair and taking her hand. His own was warm and sent slivers of light to her heart. "So glad you have come. Have you brought the stone?"

"I carry it everywhere," said Virginia, sitting down and removing it from her purse.

"That's good," God said, "very good. Would you like another?"

"Another stone?"

"Exactly," answered the man in the fisherman's cap. What do you think your next stone will represent?"

"Well, the first one is listening," answered Virginia in a quiet voice, "I can only imagine what the second stone will be, especially when it's one of David's."

God smiled. "Yes, especially since it's one of David's." He cleared his throat with a low moan. "Tell me what you've learned about the first stone," he asked. "It's important that you not only know what the white stone represents but why you should carry it with you always."

Virginia thought. "I suppose you mean 'carried' in the sense that it's carried in my heart and not just in my purse."

"Exactly right," said the fisherman.

"Well, as I said before, the stone represents "listening," and if I listen closely to the stone and to you, and even to the Son, I will not only know who I am, I will be able to tune into the power given to me because of my connection to the birthright."

"That's right. And who is the stone?"

"I suppose it's the Holy Spirit," said Virginia, although she had never consciously thought of the stone in those terms before. But standing there with God brought many things to her mind and heart that she'd never before considered.

God smiled and she smiled back.

"What have you discovered about your name?" he asked.

Virginia groaned inwardly, and she was pretty sure that God could see it.

"I know I am your daughter," said Ms. Virginia Bean. "But I'm really not…pure."

"Whether or not you agree doesn't make it any less so," said the Father. "It just is."

"But how can I be?" The words croaked out like a sick frog and Virginia in saying them wished with all of her heart that she could take them back in. In that second, she realized taking them in wouldn't have done a bit of good either—God had heard them either way.

"Why do you think the Son walked the winepress without me?" asked the Father. "Even I couldn't be there. You remember…"

Yes, Virginia remembered the time the Son spent in the Garden of Gethsemane. She remembered hearing about the blood dripping from every pore. She remembered that an angel was sent to comfort the Son but that the Father had withdrawn himself. Why had he done that? Virginia had never been quite sure why.

"Imagine my pain," said the Father now. "Imagine how easy it would have been to reach out and save my Son from pain and ultimate death."

Virginia tried to imagine, but the imagining was difficult. She thought of what it would be like to watch someone getting run over by a car without reaching out to stop it. She wondered where the Father would have had to travel to escape hearing the pain from the Son's heart and lips.

"There was no place to go," said the Father. "I could hear my Son from the farthest outreaches of eternity. But still, he had to die."

"Why?" The words were innocently asked, but in giving them Virginia could feel the answer. The Son had to die. He'd died for her so that she might live.

"How did you manage it?" she asked the Father, finally, not really sure how such a grand sacrifice in both the Father and the Son could have been accomplished.

"I remembered the purpose behind the gift. I remembered all of my children and what would happen if my Son forgot his promise. He had the strength to do what was asked of him and so do you."

"But I am not PURE!" She hadn't meant to scream the words, especially to God, but there they were, hanging above them in seeming black and white.

"But you are pure," said God. "Every time you turn to me and let go of your pain, it is as if your pain never existed."

"Never...existed?" Virginia gulped.

"My children forget this all of the time," said God, nodding his white head and turning to his desk for stone two. He held the dull black stone in his right hand and reached out for Virginia's left. Virginia felt the stone and the weight of it. She felt its smooth texture, and hoped she'd be able to carry the stone in her purse without having it weigh her down or working itself through the bag.

And you're included in that number," continued God. "Why do you think the second stone is 'trust'?"

"Trust?" echoed Virginia, wondering why a black stone could be called, trust.

"Yes, trust," God answered.

Virginia knelt. It was all she could do.

Trust

The stone called "Trust" was one interesting stone. Instead of speaking, it changed color depending on her mood, kind of like one of those old-fashioned mood rings she'd worn as a kid. Only this stone had three colors to its name; white, gray and black. The black represented those thoughts that were negative and untrusting and bleak; the white, just the opposite. At any given moment Virginia could see how she was thinking by looking at the stone. The gray, of course, meant she was on her way to black or back to white. It was a nice warning.

During the next few weeks, Ms. Virginia Bean asked God how the white stone with the silver veins worked. Sometimes he'd give her a direct answer, but most often the words would come only after she'd done some research herself. She worked on trusting God and watched the second stone change colors depending on how she thought on him.

Virginia had begun a social networking group to get the word out about her skills in factory work, and soon discovered that she had an added skill of public speaking. She took a class and was rewarded by a compliment from her instructor.

"You just might be a motivational speaker," the instructor said.

Virginia took her teacher's words to heart. She relied on them almost as much as she relied on the word of God and prayer and watching stone two for signs of change in her attitude toward him.

That didn't mean her life was easy. As a motivational speaker, Virginia had no idea what she could possibly talk about. She couldn't speak about assembly line work, could she? Or the rewards of getting to work on time or enjoying a job no matter how lousy your boss was?

It was all so depressing. The stone had turned black before she realized it, and before 11 p.m., Virginia, a.k.a. Pure Daughter of the Birthright was drowning in television and junk food and more sleep than she'd ever need or appreciate. She was sick with thoughts of getting a new job and felt as if no one cared about what she did or what she had to offer.

Virginia was in a slump and she didn't even care that the stone was black.

She felt this way for days until she remembered the meaning of the stone: "Trust."

Trust, trust, trust, she mulled the word over and over in her mind and studied it in the good book and thought about it day and night as she cleaned her house or went in search of the few groceries she needed. She was beginning to trust in her abilities as a daughter of the birthright and then it occurred to her that sometimes she was forgetting God and trusting only in herself.

She smiled and got on her knees to talk with God. He would understand.

He reminded her to study the word, "winepress."

And so, she learned of its construction—of the upper and lower vats used to make wine, how the grapes were put through the vats and then trodden under the feet of the workers. The juice was the "fat" accumulated. Virginia considered how the various processes of the winepress reflected what the Son had done. Tears glistened as Virginia thought on the Son and what he'd done personally for her.

And she wanted to thank him.

***

When she met the Son at Western Falls he reached out his hand. "You've had a disturbing week," he said, "one fraught with challenges and growth. I like that. I also see that you've been doing some studying."

Virginia smiled weakly and nodded her head. She was shown through the invisible door. It was hard for her to hear the wind but she could feel the breath of it on her face and thanked it for coming to her aid. Through the other door she found God sitting at his desk. He was writing down something on a glowing piece of paper.

"Well, Virginia," he said, "Pure Daughter," I am glad you have come."

Virginia blushed. She couldn't help it.

The man smiled over his desk and offered her a seat. "Well, what do you think of the weather?" he asked, placing the golden pen next to the shining paper.

"The weather?"

"Yes, what has been happening in your life?"

"As if you didn't know." The words were sarcastic and small and Virginia felt bad about them the moment they'd escaped her lips. "Sorry," she offered, humbly.

"Apology accepted. So, tell me about the weather."

"Do you want me to start where we left off?"

"If you'd like."

"Well," said Virginia, "I thought a lot about what you said from the good book, about trusting in God with your whole heart. I thought about the whisperings that came from stone one, about how I needed to trust in you more than I trusted in myself; that I needed to go forward in faith, not seeing what was at the other side but knowing that you stood there waiting for me and knew the end."

"That's right, and what do you think of stone two?"

"At first, I thought it was only black of course, and then it would sometimes turn a white, clear color almost as if I could see inside it…"

"Almost?"

"Well, it was still sort of foggy…"

"Kind of like trust? My dear, Virginia, trust in me is a big step, but it isn't often an easy one. In one moment you may feel as if your trust is strong, so strong it can never be broken; in the next moment, it feels like a flimsy thread that can be broken with one gust of wind or a cut of the scissors, right?"

Virginia nodded and listened.

"David's second stone was very necessary in defeating Goliath. With the first stone he knew my voice; he listened to my commands. But with the second stone, he had to completely trust in it. What would have happened if David had forgotten to trust in me in that very instant he flung that stone at the giant?"

"He might have failed."

"And he still might have defeated the giant with his own strength, but that wasn't what David was about. He knew I was by his side and trusted in that."

"Were you really there?" Virginia asked.

"Of course," replied God. "I will never leave my children completely, especially when they are confronting their Goliaths. What do you think yours is?"

"Getting this job; at least that's what my Goliath is now."

"What previous Goliaths have you had that you've had to overcome?"

Virginia thought for a moment. "Well, I suppose, getting into that old house. I wasn't sure if I'd qualify as a single owner, without a husband…"

"Yes, a husband. How do you feel about that?"

"Not having a husband?"

"Of course."

"Well, it was hard at first, especially when I was in my 20's and all of my friends were getting husbands and I wasn't."

"And you think it's as simple as that."

"As simple as what?"

"As simple as wanting one."

"I guess. At least, that's what I used to think."

"So, what do you think now?"

"I think you know best about the timing of that."

"Excellent answer, but do you believe it? Do you trust that I know the right timing for your husband?"

"Sometimes."

"Then it's like that second stone, isn't it? Sometimes it might be black, at other times it's clear, and still other times there's sort of a fog inside of it; a fog that you can't see through clearly."

Virginia couldn't help it. She had to ask. "So, when…"

The Father smiled. "Now, if I told you that, would you have to trust me?"

Virginia reached for the second stone in her bag. Suddenly it was white and light and the heaviness was not there. It was if she was holding a cloud.

"Have you studied the name Goliath?" he asked. "It might prove to be of some help."

At home, Virginia found that the name Goliath meant "uncovered," and she realized she was truly uncovering some truths that at one time had been hidden to her. She thought about both words, "Gath" and "Goliath" together and realized that the sacrifice of the Son was truly the "winepress uncovered." The Lord had faced his Goliath and so must she.

She also spent some time researching public speaking and made a list of her spiritual gifts as recorded in the Bible. She prayed a lot about what she should do and spent some time reflecting on her worth as a daughter of the birthright. She even put together a new resume. That night Virginia slept peacefully.

The next morning the second stone was clear. In ways that only God could understand, she was to re-enter Western Falls Water Company and interview for the position she'd meant to before. Indeed, she looked beautiful, but it was the shine of her countenance that made the man behind the front desk take a second look. "Welcome to Western Falls," he said. "Do you have an appointment?"

"Yes, yes, with Go…Mr. Stream," she said.

"You mean, Mr. Spurt," the man corrected.

"Oh, yes, Mr. Spurt," Virginia offered. "Sorry for the mistake."

"Sit down over here, I'll let him know you've arrived," the man said, placing a phone against his ear. Virginia retreated to the chairs. This was the first time Virginia had had to wait in the large room and she was determined to make the best of it. She enjoyed the plants and flowers and took special notice of the business magazines displayed neatly on the glass table in front of her.

Her heart was beating frantically, and so she said a little prayer that God would be with her during this visit and that she would feel calm and self-assured. She made mention in her prayer about how thankful she was for the opportunity, no matter how it turned out, though she secretly hoped it would.

In moments she'd been ushered past the main desk through a door with an actual doorknob and past hundreds of desks, computers, books and employees and through another door to Mr. Spurt's office.

Mr. Spurt stood and offered his hand. "Ms. Bean, I presume," he said.

Virginia juggled her resume to her left arm and reached for the owner's hand. She shook it firmly to show him her confidence and sat down on the chair offered. The room itself was filled with bookshelves and one of those silver ball monstrosities that clanked together on the front desk when pushed.

She'd brought both stones with her today and prayed that the second one was still a pearly white. Her purse wasn't too heavy, so she was pleased.

"So, Virginia, I see that you worked for Regal Doughnut Factory before they moved their operation to New York. How did you like working there?"

Virginia's heart thumped. Of all the questions he could have asked...why this one? She was hoping with her new skills in public speaking he would want to talk about that first. Actually, Virginia was hoping that the balding man with the blue bow tie wouldn't focus on her most recent job but would just get to the good parts.

"Well, yes, I did work for the Regal Doughnut Factory recently, but since then I have been developing my speaking and presentation skills. I would love to work with your company..."

"But Ms. Bean, it says here that you have experience in front-line work, something we're in great need of right now. What did you say you liked about the job?"

"I didn't." Virginia frowned. "What I mean to say is, I worked at that job for ten years and got to be pretty fast at what I did."

"And what particular experience did you have there?" asked Mr. Spurt.

"Checking doughnuts," said Ms. Bean.

"Did you check them by hand or were you over running the machine that supplied the work?"

"Actually, it was an eye coordination thing," Ms. Bean muttered. She'd never been so embarrassed. Her purse on her lap was suddenly getting heavy. She could feel the black stone trying to work its way out.

"What do you mean, Ms. Bean?"

"After the machine punched the holes I made sure that the doughnuts themselves had no defects." Ms. Bean stopped and looked up at Mr. Spurt.

"Are you saying, Ms. Bean, that you were in quality control; that you made sure that every doughnut made was the best doughnut that could possibly be made?"

"That's what I'm saying, Mr. Spurt."

"You don't seem very happy about it."

"Well, if you'd check over all of my more recent qualifications…"

Mr. Spurt was silent. "As I said, the job for which you are applying is assembly line work. This is where you've had experience. I'm afraid we have no need of public speaking skills per se. It's a fine skill, I'm sure, but I do most, if not all of the presentations, and I don't see here that you've had any schooling on the subject. Have you been to college, Ms. Bean?"

Ms. Bean hadn't been to college, she hadn't been anywhere but to her old job and to her old house and to this crummy company. Suddenly the second stone made its way through the bottom of her purse and clunked to the floor.

"What was that?" cried Mr. Spurt.

Ms. Bean picked up the stone as black as tar, its heaviness weighing on her more than she ever thought possible. Stuff from her purse was already plopping out the bottom; lipstick, eye shadow, a small mirror and some tissue, the last she sorely needed now. Virginia felt like even more of a fool as she carried her purse with her right hand over the hole in the bottom, and her left hand held the black stone. She struggled to open the door to the boss's office with her elbow. The boss managed the door to the foyer. She eyed the man briefly who'd first ushered her in.

Upon seeing her face, he asked, "Are you all right?"

But Ms. Bean didn't have time to talk. She rushed by the man and out the front glass doors still holding the bottom of her purse and the solid stone that had made its way through it. She marched to the parking lot and got in her car. The thing wouldn't start, and the stone, sitting on the passenger's seat next to her, was already making a hole in the center of the plastic cushion.

"Stop your foolishness!" she shouted at it. But it was too late. The rock was already making its way to the floorboards. She stopped the car and reached into the hole. The stone was as heavy as a lead weight; she was barely able to hold it in her right hand as she drove with the other.

Once home, Ms. Virginia Bean plopped the black stone in her front flower garden. It could go all the way to Hell as far as she cared, and she watched it do just that, at least for a few feet. Ms. Virginia Bean took her purse inside and fished for the other stone, but it had vanished.

"I'm dead meat," she thought but didn't say. He would hear her anyway and he'd be disgusted at what she'd done. Well, she was disgusted at him! Didn't he say he would be with her always? Hadn't he told her to have faith, and hadn't she had faith? Hadn't she put her trust in God as she went into that office? Well hadn't she?

And then Ms. Virginia Bean realized something, and that something was very powerful news. She'd been so caught up in the questions that Mr. Spurt had been asking her, she'd forgotten to listen; but not only that, she'd forgotten to trust God! She'd gone in there, thinking that she had it all handled, that she'd done all the steps. She'd actually expected God to help her without even a thought about listening to what he had to say.

She'd gotten angry at the man behind the desk because he hadn't asked her the right questions; at least not the questions she'd wanted him to ask, and she'd been so angry that the second stone had made a hole in the bottom of her purse and had almost made it through her car's floorboards, and the first stone had disappeared! Even now the first stone could be in Mr. Spurt's office and he could be turning it over in his hands!

What had happened to her?

It occurred to Ms. Bean that she'd been so unhappy at her previous job that it had been impossible for her to say anything positive about it to Mr. Spurt. All she'd cared about was the job she wanted, not the job that had been offered her. How could she be so foolish?

As these thoughts tumbled inside Virginia's head, she thought about turning on the television set and drinking ten bottles of water in succession with a bowl of pop tarts on the side, but instead she went to her room. On her end table sat the Bible. She opened it up and read about God and Mammon. Later, as she talked to God about what she'd done she remembered the Son. In prayer she asked for forgiveness and a slight glow entered her heart.

That night Virginia slept more peacefully than she felt like she deserved, and the next morning she went to the flower beds. The black stone was gone. In its place was a gaping hole.

"Where should I look?" she asked. She was on her knees in the garden. The smell of roses caressed her skin and she could feel the wind blowing against her wet cheeks. "Forgive me," she added, as she stood and went inside.

Virginia showered, put on her makeup, did her hair, and dressed for the day, but she was thinking about how best to explain her situation to God. She smiled at herself when she realized he already knew what she'd done, and so Virginia Bean decided to be honest. She drove the car to Western Falls, opened the front door, and walked in.

The Son greeted her.

"Heard you had an interesting day yesterday," he said.

Virginia blushed. "You could say that," she answered.

"Don't worry. I got your note." He smiled and Virginia smiled back. Today was the first day that Virginia had seen the Son wear anything but brown corduroy pants and a flannel shirt, but today he was wearing white. The robe he wore glowed and flowed behind him and gave him that ethereal look he deserved.

"I love your new outfit," she said, instantly regretting her easy words.

"This old thing?" he sang and turned to do something at the desk.

The door opened at her approach and Virginia walked in, but the windows, as before, were not open. The air inside felt a bit stiff, kind of like a home shut up for the summer. Still, she could see the trees in the distance and the wind as made its way through bundled leaves and branches. At the second door, Virginia hesitated. She'd never hesitated before and the thought of what he would think of her went through her mind as she stood by the door that did not open. But what he thought of her she already knew.

The door opened.

He was standing this time, looking out his own window that was open and motioned her near him. "Well, Ms. Virginia, Pure Daughter of the Birthright, you've had a terrible yesterday."

"You could say that." She stood by him, feeling of his warmth, his love, and for a moment she did nothing but listen. "I forgot," she said finally.

"I know," he answered.

"I lost both stones, I'm sorry," she said.

"I have the stones here."

"Where?"

"In my desk. But I want you to know something before I get them out."

Her heart pounded.

"You are going to make mistakes."

"How many?"

"You really want a count?"

"When I get to the end I want to know it."

"But only I know the end from the beginning."

"I forgot about that."

"You also forgot to listen and trust in me. What happened at the job interview?"

"I don't know…I mean I just didn't want to answer the questions the boss was handing out. Why couldn't he ask the questions I really cared about? Why did he have to ask me about my sorry job, the one I hated? Why couldn't he have asked me about my new training, about the person I'd begun to be?"

"And what person is that?"

"You know, the one who has more confidence and skill because she's learned how to listen and to trust; why couldn't he have asked me about that?"

"You mean, why couldn't I have asked you those questions?"

There was silence in the white room larger than the sky, and Virginia could suddenly hear birds in the distance. "Remember Noah," he said. "Remember how he sent away that dove to see if the water had dispersed from the land? It wasn't until the dove returned with an olive leaf in its beak that Noah knew the waters had subsided."

Virginia listened.

"Waiting is important in this process of learning to trust me. Waiting upon me means not being in a hurry to promote your own agenda, it means sitting silently before you reply so that you might relate my agenda."

"But don't I have a say in anything?"

"Of course, you do."

"Come, follow me. See this window? Like your heart, it can be opened or closed. You can feel the refreshing breeze; even hear the cooing of a lost dove trying to find land in the distance. But you won't know unless you're still. You didn't tell me about your other job interviews."

"I didn't go to them."

"Why not?"

"After the one I had here, I didn't dare try the others."

"Come, sit." She followed him to the desk and took a seat in her regular place. The Father reached into a drawer, pulled out the two stones and placed them in her hands. "Try not to lose them," he said.

Virginia didn't know what to say, but she was grateful and placed the two stones in her newly purchased red bag. "Thank you," she said, and stood to leave.

But the Father stopped her. "Not yet," he said. With his right hand he reached inside the shining drawer and pulled out another smooth stone. This one was brown with dark lines of black running through it. He held it in front of him.

"It isn't always easy to keep up with the optimism, is it? But David had optimism, even though he was a lad and the giant stood many feet above him. David had optimism because he'd listened to me and because he trusted in me. David had optimism because he listened and trusted in someone other than himself."

"That's why I had such a hard time at that interview," Virginia said. "I had optimism, but it had nothing to do with how much you loved me or anything to do with my birthright."

The Father nodded. "True optimism doesn't come from looking good or saying the right thing or even answering the questions exactly perfect, true optimism is a natural byproduct of listening and trusting in me. Real optimism, the kind that can fight giants, always comes when you've been tuned in to me. If a job is right, you will feel it, and the one interviewing you will feel it too. Think about this: What if you'd answered my questions in a positive way? What if you'd used your experience working at Regal Doughnut Factory as a plus rather than a minus?"

"In what way?"

"Think about it." The Father handed Virginia the smooth brown rock and at its touch the black veins within it began to glow a bright white. The sight was breathtaking. Things grow; especially people. But to really grow, to really experience life, a son or daughter must look at his or her life with optimism. There will be challenges, yes, but these challenges, if looked upon as a way of learning from and becoming better, will only create more optimism inside them. True growth can only be achieved by facing the facts while still remaining assured that all will work out as it should."

"So, I'm to learn something from my visit with you when I didn't know it was you?" Virginia asked.

The old man nodded. "Everyone on earth can teach you something, and it's up to you to be open to what they have to say."

"Even if I don't like it?"

"Especially then."

Virginia reflected on God's words. She wondered what would have happened if she'd had the optimism to think positive about her past life experiences, and what would happen if she saw them today as an opportunity of growth as he obviously did.

At home, she held the brown rock in her hands for most of the evening and made a list of all the experiences in her life that she'd always termed negative. The list was long but it was good. When she looked back at the brown rock, it was still glowing.

Optimism

Virginia was resolute to be optimistic. If all else failed, at least she knew that she could hear God and that she could trust in him. But that was the wrong way to think, wasn't it? Virginia was determined to be optimistic. She wouldn't fail because all of her life's experiences contributed to her success. Now, that was better.

Virginia had two interviews on this particular day and two more at the end of the week. One was out of the city; the others were within city limits. One particular job interested her greatly. It was working at a clothing factory as a supervisor. As the job description was laid out, most of her duties were supervising other workers; little assembly line work would be required of her. Ms. Virginia Bean was excited about interviewing for this job because not only would she be able to talk about her previous work experience, she would be able to share what she'd learned through her recent classes.

Besides her newest public speaking skills, Virginia had just begun a class in organizational techniques in business. She'd even made some new friends through her social networking group and had decided to start one of her own. They met every Thursday night at her place and discussed ways to better market themselves as future employees.

Virginia was grateful for all she had learned and was continuing to learn through the stones of listening, trust and optimism. She kept up with her visits, and this included her visits with prayer, scripture reading and making well-needed visits to Western Falls.

When the day arrived for the clothing factory interview, Virginia was ready. Clothing Tops All was located just outside the city, so the drive was fairly short. Parking her car outside, Virginia Bean walked to the front doors. Inside sat a young woman who appeared to be in her 40's behind a roughhewn desk. The place was neat but not elegant, and the building was small.

"My name is Virginia Bean," she offered.

The woman smiled. "You're early," she said. "Will you fill out these forms?"

Virginia was glad to. She sat and filled out her job history even though she'd brought along a resume as well as references and other job incidentals as discussed at her Thursday meetings. She felt well prepared for this interview.

A few minutes later, the same woman walked her down a hall. "Now, don't be nervous," she said, "my name is Katy Trim and when I interviewed here, the boss was great. Even when I gave him stupid answers he smiled as if he thought my answers were the best thing next to gravy." She smiled and ushered Virginia into the small room.

It was messy enough, but in-between all the messes were clothing swatches and color and plenty of books on the subject of clothing. Like Ms. Trim, the man was tall and slender and looked to be about her age. Virginia's heart beat a bit stronger than usual. He offered her a seat.

"I'm Mr. Style," he said, as she sat down. "You must be Ms. Bean. That's an interesting name," he added, looking squarely into her eyes. They were green.

"Well, yes, it is." Virginia was thinking of her spiritual name, the one given to her by God. She decided that this wasn't the best time to mention it, but she said a little prayer that God would assist her with the best answer. "I am a daughter of a great family."

"Is that so?" The man studied her, seemed pleased with what he saw, and reached for her resume.

"Tell me about your supervisory experience," he asked.

"Well, I haven't had any supervisory experience, per se," she said, "but I have taken some classes that I feel will make me a strong candidate for the position."

Mr. Style's eyes returned to her resume. "It says here that you've done some professional speaking."

"No, but I've taken a class. I'm also currently taking a class in organizational techniques for business…"

"But have you actually been in charge; helped others keep to their quota, inspired others to do their best work?"

Virginia thought about all the years she had spent at Regal Doughnut Factory without speaking to anyone. She'd do her shift and go home, and the next day she'd return to do it over again. But since her last meeting with God she'd made a list of all the things she'd learned from that experience. She felt good about sharing the list with Mr. Style now.

"When I worked at Regal, I learned about dedication," she said. "It wasn't always easy to stand on my feet all day, and it wasn't always easy to do the same job every day. Some would even call it monotonous." She smiled, letting Mr. Style know that she had learned from the experience and today was a better human being because of it. "I have a group that meets in my home," she said. "We discuss what it takes to become a great employee, a great leader, and I have learned a lot from those I associate with. I know that in order to inspire others, I have to be optimistic myself. Being a leader means listening to everyone's concerns. It means trusting that they have questions for a reason, and that I can assist them with the answers."

"That's a good point," said Mr. Style. "What would you do about an employee who wasn't getting the hang of it? What would you do and say to inspire him to meet his quota?"

Ms. Virginia Bean thought for a moment. She thought about everyone's role as part of the birthright. She thought about what God would say in this situation.

"I think," said Virginia, "that I would first congratulate him on what he was already doing well. For example; perhaps he always came to work on time or he was always willing to help someone else, or he always came with a positive attitude to work. I would focus on strengths, and then I would explain about the problem. I would offer my help in the form of a question: Are you having specific problems with your job that I should know about? Or, what can I do to better help you meet your quota? I think getting to the point is important. I also think that allowing the employee to share their concerns helps them as well. I would, of course, speak about this problem away from the other workers."

Mr. Style nodded, and Virginia listened intently as he spoke to her about the job and all it entailed. At the end of the interview, Virginia was happy. She felt as if the interview had been successful and that, indeed, she was a fine candidate for the position.

When she got a call a week later, Virginia was even more enthused. "We'd like you to come in for a second interview," Katie Trim said. Virginia spent the next few days thanking God for her good fortune. She thanked him for bringing Clothing Tops All into the picture and wanted to thank God in person for this great blessing in her life.

Still, despite her jubilant feeling, she returned to Western Falls only to find a grocery store in its place busy with customers. Children were crying inside grocery carts, and mothers were trying to remain calm as they stood in line at the checkout counter. Lines of men, women and children could be seen through the large window, and cars graced the parking lot. For a moment Virginia's heart saddened, but she also knew that there were other options in speaking with God and so she went home to do them.

She started with prayer and gospel reading. Her hopes still high with optimism, she asked God the question that was burning in her heart. "Is this the right job for me?" fully expecting the answer to be 'yes.' But the answer was not 'yes,' it was anything but 'yes.'

In moments Virginia was worried. She'd removed all three stones from her purse. The first was quiet, the second was turning black and the third's veins were not shining with optimism. What if she was not making the right step in taking this job? But how could this job not be the right one? It was perfect for her in every way!

Now Virginia was angry, and the black stone was making its way through her leather couch cushion. "No!" she screeched. But it was too late. The black stone was all the way to the springs.

The heaviness of the rock was almost more than she could bear, and as Ms. Virginia Bean tried to lift it from the hole, it suddenly felt like a great tree had landed on her hand. It was all she could do to keep it from sinking deeper into the floor.

But she must keep it from sinking!

"I'm sorry!" she cried, and in that moment, Ms. Virginia Bean a.k.a. Pure Daughter of the Birthright, remembered that she must trust in God, and the stone was pulled from the floor. It was sort of a muggy white, but she knew, that in time, the stone would clear in line with her mind and heart. She remembered that with all of the optimism she'd received and the knowledge that she'd been given about her birthright, that God, after all, knew all of the answers, and he had the best answer for her now.

What was it?

"This is a wonderful job, but the job isn't for you."

The words came to her as clearly as someone standing next to her. The first stone was speaking, and the words she was hearing were not her own. "Let the job go."

"Let the job go?"

Her heart began beating frantically, and as the second stone turned gray, Virginia said a little prayer, got in her car, and traveled to Western Falls. She knew God would be there.

The Son was waiting for her. "Are you terribly disappointed?" he asked.

Her look was all he needed.

"Here, go back and talk to Father," he said, opening the door for her.

God was pleased to see her. "So, your job interview went well?" he asked.

"It wasn't you, was it?" she asked.

"No, but I can see that you're disappointed in me."

"I'm sorry, I shouldn't be. I know that you know all."

He smiled. "Sit," he said. "It's difficult to remain optimistic when things aren't working your way."

"Actually, they were working my way," said Virginia. "Only…you didn't think they were right for me."

"Are you angry with me?"

"A little. It's so hard! I felt so good about the job. I felt it was the right thing!"

"Do you still want to go out for that second interview?"

"Yes. Are you mad?"

"No. I understand. It's important for you to do something you believe you'll love doing. It's important to share your talents and to help others along the way."

"Yes! You've got it! So, I can still go for that second interview?"

"You know how I feel."

"But you said…"

"I said that I understood, but that doesn't mean that the job is right for you." He took Virginia's hand. It was warm and the glow raced up her arm and to her heart. "Agency is a powerful thing. You have a choice. You can do as I command, or you can do as you want."

"But you make it sound terrible if I don't follow you." Tears accumulated in Virginia's eyes and she didn't try to stop them. "You make it sound that my choice will lead me down the…the wrong path or something."

God smiled. "Could it be that the job will take you down the wrong path—for you—that the position might be for someone else?"

"Who?" Virginia sniffed, hoping her nose wouldn't run.

"Now, if I told you that, how could you have faith in me?"

"Do I know them?"

"No."

"Well, I wouldn't want to take away a job that is meant for someone else. So, I guess there's another job waiting for me."

God nodded. "And you will like it even more than you believe you like the one currently standing before you. "In fact," added God with one of his warm smiles, "you'll like it even more than you can imagine."

Virginia had a hard time believing that another job could be any better suited to her than the one that wanted a second interview, but she tried to trust God. That week she called Clothing Tops All. She told them respectfully that she'd decided that the position wasn't quite right for her and that she appreciated their interest. She went to the other job interviews and came home discouraged. None of them fit either.

And then she remembered God. It was so easy to forget him in this world of business and busyness, and Virginia apologized once again. She sensed in the third stone, the stone of optimism, that truly it wasn't easy to remain optimistic in the world and that it took effort to remain on top. It took remembering all of the things the Father had already taught her.

As she thought on this, an idea occurred to Ms. Virginia Bean. Perhaps it was her spiritual name that gave her the courage, but whatever it was Virginia knew her job wasn't going to come through the newspaper or online. Paul, from her networking group, had lost his job almost a year ago and had just decided to start his own catering business selling some of his favorite things—desserts.

"Maybe you should look in to creating your own job," he said, during one of their Thursday visits when everyone else had left her house.

And while Virginia had listened, a part of her grew afraid. She wondered about the second stone in her bedroom, and hoped it wasn't working its way through her old-style dresser. She kept all of the stones in her purse and on her dresser when people came to her house—to keep them safe and to prevent a myriad of questions.

The fact that Virginia could begin her own business had occurred to her once before, but she'd quickly let go of the fact. She was living in the real world, wasn't she? She had to find that steady job, and a job she'd create for herself couldn't be right, could it?

Though the thought of planning and implementing a new business made her nervous, Virginia decided to call her new friend and talk to him about it again.

"Well, I know you're a go-getter," he said. "Didn't you say in one of our last meetings that you paid for your house with cash and that those new classes you've been taking came from the funds you saved up all those years you worked? And isn't the money getting you through unemployment now?"

Of course, Paul was right. She'd done all of these things, and with her renewed optimism, trust in God and her newfound listening skills, Virginia felt as if she had made some real progress in her life, but could she start a new business, and if so, a business doing what?

Paul was little help here. Sure, he'd brought along a beautiful sunflower to "light up her life" he said, and she'd loved the gesture, but he seemed to think she could start her own doughnut service or something. He felt that her skills would help her to set up shop, so to speak.

"But you're crazy! I've never made a doughnut in my life!"

"But I have!" said Paul.

"You have?"

"Okay, I've never had my own place or anything, but I have experience making the stuff."

She couldn't believe it! Of all things, Paul made doughnuts! And then a sudden thought occurred to her: "What about teaching a class on doughnut making?"

"That would be fun. Like you, I don't know many people that have that skill."

Virginia thought. "I don't know if I want to open a doughnut shop or anything like that," she said. "Don't get me wrong, I've just seen too many doughnut holes in my life to keep me going for a second life."

Paul laughed. "You're so funny," he said. "Maybe you should start a class on positive thinking."

"About doughnuts?"

"Everyone thinks positive about doughnuts. Your first class could be, "You'll go nuts without these doughnuts!"

Now it was Virginia's turn to laugh. "What if the doughnut was our symbol? Kind of a sweet way to say, 'You need to treat yourself sometime?'" Or, come and get your just desserts. We could call the place, the store, the catering business, whatever, 'Just Desserts'"!

"We? What do you mean, we?"

Now Virginia was getting excited. "I think we may have something here. I'm looking for a job and you want to begin your own business, in catering, right? Why don't we combine forces and come up with something?"

There was a pause, a pause much too long for Ms. Virginia Bean to handle. Finally, she said, "Paul, are you still there?"

"Yeah, I'm just thinking."

"About what?"

"About our new business, of course."

After her visit with Paul, Virginia headed over to Western Falls, the three stones still in her purse, something she was glad about. She and Paul had planned to meet the following Thursday before the group met and Virginia just couldn't wait to tell God all about it.

The Son met her at the front desk as usual.

"So, you're back," he said first. "And you seem unusually happy today," he added, grinning at her as if he already knew her secret; but of course, he already knew it.

"So, what do you think?" she asked.

"What do you think?" he offered.

"I think I may have just come onto something grand," she said, and the Son opened the door for her. She followed the path to the next door, enjoying the sound of birds through the windows, and taking in the sweet scent of the trees in the distance. The second door without the seam opened, and Virginia walked in. As usual, God was waiting for her and for the first time Virginia wondered how many others visited this place. She never saw anyone in the foyer, and, as far as she knew, she was the only one who visited. Her surroundings here were a far cry different from the surroundings she met up with when she arrived at the grocery store.

It provided her a way to begin the conversation: "So how come I'm the only one who ever visits you?" she asked. "You have other children."

"That's true," said God, standing. He directed her to the window. "And they come as well."

"But why is there never anyone out in the foyer, waiting?"

"I have time for all of my children. No one has to wait."

"But how can you do that? I mean there are thousands! Millions! Someone at some time needs to be waiting out in the foyer!"

Virginia felt her face flush.

"This may be another trust issue," said God. "I am here for all of my children whenever they need me."

"But what if they call on you at the same time?"

"Time…now that's a worldly issue. In the heavens there is no time."

Virginia gulped. "No…time?"

He took her hand. "I don't expect you to understand, but I do expect you to keep asking me questions." He smiled, taking her in. "How about that business idea you had?"

"Well, it's not completely formulated yet, but I have this idea about combining businesses with Paul."

"Paul, he's a good man. Do you like him?"

"He's nice enough. He's been out of work for over a year now and wants to combine his expertise in desserts with my…" It was there Virginia stopped. What was it that she was bringing into the picture?

"I think Paul's right about your 'get up and go' attitude. I also see something in the arena of classes to help folks think more positively about themselves and their lives…"

"But how does that meet up with desserts?"

"You might think this is a bit funny," said God, "but did you know that desserts spelled backwards is 'stressed'"? And did you know that many people come to me with this very issue on their plates? Every day there is a million somebody's that feel as if their life is too much to take, and they want me to take it all away."

"That would be nice."

"Most people think so, but if they really thought about it they'd realize that an easy life without trials, is a life not really worth living."

Virginia pondered on God's words. "So, there must be a purpose to our existence," Virginia said, "and our purpose has got to be unique to each of us."

"Why do you think that is?" asked God. He'd removed himself from the window and instructed her to take a seat.

Virginia sat and placed her purse on the floor. "Do you think that my work at the Regal Doughnut Factory, and not marrying yet, and buying my first house without a husband was really necessary to get me to where I am now?"

"What do you think?" asked God.

"Well, I have learned to be independent," Virginia said, placing her hands on the table and folding them together. "And being independent, I've learned about my gifts; if things had been easy for me I probably wouldn't have discovered them."

"You definitely wouldn't," replied God. "Stretching is important for all of my children. It's like this; I give my children determination to fulfill their purpose in life, but along with determination comes submission. Submission is what you do as you fulfill your purpose in life. You listen, you trust, you carry that optimism I have given you, and if you're especially smart you're tenacious in what you do. You never surrender. You never—give up.

"Tenacity. I have a feeling that tenacity is the next stone."

"You're right of course." God smiled, reached into the drawer, and handed Virginia the fourth stone. The stone was white like the first, but this one had writing on it—actually, the rock looked as though it was engraved. She touched the words across its surface: words like, "Keep Going," "Keep swimming," and "Keep Writing."

"Writing things down is important in remembering them and moving forward," God said. "A written word kept for all time, and perhaps even for eternity" (he winked at Virginia) "will help you to keep that tenacious spirit that Paul is always talking about."

"Paul?"

"You know, your friend."

"Oh."

God placed the white stone in her hand. "Remember I am here," said God. "Remember that you are my child and that I am here to help you through all of life's experiences."

The stone in Virginia's hand was warm with energy. If it had had legs it would have jumped from her hand and led her out the doors to the Son, but as she carried the stone home, Virginia couldn't help thinking about the power that it held. And she was more determined than ever to live her life full of purpose.

She placed the fourth white stone on her end table that night so that she'd remember to write, and during the day she carried the words within her purse along with the other stones. It just seemed the right thing to do.

Tenacity

At first, Virginia recorded her plans for the business, and she took notes when she and Paul met, but later the words written in her journal extended to her thoughts and dreams and wishes for her future. As she recorded her thoughts she often spoke to God and recorded the answers he gave her and in time Virginia realized that communication with God was actually a two-way fare. She would speak. He would listen. He would speak. She would listen. The importance of this revelation meant so much to Virginia that she thanked God every day.

She and Paul became great friends and fine business partners, but the day Paul asked her out on a date, Virginia wasn't at first sure what to do. She hadn't been on a date in at least five years! What would she possibly say and do? She'd felt so awkward on dates, almost as if she had to be someone she wasn't, to fit into the picture of dating. But this was a date with Paul! How hard could it be?

Virginia laughed at herself and reflected on the words of God: "Your birthright gives you ample opportunity to set out into the world and do all that will be required of you." The words gave her peace and Ms. Virginia Bean accepted the invitation.

But the date wasn't easy even though he'd brought along a single sunflower to "set the mood."

She spilled her water once and dropped spaghetti noodles and sauce on the linen tablecloth three times.

Paul laughed. "You're even funnier on a date," he said, as if spilling was now a part of her "funny" repertoire.

She smiled back, wishing she'd ordered something other than spaghetti. A piece of toast would have been nice.

"I don't want to talk about business tonight," said Paul, wiping his chin with a napkin. "I just figured it would be great to get to know you on a more personal basis."

"Personal?" The words croaked. He probably thought she was a giant frog.

"Yeah. Tell me more about yourself. What do you do for fun?"

The restaurant had an air of old-time Italian about it, almost like they'd left Idaho and traveled across the world to Italy. There was something about the atmosphere that felt good, almost relaxing, as if, in walking out the front door one would be right there. So why couldn't she stop dropping things?

Ms. Virginia Bean laughed. "You know," she said, thinking about the question Paul had asked that she didn't know how to answer, "I wouldn't be a bit surprised if I walked out the door right now to find something surprising on the other side."

"Like what?"

"Well, you know..." It was then Virginia realized that Paul didn't know that she had often stepped out of doors to find—what was Western Falls anyway but an otherworldly place? But she couldn't tell Paul about her visits with God, could she? She couldn't pull out the stones from her purse for some sort of proof that he existed, could she? The thought made her stomach turn and she felt the stone of trust warming inside her purse.

What would God want her to do?

The answer was easy.

"Do you believe in prayer?" she asked.

She could see Paul swallowing hard. "Yeah," he mumbled, "why do you ask?"

"I believe in prayer," Virginia said, stroking her linen napkin like a small pup. "And I believe we can get answers." She looked over at Paul. He wasn't smiling. Instead, there was a look of recognition in his eyes.

"I'm glad you told me," he said. "I haven't always prayed..." He hesitated as if trying to figure out what to say next, "but I know it works like you said."

"What do you think about faith?"

"You've got to have it to know that God answers you," Paul said. He looked past her to something far beyond, and then his brown eyes refocused on hers. It was the first time Virginia had noticed the color of his eyes; the color of optimism.

Following dessert (chocolate layered cake with fudge icing) she and Paul took a walk and he thanked her for opening up and sharing her heart. She thanked him as well—something miraculous had happened on this first date, and she had a wonderful feeling that God had something to do with it.

As she sat in her room with her stones laid out on her bed, Virginia Bean, a.k.a. Pure Daughter, thought about the conversation she'd had with Paul. No, she hadn't mentioned her personal visit with God or the stones, but there had been a connection that Virginia couldn't possibly deny.

The following morning Virginia left her home and went to visit God at Western Falls. Once there, the Son took her aside. "I'm happy for your success," he said. "And I see that you've been journaling."

"Who knows, maybe it will hang on for eternity," Virginia said, smiling.

The Son took her in his arms and they embraced. Ms. Virginia Bean couldn't deny the warmth and light penetrating her heart. It was as if she'd been transported to heaven while still remaining on earth. The Son's white robe brushed against the shining floor as he led her to the first door.

"I am so pleased with your success," he said again.

Virginia was pleased too. As she walked through the first door and on to the second, she thought about the Son and his special role in her life. She thought about the door without even a crease, without even a doorknob and she was glad that the Son had the power to open it. But then Virginia thought of something else. It was her desire to learn more by following the Son that she'd been able to get through the door in the first place. She thought about his role as the winepress and thought about what that had always meant in her life, even when she hadn't been consciously aware of it.

"Thank you," she offered, before the second door opened.

God was sitting at his desk. He smiled over at her. "Hello, Pure Daughter," he said.

"Hello, God." It was the first time she'd used God's name out loud and the sound of it brought unmistakable warmth to her mind and heart. She thought she climbed to a high mountain and could feel the breeze and the caressing way that the branches from the trees played against the sky.

"Please, sit," he said.

Virginia sat, and placed her purse on the floor. "Am I ready for another stone?" she asked.

"Not quite," said God. "There's something you need to do first."

"Do?" asked Virginia Bean.

"Things are going to get tough for Paul," God said, "so tough that you're going to want to leave him."

"Leave him?"

God took her hands. "He's been on a similar path," he said.

"You mean he's been talking to you too?"

"Does that surprise you?"

"Well, yes, and no," Virginia said, placing her hands together on the table. "Paul seems more assured, more confident than me. You know, when we talked about prayer he only hesitated once in his sharing with me. After that, it was smooth sailing."

"But the sailing is going to get rocky," he said.

"What's going to happen?"

"I can't tell you that but be assured that you are the woman to help him."

Virginia's heart burned. "What if I mess up?" she asked.

"You will use prayer and scripture study and journaling to get you through this, and you will help Paul to see that through listening, trust, optimism and tenacity even his life can be a life full of purpose."

Virginia opened her purse. She placed the four smooth stones on God's magnificent desk, for suddenly she could see a bright light within the white wood.

"You must trust me on this," said God. "You must not lose hope; your optimism must shine through the barriers presented to you, you must be determined in your mind and heart that this is your purpose as well as the purpose for Paul."

Tears fell down Virginia's cheeks. She felt lost and shy as if God wasn't with her at all. "What's going to happen to him?" she cried. But God said nothing and so Ms. Virginia Bean looked down at the stones for answers. Nothing came, so she gathered them in her hands and replaced them inside her purse. When she looked up, God was gone.

Virginia drove home in her old car and once there called Paul.

"Hi!" he said cheerfully, "reneging on our second date?"

He'd asked her out to a movie; some "romantic thing" that would "take her breath away," he said, and she'd been excited to go; but not now.

"No, nothing like that," she said. "Is everything all right?" she asked.

The phone was silent for a moment. "Well, yeah," he said cheerfully, "why do you ask?"

"No reason."

"Then you're still up for Friday night? I can splurge for a dollar show at the Cineplex."

She smiled, though he couldn't see it. "I'll be ready."

"Did you just want to hear my voice, is that why you called?" he asked.

"Sure," she answered, though the worrisome words of God still tumbled in her mind.

***

She didn't like the movie. It was too gushy and too unbelievable. What was romance anyway but a way of getting men to do something they didn't really want to do? Virginia regretted her thoughts the moment she thought them.

Paul was different. He treated her as an equal and wanted to hear her opinions and thus far hadn't fussed about anything romantic other than the sunflower that kept popping up whenever she saw him. But when they got to her door he leaned forward to kiss her and she let him. The feeling was good and transported Ms. Virginia Bean far away from her front door. Was she falling in love with Paul? Perhaps God was wrong about her wanting to leave Paul because right now she wanted to do just the opposite.

But a week later Paul called her on the phone and he sounded different, almost too quiet.

"How is the business plan coming?" he asked.

"Great! It's almost done and I can't wait for you to see it!"

There was a pause on the other end. "I've been thinking, maybe it would be a good idea to get you practiced up on doughnut making…"

"I thought you were going to do that."

There was another pause. "It might be a good idea to have you learn a bit, just in case."

"In case of what, bad weather?"

Paul laughed. "I just think it might help both of us if you knew how to cook."

"So, I don't know how to cook now, is that it?"

Paul was silent again, and Virginia thought about all of the real reasons Paul would want her to learn to cook. The only one that made any sense was that he wasn't going to follow through on their partnership after all.

"Are you having second thoughts about our business?" she asked.

Another hesitation. "Oh, no, no. Can I come over today for a first lesson?"

"Sure."

"How's 1:00?"

"Why don't you come for lunch? I can prove to you that I can cook and you can let go of the idea that I have to learn how to make doughnuts."

"Sounds good; but I'll bring my supplies just in case."

In the end Ms. Virginia Bean had fixed tuna sandwiches and tomato soup for lunch, something she couldn't mess up, and Paul had taught her how to make doughnuts. By evening, her counter was filled with a variety of doughnuts; chocolate, sprinkled, even jelly filled.

"What are we going to do with all of these doughnuts?" Virginia asked.

"I've already thought of that," said Paul. "Let's distribute them around the neighborhood with our new business cards."

Virginia had received the new cards just yesterday; they were glorious things that made a person feel more like eating the card than anything else. "Stressed? Come and get your just Desserts," the card read. A luscious looking doughnut was on the front and on the back the contact information was displayed in glittering pink.

They'd decided to start the classes in Virginia's home and as the interest grew, so would the space. Although Paul's name was on the card as partner, it was Virginia's address that became their new place of business—at least for now.

By late that evening the doughnuts with their respective cards were ready. Paul left her home with a promise to call her in the morning for delivery. But the following morning, Paul didn't call, and so Virginia called him. He didn't answer. She tried him again at noon and again and 2:00 p.m. When he still didn't answer, Virginia grew worried and drove over to his house.

On the way over, her car stalled. She'd been having trouble with it off and on for weeks, but now the thing wouldn't budge. She called a tow truck and the car was wheeled off to the nearest repair shop. She was only two blocks away from Paul's by then and walked the rest of the way over.

She knocked. His car was in the driveway but he didn't answer the door. The door was beautiful; it was painted a burgundy pink and there were sunflowers growing near both sides of the doorframe. The flowers reached almost to the windows.

The words of God entered her heart: "The sailing is going to get rocky."

She felt like she should walk over to the neighbor's house. It was the stone of listening. A woman answered. She was petite and a small child was hanging onto her left pant leg.

"Hi," she said, "I'm a friend of Paul and…"

"Are you Virginia?" the woman asked.

Virginia nodded, taking in the woman's brown hair and hazel eyes.

"He was on his way out to the car this afternoon, said he had overslept, said you two had a great business going and he wanted to get to your place so you could get started on your deliveries…" The woman took a deep breath as the little girl clung to her leg. "He fell right there in the yard. I was with June and he just collapsed! I called the police and the ambulance came. He…he left just a few minutes ago…"

"Is he okay? I mean, do you know what's wrong?"

"I have no idea," said the woman who had never introduced herself. "One minute he was talking to me, the next, he was on the sidewalk. But I have one of his extra car keys…" She raced into the house. "Here," she said," handing the single key on a ring to her. "I didn't see that you had a car."

"It's…what hospital is he at?"

"St. Joseph's. I'm so sorry," the woman added, picking up the little girl.

Virginia thanked her and ran to Paul's car. It was in pristine condition; even the driving wheel looked polished, but all Virginia could think about was Paul. What had happened to him? She tried not to worry too much—the stone of trust was still in her purse—but the thought of him at the hospital begin to fill her mind with fear. How could she trust God now, when the only man she had ever loved might die?

At the hospital, Virginia discovered from a nurse that Paul had had a heart attack, but it didn't make sense—she didn't learn about the heart murmur until later. In moments she was with God in her mind and she had a myriad of questions to ask him, like, "Why him?" and "Why now?" And "Why me?"

She'd never been in love before. Did God care about her at all?

Paul had been moved out of intensive care and was in one of the recovery rooms near the east end. When she came through the silver door he had his eyes closed and she could tell that he was breathing by the rise and fall of his chest. A white sheet covered his body, and his head and arms were exposed, but his left arm was hooked to a machine. It bleeped numbers that Virginia couldn't begin to understand. The air felt sick, almost as if the regular stuff had been mismanaged somehow, and Paul was getting the stuff that came cheaper.

She sat on the chair next to him and placed the four smooth stones (the second stone was gray and the veins of optimism were as cloudy as her thoughts) on his end table next to his water. The call button and the light were currently off, but it was early yet. She waited until almost 6 p.m. and voiced her concerns about Paul's health to the nurse that frequented the room.

When his eyes finally opened she was holding the rock of listening.

"Hi," he said drowsily. "I'm sorry."

"So am I; the doughnuts are probably going stale on my counter." She wiped at her eyes hoping he hadn't seen the tears that had accumulated.

He smiled, though his eyes smiled more than his lips. "I guess you heard," he added.

She nodded.

"So, what do we do now?"

"Punt, I guess." He reached for her hand; she took his in hers and thought about their last date and the sweet kiss and the many things she'd already learned from him about doughnut making."

"You're a sweet man," she said.

And he smiled back.

"I want you to practice," he said. "I have all of my dessert recipes to the right of the sink. I want you to keep practicing until you have doughnut making down pat."

"But you'll be here to help me."

"I might not."

"You have to be here! We have a business to run!"

He smiled at her wearily and kissed her hand slowly, the warmth of his lips traveling up her arm and to her heart.

She stayed with him until he fell back asleep, grabbed some late dinner in the hospital cafeteria, and returned to the room. She slept in a chair the entire night, and the next morning had a crick in her neck the size of Alaska. Her legs felt stiff and she felt more miserable than she ever remembered. But she loved him.

His eyes were already open. "I've been watching you," he said.

She blushed.

"You're beautiful when you're asleep," he said.

"As opposed to when I'm awake," she teased.

"Even then. Come closer, I want to talk to you."

She didn't want to come closer. She was afraid. But he was looking at the stones now and probably wanted some sort of explanation. How could she explain what the last few weeks had meant to her; to be with God, to hear his voice, to follow his direction? He would probably think she was crazy, she laughed silently to herself, well, he already thought that...

"So, what about these rocks?" he asked.

Her hands trembled.

"Actually, they're stones," she said, and then she remembered what God had told her about Paul meeting with him just as she had been doing. So, he had to know about the stones!

"The first one is listening. God gave it to me when I began searching for a new job."

"I didn't know stones had names," Paul said.

"And the second is trust."

"Trust in what?"

"Actually, it's trust in God."

"And the third?" He was grinning at her in a funny way and Virginia felt a bit uncomfortable. She could hear the moaning and ticking of the machines as she looked into Paul's eyes. What was he trying to tell her?

"Optimism."

"Wow! And to think all of this time I thought you were being optimistic on your own."

"That's not funny."

"So...what's the last...stone?"

"It's tenacity and it's not the last stone it's..."

"How many stones are there?"

"Just one more."

He laughed. "Of all the hair brained things I've ever heard, this one takes the cake, Virginia. You are a hoot! I was wondering how you were going to cheer me up, but I could have never thought up this!"

Virginia was silent as she looked down on him.

"Well?" His eyes took on a hazy look almost as if he was only partially with her.

"Well, nothing! I was serious, do you understand? These, these stones are important to me!" She left his side and walked to the window. She couldn't believe she had told him, and she couldn't believe he hadn't believed her. A joke? How could he think that she'd joke with him at a time like this? And then another thought entered Virginia's heart. She was always joking, why not now?

"I'm sorry," she said, and turned to face him, but Paul's eyes were already closed. In moments his breathing grew heavy and Virginia knew he was asleep. But she didn't care suddenly about anything. She turned again to the window. It was the middle of July, almost a year following the loss of her job at Regal, and it was raining.

***

The next morning Virginia tore off all of the business cards from the doughnut gifts and visited her neighbors without the cards. Some had heard about Paul and they offered her comfort. Others seemed pleased that she was offering them a gift when it was she that needed one. By noon, every doughnut had been distributed, and Virginia sunk down in her black leather couch to rest.

That's when she saw the hole.

She'd forgotten all about the hole but it was still there. She bent to touch the burnt fabric and leaned in closer so that she could see to the floor. Funny, she'd never replaced the orange shag carpet and it glared up at her through the hole as if trying to tell her something—maybe to cheer up—or get it replaced. It was a fuzzy blob and all Virginia could think about was the fuzzy mess she'd gotten herself into.

It was dinner time when Virginia remembered that God had warned her about leaving Paul and that he needed her now, and hadn't God said something about she being the only one?

The rain had stopped and, in its place, fresh air and clean streets. But Ms. Virginia Bean didn't pick up the stones; she went to the hospital without them. She couldn't see the stone of trust anyway. She smiled weakly thinking of God

77

holding it. "I'm going," she said to him, though she was still in the car, "I'm going."

When she got to the hospital, Paul was gone.

"His father came to get him," said a nurse.

Virginia returned to Paul's home only to see a vacant driveway. She parked and walked up to the sunflowers. Somehow, they'd grown a few feet since her last visit and now reached the top of the roof. Strange, Virginia thought as she knocked on the door.

When no one answered, Ms. Virginia Bean tried the handle. The door was not locked and so she walked in. She'd never been inside Paul's house before and was intrigued with the waterfall in the corner and the sunflowers gathered in almost every room. The smell of freshly baked doughnuts wafted from the kitchen.

She peeked around the corner, but she didn't see Paul; it was God.

"It's amazing how doughnuts can enliven a perfectly stressful day," said God. "You wouldn't believe all the folks asking me to fix things for them, as if I don't help them already."

"God?"

"Hello, Virginia. I thought you might need me today."

Virginia's heart pounded. "For what?" she asked.

"Paul will be dying soon."

Virginia didn't say anything else. She raced to Paul's room. The door was open and sunflowers were blooming everywhere, even on the window sill and clothes hamper in the corner. Paul opened his eyes and looked at her. "So, you forgive me?" he asked.

"Of course." The words sounded froglike but she didn't care.

"Come and sit by me," he said.

Virginia sat but the words didn't come. Paul's face was pale, his movements slow. "Sorry about what I said. I was just jealous."

"About what?"

"All I got were these stupid sunflowers." He hesitated, and then smiled. "I knew the stones when I saw them that they had been some communication from God as the sunflowers have been for me. I'm not sure how I knew, I just knew."

"So, what do the sunflowers represent?" Virginia asked.

"I have known for a long time that I was going to die," Paul said, "but I haven't always made the best of life. When I met you, I thought God had changed his mind, that somehow, he would spare me because of you. But I don't think that's the plan."

"I don't care about the plan."

"Well, you should," said Paul, "God must care about you very much to give you those stones. Imagine having a gift like that to take you through your life. I'm ready now."

She touched his hair.

And so, Virginia taught Paul, the man she'd grown to love with all her heart, what she had learned from the stones that God had given her. She told him about the first time she'd entered Western Falls, about her meeting up with the Son and how God had instructed her in the ways of the stones. When she finished, Paul asked, "Did you say, Western Falls? I know that place!"

Virginia rolled her eyes. "Of course, you do! It's where we both met with God."

Paul wiped a white hand against his forehead.

"Would you like some water?" she asked. It was then that Virginia noticed the bottled water sitting on the end table: "Western Falls," it read. She picked it up. "Well, I'll be!" she said, turning it around to read the back label.

"I could use a drink," said Paul.

Virginia opened the lid and leaned closer to Paul. The clear liquid reached his lips and he slowly drank. When he was finished, Virginia continued to study the label.

"This looks like normal bottled water to me," she said.

"That's why I find it strange that you met with God at the Western Falls bottling plant."

"So where did you meet up with God?"

"At Richard's Grocers. You know the one."

"On North Shore Main?"

"Yeah, that's the one. I found God first when I purchased a Bible. I read his words and I began praying. I had very little hope then; I sort of drifted. I knew as a boy that my heart was weak and as I grew older things just got worse. When I met you, I thought, maybe God won't take me yet. I was filled with so much optimism! I thought God couldn't possibly take me now!"

Virginia noticed that Paul's eyes were glistening wet and she knew hers were following a close second. She thought about the stones and how they mirrored just what Paul had been going through.

"You were such a go-getter!" Paul continued. "When you set up that Thursday business meeting I thought, maybe I shouldn't give up. The first time I saw you my thoughts were confirmed; I knew that you wouldn't steer me wrong. When you asked me about joining you in your business, I could hardly believe my great luck! And then I thought of God. I had to thank him, and so I did. But the answer was the same that I didn't have much longer. By this time, I was not only praying and reading my scriptures but the sunflowers kept growing like wildfire! You should have seen me trying to explain them to my neighbors this last winter!"

"They grew in winter?"

"My neighbor, Ann, thought I was the next best thing to the gardener club! She was always over here picking sunflowers for her dinner table, to take for the next family event, to bring to a sick loved one or a neighbor. Her little boy had died and it was all she could do to keep going…and then the sunflowers came. Many of the neighbors would look at me strange; others would say they were fake flowers that I had stuck in the ground and that I was trying to prove something. Now that's its summer, the talk has diminished…"

"But what do the sunflowers mean?" The question was burning on Ms. Virginia Beans lips.

"Flowers die, and I think what God was trying to tell me was that I would die too, but not now. Keep moving forward," he seemed to be saying. "Keep growing!" "You didn't hear him?"

"Not really. But I could feel his words."

"But I have talked with God," she finally said, "I have heard his voice."

"I know that too. What a great blessing!"

"So, you haven't actually talked with God?"

"Well, sure. I have prayed and have felt good as I have done so. I have felt good about the direction I have taken in my life, about meeting you, I know that it was God's will. I think you just scared me a little when you began to speak of the rocks, I mean stones, as if they'd actually spoken to you."

Her hand was moist; he'd been holding it for some time. Now he let it go. "I am no longer afraid. I know now that you talk with God and its okay for me to die."

"Did you know that God's in your kitchen?" she asked. By the look in his eyes, Paul seemed more than surprised. "Maybe he can come in right now and heal you! What about that?"

"God, he's in the kitchen?"

Virginia stood. "I'll prove it to you," she said. Paul blinked.

But when Ms. Virginia Bean reached the kitchen, God wasn't there. There were plenty of doughnuts, however. They filled every counter, every table, every surface that a doughnut could grace; even on the chairs that were usually reserved for sitting. Those, God had covered with plastic wrap.

Virginia was momentarily taken back; she was even a bit angry. And then she realized it didn't really matter anyway. She could prove that God was here just by showing Paul the doughnuts!

Virginia felt a light in her heart that was brighter than anything she had felt before; a light that was brighter than the stone of listening, brighter than the black and white stone of trust, the brown stone of optimism or the glittering veins of tenacity.

Paul laughed. "I can't believe you did this!" he exclaimed. "We must package these up and you must get this other batch out! Just leave me in the car, I can watch from the window!"

"What?" she gasped.

"Come on! It's the least you can do for me after stealing my car!"

"Stealing your car?"

"I'm kidding! I'm glad you borrowed it; after I'm dead, it's yours!"

"Come on, Paul."

"Well, if I hadn't already taught you how to make doughnuts I would have believed that God had made each and every one of these!" He grinned, walking wearily to a kitchen chair. "But since you've obviously had time to practice...Can you get this off of here so that I can sit down?"

The pan's plastic wrap was removed and Ms. Virginia Bean tried to explain. "Really, Paul, God was here! Here! He made all of these doughnuts for us!"

"And why would God do that?" Paul asked. "Isn't he too busy answering everyone's prayers?"

"Yes! That's why he was here! Besides, he was the one who brought you home from the hospital!"

Paul hesitated. "You mean the guy in the fishing hat? I wondered who he was."

"And you went with him anyway, you're crazy!"

"Evidently not if you're telling me he's God." He reached for her. His arms felt warm and humbling at the same time. "Do you know you're the greatest person I have ever known?" As he held her, Virginia cried, but her tears weren't for what he'd told her, they were for what she was going to lose.

***

The doughnut delivery was a success, and Ms. Virginia Bean opened her new business two months later. The only problem was that there was just not enough space to hold the classes.

Paul was with her for an additional four months. He traveled with her as she delivered doughnuts; sat near her while she cooked and attended her classes when she taught. By the end of the sixth month since the unwelcome news had met her ears, Paul passed on. He was in the car and they were delivering desserts to the next neighborhood and nearby businesses. She looked over because the pan of freshly baked jelly doughnuts had suddenly toppled to the floor.

"Paul?" she asked, but he was already gone.

A year later, the tallest sunflowers by the front porch near Paul's door had grown as tall as the trees. A new family of children had moved into the house; members of his extended family, and there was no stopping the flowers' growth. Ms. Virginia Bean hadn't seen Western Falls for a long while, but she still spoke to God and her prayers were still answered. She gloried in those things she learned and shared those things that God wished her to share. She was never alone and knew that Paul was happy.

And then one day while delivering to Richard's Grocery, she spied a familiar face staring at her from across the bakery counter.

"Don't I know you?" the man asked.

"You look familiar," said Ms. Virginia Bean.

And suddenly the man reached under the counter and grabbed something. He stood, and leaning over the bakery counter, handed it over to her. It was a stone—a clear stone without mark or color or blemish. "I am so glad to see you again," he said. "You wouldn't believe the trouble I've had trying to hide this rock from my customers' prying eyes."

When Virginia looked over at him with concern, he winked at her. "I was the man you met at Western Falls. I worked there."

"You what?"

"You're going to think this strange, but this elderly man wearing a flannel shirt and brown corduroy's, he asked me if I could get this to you."

She waited.

"He was dressed for winter even though it was summer, and he handed me this rock. He said, 'Now when you see Virginia, I want you to give her this stone. I want you to tell her that the stone's name is Constancy, and that's she's to carry it throughout her life along with the other stones she's received.' Have you ever heard such a strange thing?"

Virginia smiled, unmistakable warmth flowing through her. He hadn't forgotten. "Anything else?" she asked.

"Well, I remember when you came in that day for an interview, and…excuse me for being so blunt…I noticed how beautiful you looked and I was hoping to see you again…and so when the man in the corduroys offered me the rock and told me to hold it for you, that you'd be by…"

Virginia was still smiling.

"Well, I held onto it. With this note."

He reached over the counter and handed her a note sealed in a crisp, white envelope. Virginia turned it over to discover a golden seal on the back. "What do you think it says?" the man asked.

"Well, I think it must be good news."

"That's good." The man continued to stare at her.

"But I have one question," said Ms. Virginia Bean, "I thought Western Falls was at this location, what I mean to say is…"

"Well, of course one business had to burn down first for the second to be built," said the man. "I had no idea what

I was going to do for a new job. It was the strangest thing, a bottled water company burning down, but one morning, I got up to go to work and the place looked like my grandmother's drawing room."

"Your grandmother's what?"

"She smoked cigars, and when I was a kid, we found the drawing room burnt to smithereens—grandma was safe in another room, of course."

"Of course. And so, you built this place?"

"Why sure, it's been here for over a year."

"Over a year?"

"Yeah. What do you think?"

Virginia looked around. She saw what she had always seen, with one exception. "Where does that door lead?" she asked, "the one to the right side of the counter there?"

The man smiled. For the first time Virginia noticed his badge: "Richard Stone—Owner."

"Let me show you," he said. "Come this way."

She followed Richard to the door. "It's funny," he said, looking into her eyes. "Most people don't notice the door here without the handle. It's a great place to come and hide when you need to."

The door opened with a push of a small button under the counter and Virginia followed Richard inside, the stone in one hand and the letter from God in the other. The doughnuts had already been shelved by Richard. Although white tables and chairs were placed strategically throughout the room there were many windows that overlooked the garden. She could see large trees in the distance and could hear the voices of birds.

A lone tear escaped her left eye.

"It's beautiful," she said.

"Western Falls had a place like this," he said now, taking her closer to the window. "And when the place burnt down I suggested that we rebuild the area. We've just been looking for a replacement, someone who can be trained in doughnut making. I'm just helping out until then."

A replacement? Now Virginia was silent. How could she tell the man that she was just the woman he needed? Had the old baker told him anything about her?

"Where's Frank?" she asked.

"He decided to retire, can you believe it? I wondered how I was going to get the stone to you—all I knew was your first name—but then I discovered that you were one of our doughnut vendors. A few days before Frank left us he let me in on his little secret. We already have a large vendor, but he'd been secretly taking in your doughnuts for a couple of months without my approval."

Virginia's heart stopped. "I'm sorry…" she said.

"Don't be sorry, I'm not," Richard finished. "I don't know how the man in the corduroys knew that you owned Just Desserts, or how I would be building a new business…maybe he burnt the place down…or how you'd find me…" Richard smiled, small dimples caressing his cheeks. "But he knew you'd be coming."

She blushed. "Tell me, what usually occurs in this room?"

Now it was his turn to color. "It's a quiet place. I use it mostly for reflection, although some of the employees that know about it tell me it's a wasted piece of space. But I don't think so." His face glowed as he said the words. "Are you all right?"

Virginia had been daydreaming—how long she had no idea. The thought of her dream coming true in just such a place where she'd spoken with God made her throat tighten up and tears well in her eyes. But how could she tell Richard? How could she not tell Richard? How could she not share with him at least her desire?

Placing the last stone in her purse along with the letter, Ms. Virginia Bean a.k.a. Pure Daughter of the Birthright walked even closer to the windows. She touched the glass of one pane with her hands and felt the power of God as the warmth caressed her fingertips—and she listened. She trusted God more now than she ever believed possible, and she was optimistic that her next words would be received with gladness. She would not hesitate now, couldn't hesitate now. It was her greatest desire to live in constancy—to be constant in her desires to serve God and those around her. And in return, her dream would finally be realized.

She turned to Richard. He was a tall man with wispy blond hair the color of sunflower petals and blue eyes that spoke to Virginia of the sky. All the talking had stopped. Instead, Richard stood waiting, as if somehow, he'd been made aware that something important was going to happen— something that was going to change her life as well as his. And it was as if, in that very moment, God stood watching.

She couldn't see him with her eyes, but Virginia knew.

Constancy

My Dear Virginia,

     I'm sorry I couldn't deliver the stone of constancy to you personally, but I know that you'll understand when I tell you that receiving this particular stone from my son Richard was the better solution.

     Constancy is an important stone. The clear stone will help you remember what matters most. If you spend time with me in the morning and take me with you through your day you'll find that when problems come up they will be easier to handle—they'll be clearer to your eyes and heart.

     Constancy is that true grit that holds everything you have learned together; it keeps you close to me and allows for growth.

     As always, know that I love you. You are my child and I am here for you. Remember that my words will never end and that you will continue to receive from me as you continue to listen, trust in me, have an optimistic heart, keep determined in your tenacity and constant in your direction. Remember that David had to practice at stone throwing; he wasn't an instant expert, and I don't expect anything less from you.

To aid you in remembrance of your duty, I have included with this letter a quick guide. Use it every day to remember what you've learned.

I look forward to seeing you again when you pass from this world to the next. No, I won't tell you when that is; but know that the moment has been chosen especially for you. Until then, remember me as I remember you.

Your Loving Father,

Conquering your Goliaths—a Spiritual Guide

LISTENING

❖ Things are not always as they appear.

❖ Silence is the question, listening is the answer. We all need a room of light where we can see and hear.

❖ You are beloved. Knowing you are a pure daughter (or son) of the birthright gives you ample opportunity to set out into the world and to do all that will be required of you. Your birthright is a gift. It's at the heart of a successful life.

❖ Daily prayer, scripture study and journaling will help you to listen and to keep listening.

❖ I will wait until you're ready to hear.

❖ Focusing on heavenly pursuits will keep you away from distraction and forgetfulness.

❖ Questions bring answers.

❖ The knowledge of specific words from the scriptures will increase your understanding of life.

❖ Conversations travel both ways.

❖ Do what is right; the money will follow.

❖ The stone of listening is best carried in your heart.

- Your given name is important to who you are as a spiritual being.
- Death is necessary. Atonement is the gift of life.
- Repentance and forgiveness are necessary for
- continued healing.

- TRUST
- Our thoughts create a negative or a positive reaction.
- Research precedes knowledge.
- Strength comes from reaching out to others.
- A righteous life is not always an easy life. Slumps in life will happen.
- Trusting in me always trumps trusting in yourself.
- Reflection is key to remembering. Review what you have learned by writing it down.
- Trust comes slowly and will be stronger at certain times in your life than others.
- You are never alone.
- Overcome by doing.
- Timing is everything.
- Turning to me lightens the load.
- Spiritual truths hidden are uncovered through time.
- Trust your past; use it to improve your future.
- The future isn't always clear.
- Take me with you everywhere.
- I know everything; you don't need to hide your mistakes.
- Anger causes the windows of revelation to close.
- What is lost can be found again.

OPTIMISM
- ❖ Look at your life with optimistic eyes.
- ❖ Take the initiative. Begin something new.
- ❖ Some things need to be let go of to make room for better things.
- ❖ Use your talents. Love what you do. Get my help.
- ❖ Work with someone else. Brainstorm your ideas.
- ❖ Don't let fear stop you.
- ❖ I always have time to listen.
- ❖ If something is difficult, do it anyway.
- ❖ There is a purpose to your existence.

- ❖ TENACITY
- ❖ Keep writing. Keep praying. Keep reading.
- ❖ It's important to share your faith in me.
- ❖ Spiritual success is a rewarding journey.
- ❖ Everyone has their own road to travel.
- ❖ I work in mysterious ways so be open to them.

- ❖ CONSTANCY
- ❖ Remember what matters most.
- ❖ Constancy is the grit that holds everything together.
- ❖ Constancy keeps you growing.
- ❖ Constancy takes practice.

Kathryn Elizabeth Jones

Notes

Notes

Kathryn Elizabeth Jones

Notes

THE FEAST

ACKNOWLEDGMENT

To my husband: The bearer of many gifts including the nudge that this book needed to be written.

Preface

In *Conquering Your Goliaths: A Parable of the Five Stones*, Ms. Virginia Bean meets God and through the five stones: **Listening, Trust, Optimism, Tenacity** and **Constancy**, she learns a few things. About herself. About her relationship with God. About her relationship with others.

Listening teaches Virginia how to keep still long enough to listen to God.

She Learns to **trust** in God always, even if she doesn't agree.

Optimism keeps her thinking positive no matter what she faces.

And **Tenacity** plays a big factor in moving her forward despite the obstacles.

Constancy, well, let's just say that it teaches her the importance of walking with God always. In good times and in bad.

Consider that even in the best of circumstances and the most difficult of trials, a person has a way of drifting away from the source of all happiness.

Like now, for example.

The End

Her marriage with Richard was over. This was something Virginia knew for sure. She also knew she must have imagined the stones' supreme power and her awakening with God.

As she sat on the couch that still sported a hole large enough for a rock to pass through, she smiled at it sadly, touched the worn fibers of the cloth filling its gap and thought of Richard and how much she missed him. She thought of her life, alone again, without a husband, without a child.

They'd been married five years and during that time Virginia had used the stones and what they represented in her life with Richard. He'd agreed that they held a power, and they'd displayed them on the mantel for all to see.

Except the stones hadn't given them a child, and after three years of relentless doctor visits, tests and more tests, Virginia was tired of it all and Richard was gone.

He said he loved her. She said she loved him, but without a child their marriage seemed a void, a mistake. She thought of Richard, imagined him alone in a hotel room outside of town. It was winter and the air was bitter, icy and dry to her skin. Her skin felt like sandpaper and her throat practically closed off at night as she breathed in the stagnant air.

Just like her life.

Virginia walked to the bedroom and to her side of the bed. A tear dropped onto her pillow. The side next to hers still held Richard's pillow. She reached for it and pushed it against her chest, breathing in the scent of him, sort of an Irish Spring with a smattering of spruce.

It was the trees he loved best, and they'd spent many days following their wedding hiking the mountains and sitting next to plants and communicating with them.

It didn't seem so natural now, but then, right after she'd discovered it, it was like the power of the stones enveloped everything and everyone she knew. At the wedding, long lost friends and family who never dreamed she'd wed, and even the flowers and other natural growth near the lake, breathed in their love and she could feel their presence.

She knew God was there. She'd felt him too. In the days following her wedding she hoped he'd come to her again or direct her to meet with him, but he never did. The stones sat on the mantel, and although she was reminded of their glow or colors from time to time, life caught up with her and her business began growing faster than she could keep up with it.

Just Desserts. Using Richard's place, a log cabin built only 10 minutes from the city, she'd grown her business both in clientele and opportunity. Many people taking her awakening courses had found their lives improved and their own businesses and personal life, soaring.

But the fights and lonely nights without Richard had finally taken its toll. He hadn't returned and it had been a week.

She dared not teach, for in teaching she would see him. And so, she'd cancelled her classes and hired a runner to take what she had baked from home to Richard's place on the corner of *North Shore* and *Main*. Though she'd done plenty of baking there since meeting Richard, now it just seemed awkward.

What would she do now?

She stood and reached for the white stone but as she stood there, feeling the veins in the rock's surface, it didn't speak to her. She wanted to hold the black rock, but hesitated. No, she'd leave it there. She wouldn't reach for the other rocks, she couldn't.

All was lost.

The Ring

Richard had never loved a woman as much as he loved Virginia, her weirdness included. He'd accepted the five stones, had lived with her desires to be perfect, had even helped her work through the pains of her doubting heart, but the one thing that they lacked together had reached forth its tentacles and pierced his soul as well as hers.

Why wouldn't God allow them to have a child?

The doughnuts had arrived again in perfect order, though he knew that his wife was faring much worse. Her classes cancelled, folks coming to the bakery had dwindled until even the bakery sales hadn't given them a reason to return.

He couldn't reach her. Heck, he couldn't reach himself. God had brought them together, he knew that. As he stood in the center of the room where he'd first gotten a glimpse of her, the stirring returned. Tears welled in his eyes as he thought of her standing by the window. He could almost see her, could almost hear the doves in the distance, but the windows were iced over and the room felt too heated, too dark.

He turned when he heard the bell.

An old man stood before him.

"What would you like today, Sir?" he asked.

The old man shifted his shoulders. He wore a black and white checkered shirt, corduroy pants the color of wet dirt and a fishing cap.

"My wi...I mean these doughnuts are terrific," Richard said when the man said nothing.

"What makes them terrific?" The man leaned closer to the counter and took a deep sniff. "It's hard to smell them through the glass."

Richard tried not to smirk. The man must be deranged or something.

"Do you like chocolate?"

The old man touched his white beard. "I like chocolate."

The man was silent for some time and it seemed to Richard that he was looking at each doughnut individually, sort of examining each one with his eyes. Virginia had not only made chocolate but chocolate with sprinkles and the heavy duty filled kind. Today there was raspberry, lemon and meringue.

"What do you think of the colors?" the old man asked. "Does the color of the doughnut make it taste better?"

Richard thought the question odd. It was like asking if a brown doughnut was better than a pink, frosted one. "Do you have a favorite color?" he asked.

"I like all colors," said the man.

Richard wondered if the old man was just speaking about doughnuts. Just then a young girl came up to the counter. "I want a cupcake," she said.

The old man smiled. "You'd better get her that cupcake. I can wait."

Richard walked over to help the young girl. She was a tiny thing, probably only five or six. "Where's your mother?" he asked first.

"Down that way." The girl pointed in the direction of the dairy department.

"Would you rather have a doughnut?" he asked. Virginia hadn't delivered any cupcakes today and he was out.

The girl peered inside the glass. "The pink one with the diamond in it," she said.

Richard smiled, he couldn't help it. The young girl had cheered him up. Unfortunately, there wasn't a cupcake with a diamond in it.

"I'm sorry..." he began, but the girl was pointing. "There, in the corner."

Sure enough, when Richard looked to the corner of the case he could see something glittering a- top a bright pink cupcake. He reached inside the case and pulled it out. The ring was fake but it still glittered against the countertop glass.

"That's it!" squealed the girl, reaching for the bobble. She took the cupcake from his hands. He could see her pulling the ring from the pink frosting and licking it off. He thought of pink, the typical favorite color for a girl, and watched the young girl until she was out of sight. Hopefully with her mother, he thought. But when he turned to help the old man he was no longer there.

Richard thought more about the pink cupcake with the ring on it that night at the hotel. He wondered where it had come from and hoped the little girl had been safe in eating the cupcake. He decided to call Virginia.

"So, you say that I must have made some pink cupcakes?" she asked.

Richard nodded, though his wife couldn't see the gesture. "Yes," he added wearily into the phone. "You must have made some, I'm just having a difficult time remembering."

"But I haven't made cupcakes for at least...oh, two months or so. They sell better when it's warm out. Are you taking in a new vendor?"

Richard didn't even have to think about that one. He hadn't had a new vendor since she'd joined him five years ago; hadn't a need of a vendor. Her stuff was great.

"No new vendor. It's funny, you know. This old man came up to the counter. Pretty strange, if you ask me, and then there was this little girl pointing to a pink cupcake with a ring in it."

"Did you say a ring?" Virginia asked.

"Yes. It was right there on top of the pink cupcake, glittering away. The ring was fake, of course."

"Of course. So where do you think it came from?"

Richard had no idea. It suddenly occurred to him that they were speaking for the first time in a week; actually speaking, not yelling or blaming the other person. It was nice. "So, when will you be returning back to work?" he asked.

There was sudden silence on the other end. "I don't know. Maybe when I'm feeling a bit better."

"Are you sick?"

"Of course not, especially in the way you might be thinking," she countered.

Her voice sounded strange, almost foreign to him; so, it was going to end the same way. "Take your time," he said.

"I'll do that."

There was a sudden emptiness on the other end of the line and Richard knew that she'd hung up.

That night Richard dreamt of the ring. It floated above him like a glittering specter. He saw it again atop the pink cupcake as the girl licked the pink frosting off the ring on her forefinger.

***

Virginia tossed and turned. Why had Richard called her for such a stupid reason? A pink cupcake? It just didn't make sense. She got up, and although it was near 3 a.m., started on a batch of cupcakes. If this was his way of getting more work out of her, well, she'd do it. She couldn't sleep anyway and thoughts of creating strawberry cupcakes with pink frosting and a sweet ring on top did something to her; something she just couldn't put her finger on.

She laughed at her own joke and got busy. In time, the smell of strawberry jam filled the space in her kitchen and all she could think about was getting her hands on those fake rings that Richard had spoken about.

She knew of a craft store nearby that might have them, and as the batter swirled and became a luscious pink, she thought of him.

Richard had won her over early on. But it had never been about the ring. It had been more about the heart. He'd only been able to afford a small diamond; she looked at it now on her third finger and smiled. The band was silver, and a small, white stone was tucked into its center like a warm blanket. It had been enough.

He understood her and had loved the way she loved life. The hikes were magnificent; almost as if she was reaching God by hiking to the mountain's peek... A sudden thought came to her mind of a tall tower reaching to the heavens but she shrugged it off. It was just like her to ruin a good thought with a bad one.

The cupcake papers ready, Virginia poured the mixture inside, making sure to leave enough space for rising. She laughed at herself again, remembering the cupcakes she'd first made with her mother, now gone. She recalled how her mother had scolded her for filling the cups too full. She'd made her scoop up the goop on the pan and reuse it in other cups. And then she thought of Paul and God. For it was Paul who'd persuaded her to begin *Just Desserts* in the first place and it was God who'd kept her going.

And now?

She remembered the first time the stones had sat still without working and how alone she'd felt. She was frustrated, yes, about the baby she would never have, but she'd felt assured that God would help her. Hadn't he always?

She placed the pan in the heated oven and sat down on one of her kitchen chairs. The legs scraped momentarily against the hardwood floor as she pulled the chair to the table. With nothing before her but her memories, she placed her hands on her head and cried.

It had been just yesterday since she'd spilled a tear and now it came in a rushing stream. It just wasn't fair, none of it! She was alone, again! And God had done nothing to help her!

The sobbing was followed by an embarrassing runny nose. She stood and walked to the bathroom, grabbed a tissue and returned to the kitchen. Just 10 minutes left.

***

Richard got up from the hotel bed and took a shower. He briefly thought of the stones but shrugged the thought aside. They'd worked for Virginia for a while, so long that she had grown so accustomed to their help that something had happened to her; a drifting of sorts had occurred. It was a natural drifting, he thought. Sort of like she figured the help of God should come to her without her having to work for it.

He'd called it a stronger focus on change, a step-up, and Virginia had yelled at him. "What do you think, that I'm a loser or something?" she'd shouted. As if not getting pregnant was suddenly her fault when they'd discovered months before that it was his.

They'd spoken of adoption, but Virginia had wanted her own child. And she'd said it like having a baby finally made things perfect for her; having a child of her own.

Richard just didn't get it. Wasn't it bad enough that it was his fault and that she'd probably married the wrong man? He could hardly live with himself knowing that he was the cause of her unhappiness, and it was no wonder that she couldn't live with him either.

He stepped out of the shower, toweled off and got dressed, still thinking of the woman he'd fallen in love with. He wished they'd never spoken about having children.

***

By 5 a.m. the cupcakes were finished and Virginia was exhausted. She loaded the cupcakes into the cardboard carrier, wrapping the plastic loosely over the top, and carried the carriers one at a time to the car. No, she still didn't have a van--that one had been next on the agenda before Richard left her. But Paul's old car, which still looked as new as the day it was driven off the lot, would work. She'd promised him that she'd take care of it and she had. She had the detailing done on the car once a month and kept the outside to a spit shine. He would have been proud.

She was a few minutes early but had a key to the bakery area. Once inside, Virginia avoided the secret room (although she had to walk through it to get to the counter) and placed the cupcakes on the other side of the glass. The rings weren't on the cupcakes yet, but that didn't matter. As soon as the craft store opened she'd run over, pick up what she needed, and add the last bit of decor to the fluffy pink tops.

As it was, she'd have to deal with her husband. Much better to get the cupcakes shelved than have him offer to carry them for her. Once in place, Virginia looked around. There were a few food stockers in the small, country store, but no one else. Boxes filled the few aisles as they were opened and their treasures deposited on various shelves.

Shutting the glass counter door, she turned, made her way back through the secret room where she'd held many classes and shared her thoughts about growth and the power of God. But when she reached the door she was not alone.

She wanted it to be God with everything that was in her; wanted him to see her, embrace her. It was so

112

unlike her to be dreaming about something that hadn't occurred in years but yet that's what she was doing; thinking of him in those awful corduroy pants and tattered fisherman's hat. Tears were suddenly welling as Richard opened the door.

"So, you've decided to show up," he said. It appeared that he was embarrassed, but he didn't recall his words. Instead he added, "I can use all the help I can get. Baking today?"

Virginia shook her head. "Not today. I've got some cupcakes in the cabinet. Just heading to the craft store." She noticed that his hair wasn't brushed, and that his blue eyes appeared clouded over. He was suffering.

For a moment she stopped but no words came. She felt the warmth of the room and the way her skin tingled at the thought of him touching her. But she couldn't speak.

"Cupcakes. What kind?" he asked.

"Pink ones just like you wanted. I just need to go and get the rings."

Richard appeared to consider her words. He directed her to the window. "Have you noticed how icy the glass is?" he asked.

She nodded. "Nothing like summer."

"But look how beautiful it is. See that long icicle?"

There was a large one that reached from the top of the room, well past the window, and almost to the snow below.

"I know things are tough, but I think it's going to be okay."

"What do you mean, okay? I want my life to be better than okay."

She felt the smell of spruce next to her, like Christmas that was still there, but he didn't touch her. "I'm sorry," he said.

"So am I."

"Since that little girl asked for that pink cupcake, I've been thinking a lot about you."

"You're kidding." It seemed funny that her husband would associate a pink cupcake with anything having to do with her.

"You know, that old man with the fisherman's cap and old corduroys scared me a little, I think."

"What old man?"

"The one at the counter."

She touched the glass with her forefinger thinking of the ring. Perhaps all hope wasn't lost after all. He was going to apologize now, tell her it was all his fault, ask her to forgive him.

"The old man. You know, he sort of reminds me of the old guy that came to the counter years ago and handed me that constancy stone that you no longer use."

She was angry. How dare he... and then she noticed that her heart was racing. An old man who looked like God? Impossible.

"You sure it was him?"

"I didn't say that."

She turned. His blue eyes had cleared and he was looking deeply into her own. She thought she saw love there. "So?"

"I said that he reminded me of him."

"So, what did the old guy look like? What was he wearing?"

"He had a beard, a checkered shirt, some old pants, a fisherman's cap, like I said, why?"

"You're kidding." Her heart stopped and, in its place, a small light began to glow. "Are you sure?"

"I'm sure about what he was wearing."

"But what if it was God? Did you feel anything different when he was there? Did you notice anything, anything at all?"

Richard shrugged his shoulders. "Not really. Well, except..."

"Except what?" The glow she'd felt in her heart had suddenly changed to something akin to excitement.

"That pink cupcake with the ring on it appeared seconds after he arrived."

KATHRYN ELIZABETH JONES

The Vow

After a quick trip to the craft store, Virginia returned with the rings. She placed each glittering stone atop a single cupcake. Once finished she looked over at Richard.

"What do you think it means?" he asked.

"I have no idea," she answered, but her heart was still pumping with excitement. After all this, all these years, she'd finally be able to speak to him again. And then a new thought occurred to her. "So, why do you think he came to you first?"

Richard shrugged. The store had just opened and he was busily putting the new batch of cookies into the case. "Maybe I was at the right place at the right time."

"What's that supposed to mean?"

"Just what I said. I was here, he came--if it was him." He turned from her and went to the cooling counter.

She considered his words. It was God and she was going to reach him if it was the last thing she did. There was that tower again to heaven. She looked back at Richard. He was gathering another sheet of cookies.

"Really, Virginia, I'm here all of the time serving customers."

"While I'm at home feeling sorry for myself, is that it?"

"Now you're putting words in my mouth." He slid the second batch of cookies inside and turned to her, placing his hand on her shoulder. She flinched.

"Sorry. Maybe you're just making a mountain out of a molehill. Maybe it was just some old guy."

"It was God," said Virginia.

And so, she decided to stay and work with her husband the entire day. They sold doughnuts, a few pink cupcakes and plenty of cookies, but God didn't show up and Virginia went home miserable. Still, she wasn't alone.

In the car Richard spoke about getting the classes started up again. But she couldn't do that. He inferred that it would help her. That it would probably assist her in connecting again with God. "When was the last time you prayed?" he'd asked, before she'd become angry and threatened to leave him for good.

He knew she hadn't prayed ever since the final results had come in. She hadn't prayed because she was too angry to pray. She hadn't prayed, because God knew how she was feeling. Why wouldn't he just step in and fix it? No, she hadn't prayed, and she wouldn't be praying now.

***

Richard snuggled on the old couch as best as he could, trying to avoid the hole. Amazing, really, how they'd kept the couch with the defect for so many years, but it was comforting to him, somehow. Virginia had told him all about the stone of trust, how it had burned through the fabric and to the floor, and Richard wondered if that was what was happening now. Trust, or lack of it.

He wondered if he was partially to blame. Sure, he believed his wife, but she put so much stock in the stones that it had been difficult, if not impossible, for her to think about anything else. It was like she was waking and sleeping stones, and it was unlike him not to believe her, he just didn't get it--at least not all of it.

And then the business had grown and things had changed for his wife. She no longer held the stones. Some days she didn't even look at them. And then came the day she no longer spoke about them; it seemed to him that it was just easier for her to get up, shower and go about the day than to think about them.

Richard wondered if that had caused it, or if he was only imagining the change occurring then and not when they found out that they couldn't have a baby. They'd completed the nursery, had purchased clothing that could be used for either a boy or a girl, had purchased a crib and all that goes with it, painted the room an *either way* yellow, but nothing had happened. Virginia had been sure about that, just as she was sure about most things in their marriage. *If we buy the right stuff, then the baby will be conceived. If we do all the testing required, the baby will come.* But the baby hadn't come.

The night was a long one as Richard slept on the couch, his home away from home without having to go to the hotel. Well, at least he was making progress.

***

Virginia was questioning everything and it didn't matter that her husband had already picked up his things at the hotel and had made his way to work. She knew this because a matted lump of blankets caressed the couch and floor and dirty socks, shirts and pants lay near the hamper--though not directly in it.

If God had reached out to her husband, and she had no doubt that he had, why him and not her? What was she doing wrong? She'd long since wondered if God had merely forgotten about her; he had millions of children after all. Perhaps what she needed was a swift kick on the backside, but her heart still ached for the companionship she'd once had.

The door to the nursery was open just a crack. Either she'd forgotten to shut it or her husband had been there just that morning. It was 6 a.m. and he was already at work; the man was quick in the morning, but sloppy in the process.

The glow of the sun coming through the window made her think of God, if only for a moment, and then she was folding and refolding the blankets, straightening the little diapers and nightshirts, and winding her way to a small bookshelf that housed all of her favorite children's books. She sat in the wooden rocker and opened the first book her hands reached but it didn't take long for her eyes to cloud with tears. In only moments she couldn't see the words, but she could feel in her heart the emptiness of the child that would never be hers.

It wasn't fair!

Tears formed in her throat. She couldn't breathe. The sun, it's rays piercing the thin draperies, filtered to her eyes and made her blink. But even then, she didn't hear him, she didn't hear him.

This was her daily routine after Richard went to work, and it was just easier for him not to know. She didn't blame him, not really, she just ached so much for a child. It was like she was missing a part of herself. The book sat opened, and as Virginia rocked in the chair that held no child, she wrapped the small yellow blanket around herself. It was warm, and in moments she imagined her child was there.

***

The old man stood in front of him, his long beard as full as he last remembered it, the same checkered shirt and old brown corduroys reminding him of a muddy lake in April just before the thaw. And he had on that old hat as if he was just stopping by before doing some fishing.

"So, I see your wife made some pink cupcakes," he said.

Richard's heart was already pounding. If Virginia was right he was talking with God and it was one thing to talk with him when you didn't know it and quite another to speak with him when you did. He felt his legs growing soft and the tips of his fingers tingling.

"I... ah...yes, my wife."

"They look nice," the old man said, looking down. "Only, the rings, they don't quite glitter as much as the one you had in the case the other day. "

Richard looked into the case. God was right. They were all rings with a fake diamond like before, but the rings didn't glisten this time.

"Well, they're pretty cheap," he said. "The one that was in the case the day before yesterday may have cost you more."

"Me?" asked the gentleman, touching his beard.

"You...did bring the cupcake with the ring on it yesterday," stumbled Richard.

"Why would you think that?" The old gent stopped looking at the cupcakes and his blue eyes warmed Richard's. Perhaps...this was God.

"I just know...the child...ah...I didn't have that cupcake in the case until...after you arrived."

"Well, I'll be," said God. "You are correct."

"I am?" stammered Richard. "I mean, why would you bring me a pink cupcake with a fake ring in it?"

The old man smiled. "Well, if I told you that, that would take away some searching on your part, wouldn't it?"

"I imagine so." He suddenly knew that God could read his mind, and if he was reading it in this very moment God had to know how petrified he was.

"But I'll give you a clue," said God. "I like giving clues when my child is especially afraid. That way, you don't have to faint and you don't have to feel as if you're losing your stomach."

Richard nodded.

"The diamond was real."

It took a few moments for the comment to register. "You mean, that little girl got a real diamond ring? She didn't even pay for the cupcake!"

"That's right," said God. "She didn't pay, but her family needed it or, you could say, the money that was needed that only that cupcake could deliver, was offered."

Richard couldn't believe it. And yet, God was standing right there telling him that it was true. "So, my wife didn't really need to make all of those pink cupcakes then?"

"What do you think?"

Richard blinked. What did he think? Was this really God? Had he provided the pink cupcake with the ring on top to teach him something? And if so, what?

"I think I need to talk with my wife about this."

Richard looked *away* for only a moment. He imagined the young girl leaving him, the ring on her forefinger, her tiny fingers wet with pink frosting. But he shouldn't have looked away.

Looking back the man was gone.

In that moment he wanted to call Virginia on his cell phone, but that didn't feel like the right way to talk about a communication with God so Richard waited the entire day to tell his wife what had happened. When she didn't show up for work in the afternoon he wanted to close up shop but knew that he couldn't, and when the evening arrived and she was still not there, he took a few deep breaths and anxiously awaited their time together at home.

For moral support or for use in his imminent object lesson of sorts, he brought along one of her pink cupcakes. It sat next to him in a small box.

***

"You what?" Virginia shrieked. She couldn't believe it. God had come to him again! Again! "So, what did he say this time?" she asked irritably. A distinct impression came to her mind that she'd been through this one before. It was sort of like explaining the power of the five stones to her friend, Paul, all over again. He hadn't believed her at first, and she was having a hard time believing her husband.

"He admitted to bringing the first pink cupcake."

"The one you gave to the girl."

"He said the diamond was real."

"What?"

"The ring that I gave to that girl. The ring, it was real."

"Virginia was silent."

"It was hard enough that I knew I was talking to God, and then he told me that the little girl got that cupcake with the diamond ring in it because the money was needed for her family."

"Unbelievable! said Virginia.

"Believe it," said Richard. "So, what do you think it means?"

Virginia couldn't do anything but shrug. "Well, how should I know?" she finally said. "I mean, God isn't speaking to me anymore. He obviously prefers you." She hesitated. "You must be doing something right."

"Just listening," said Richard.

"Don't throw that one in my face." Virginia felt her face grow hot. She shouldn't have said it, but it was exactly how she felt. She placed her hands on her head, and just like the morning she'd made the pink cupcakes, she began to cry. Small tears fell at first and then the sobs arrived in all their glory. Before she knew it, Richard had reached for her and was holding her close.

Later, he withdrew the pink cupcake with the fake diamond setting on top and they talked for hours about its possible meaning. Rings sometimes meant friendship, but a diamond ring usually meant marriage. In the case of the little girl, however, it must have meant 'means'--having the means to provide.

The next morning Virginia cooked her husband breakfast. It was 5 a.m. but she felt that she needed to do this. The night before he'd been tremendously supportive. She must have cried 2 hours--at least. It was his favorite: scrambled eggs, bacon and pancakes. She was just finishing up the last dollop when he walked in.

"I knew something good was in here," he said, looking at the feast and kissing her neck. She wasn't sure if he meant the breakfast or herself. It made her happy and tingly.

"The juice is already on the table."

He sat and poured a glass. "Do you know," he said, "we haven't had breakfast together since I can't remember when."

But she remembered, though she didn't want to bring it up. "Do you think we should take the nursery down?" she asked.

He chewed for a moment. "I don't know. I kind of like it." She didn't want to tell him that she had spent every morning for months in that room, rocking with no one, reading to no one, but she just wasn't ready to tell him her secret.

"I like the room, too." She dished up her plate and sat across from him at the table. It was especially cold out this morning and so she'd worn her old robe and slippers. He already had his working duds on; cream colored pants and a navy button up shirt. His hair was combed like she liked it and he wore a smile larger than she'd seen in months.

"This is good," he finally said. His plate was almost empty. She'd taken two bites.

"Would you like some more?"

"Pancakes if you have them." She felt suddenly as if they were in a restaurant, but after five years of marriage she knew Richard's ways. He was thoughtful, serious for the most part, and used proper etiquette when the occasion warranted.

She got up and reached for the pancake plate. He took his fork and stabbed the first two gems from the stack. "Have you thought any more about the meaning of the ring?" she asked.

He chewed, swallowed and then said, "I have, and I'm wondering if we're right in both cases. In the first case we have a young girl with a poor family. She gets a cupcake with a ring. When her mother discovers the prize, she realizes the ring can be sold and the money provided. In the second case, the ring is for us. We made some pretty heavy-duty commitments to each other the day we became husband and wife." He paused, and Virginia wasn't sure if he paused for effect or for something else.

"An all-knowing God might just teach two things at one time," he added.

It was an interesting thought. Give the little girl the money she needed; remind them of the commitments they'd made to each other--the ring, a symbol of that commitment. "It feels right," said Virginia, "but how can we be sure?"

"I prayed about it last night," said Richard.

"You what?"

"Prayed. And I think it worked. I think God is trying to tell us something."

***

Virginia wasn't going to miss out on seeing God ever again. She traveled to work with her husband the entire next week and the week following, and though sales began to increase, the old man in the corduroys had not made an appearance. In addition, she still hadn't begun her classes and by the third week she just couldn't go back. Richard was disappointed. He told her not to worry and to let God take care of it, which only made her angry enough to stomp out of the hidden room and to her car.

Once home she cloistered herself inside the nursery, though it was noon, and read and rocked the child that wasn't there. This time, however, the experience was hurtful. It didn't feel the same. It was all fake, this preparing for a baby that would never come. She couldn't do it anymore.

Anger coursed through her. She reached for the thin draperies and tugged them from the window. She attacked the walls next, breaking the lamp and small end tables in the process. As the heat erupted within her, she took apart the crib, bit by bit until all that was left was spindles, box springs and side pieces. These she shoved out the nursery window. They clanked against the house and fell to the icy snow beneath. She didn't even look out the window to see how they'd landed. She didn't care.

Turning from the window, Virginia reached inside the closet and pulled out the little outfits from their hangers. Sobbing, she tossed them out the window. They fluttered and were gone. She attacked the dresser and the changing table next, withdrawing anything inside and tossing the contents out the window with the other things. The books were last.

As she held the last treasure in her hands, a book her own mother had read to her as a child, she tore the pages one by one from the book's spine. This was the hardest feat of all. It was as if she was telling God that not even the relationship with her mother mattered.

As the tears fell, she watched each piece coast to the floor like a paper bird. Now she was finished. She could go on and she didn't care if God ever spoke to her again.

Virginia slammed the door.

***

Richard was beyond angry. He looked at the disheveled nursery and thought about his wife already asleep in their bed. He'd known something was wrong the moment he'd driven up. Not only were the baby's things all over the snow, but most were broken or torn.

He left the nursery and entered the bedroom. Whether his wife was faking sleep or not it did not matter. It was time to talk.

***

"I don't care!"
"But I do!"

Virginia wrapped the pillow around her face and tried to go back to sleep. It was late and she was tired but he wouldn't stop bothering her. She'd probably reacted without thinking, she knew that now, and Richard was going to tell her what she knew already.

"Virginia." The words were soft and she almost missed them under her pillow. But they were there. "Honey. We need to talk."

"Why?" she mumbled behind the barrier. "Why?"

"I know you feel bad about the baby."

"Bad doesn't even touch it. I'm miserable."

"Remove the pillow so we can talk. Okay, honey?"

From the corner of the pillow she peeked out. Large tears were running down her husband's cheeks. And he wasn't wiping them off.

"I love you, you silly," he said, removing the rest of the pillow from her face. "Don't you know that?"

"I just can't believe," she sniffed, "that we're not going to have a baby."

"I know, I know." Richard caressed her hair. Before she knew it, he was lying beside her and holding her close. The feeling was nice.

"Don't hate...me," she wheezed. "I did a...stupid thing."

"It wasn't stupid. You were angry, that's all."

"Angry enough to wreck everything in that room."

"We can clean it up."

She wondered where the lecture was but it didn't come. Instead, Richard lay by her. He continued to stroke her hair. "We will get through this."

"How?"

"With God's help."

"But how do you know he'll help us? I mean, he won't talk to me and he'll only talk to you when I'm not there."

Richard wiped away another tear from her face.

"Why do you think that is?" he asked.

"I don't know, because I'm a grump." She sniffed again. "I'm angry at him. He has full control over giving us a child, but somehow he doesn't think we deserve it."

Richard remained silent. For a time, Virginia wondered if he'd fallen asleep. And then he said, "I don't think it has anything to do with deserving something. Did you deserve to be single all of those years? And your friend, Paul, did he deserve to die?"

"Of course not."

"Then why would you think that you don't deserve to have a child. Remember it's my fault. I am the one that can't get you pregnant. You should be angry with me."

"But I am angry at you!"

There was a slight loosening of the hug, but Richard didn't move away.

She continued, "I mean, all this time. I was single for so long and when I found you I thought, well, now I can finally get my life started! I'm married to a man I love and now it's time to have children."

"Is that the only reason you married me? For children?"

"Of course not. I... I just want children, that's all." She was wetting the pillowcase with her runny nose but she didn't care.

"What if we're not supposed to have children? What if God has another answer for us?"

Virginia thought about that. Nothing could be better than bringing children into the world and if she couldn't have any of her own, what was the point?

"You remember our vows." His voice was quiet, almost as if he was struggling to keep his tone in check. "I remember that we promised to love one another through sickness and health and for better or for worse. If we never have a child would it really be such a bad thing?"

Virginia's tears had dried. She wiped her nose with her shirt sleeve and thought about her husband's words. She remembered that moment at the altar and what she'd promised him. Still, it didn't make things any easier. She wanted a child and there was no way that she could see to work her way around that feeling...

***

"Richard!" Richard sat bolt upright. His blond hair had taken a beating from the night before; it went every which way, and he was still wearing his clothes and shoes.

She laughed. She couldn't help it.

"What?" he bumbled. "What?"

"You slept in your clothes. You never do that."

He laughed back, licked his hand, and tried to flatten his hair.

"You never do that either," said Virginia.

"Well, maybe it's about time that I did. I'm sorry. You needed someone and I just didn't know how to be there for you."

She thought about the night before and wondered what he could mean. He'd done all of the right things, but then again, she'd finally been ready to receive them. To receive. Her mind caught hold upon a thought, a reoccurring thought that had never really left her. The tower. It was always about building the tower to God or climbing the mountain, or something.

She sat. "You need to get to work."

"I know, I just wanted to make sure you were alright. Are you coming today?" He stood and walked to the bathroom, tugging at and dropping his clothing and shoes as he went. She heard the faucet turn on.

Was she going to work with her husband? Of course, she was. How could she go anywhere else?

***

Richard stood by the bakery shelves. There had been a call for chocolate the last few days and Richard had said nothing to Virginia about it. But now, somehow, he felt it would be okay.

"Do we need cookies, or what?" she asked.

"Chocolate. Can you go to Wholesale Max's? I probably shouldn't leave."

With their late arrival had come a fair share of strange looks and a few put out customers. Richard had tried to make it up to them with a free cookie but this had caused even more emptiness within the shelves.

"Sure," she said. "I'll be back soon."

Virginia went through the secret doors as usual, but this time, she thought seriously about getting her classes started again. After work she'd clean up the mess she'd made at home and then make some calls. Previous students might be interested in a new class, and even if they weren't they might know of someone who was.

In the car, Virginia traveled north. It took about 15 minutes to get to Wholesale Max's. She picked up the chocolate, packaged in bulk, and had almost reached the door when she saw him. Unbelievably he was at the magazine stand, and if she hadn't looked in his direction at exactly the right time she might have missed him.

He was the same as she remembered him. Brown corduroys, a flannel shirt, white beard...

His eyes turned in her direction and he smiled. It was like the sun had come out in just that moment. She walked toward him, bag in hand. "So, what are you doing here?" she asked.

"Just shopping."

"Oh."

"Don't worry, there is a young man here who needs my help, only he doesn't know it."

How familiar that sounded!

"Thank you for the gift," she said, looking into his eyes and finding nothing but love there.

"You're welcome, daughter. How are things with you and Richard?" He grinned mischievously at her. "Now you know, Virginia, that everything happens for a reason. "

"You mean finally meeting you here has its purpose," she said.

"That, and other things."

"I want to have a child," she said suddenly. She knew it sounded abrupt, but she also knew that he would understand. He had always understood her, even when she wasn't thinking right.

"For what reason do you want a child?" he asked.

"What do you mean?" She hoped he wasn't reading her thoughts.

"I mean, a child is also a gift, a precious gift."

"And I deserve one."

"Be careful, Virginia."

133

Virginia could feel her face getting hot. If she'd touched it, it would have probably scalded her hand. She tried to remain peaceful, but the anger was seeping through her heart and out through her skin.

"Just remember what you've learned before."

"You mean about the stupid rocks."

God raised his left eyebrow and looked down the aisle. At the end of it stood a young man stocking the shelf. "I must go to Trevor now," he said.

"But what about me?" It sounded wheezy and whiney but Virginia was bothered by God's treatment of her. It was if he didn't care. But that couldn't be it. He was still watching Trevor. She reached for him.

"Please, God, you've got to help me," she said.

But God didn't turn and she couldn't help watching the man in the brown corduroys and fisherman's cap walk slowly to the young man at the end of the aisle.

***

Virginia tossed the chocolate to the table. "I can't believe it," she said.

"Can't believe what?" Richard was just finishing with the last tray. "You got the chocolate."

"Of course, I got the stupid chocolate!"

He didn't even have to turn. Virginia was angry about something...something else maybe, but possibly the same thing she'd been upset about for years.

"God, he's not going to help me."

Richard eyed her carefully. Had God finally come to her then? He was glad, but why was she so angry?

"I asked him for a child, to his very face, and he still wouldn't do it."

"Did he say why?"

"Something about a child being 'a precious gift' and that I needed to be 'careful.'"

Richard couldn't have been more shaken. Sure, he'd fully suspected that a child would never be in the realms of possibility for them, but now after Virginia's visit with God, things seemed definite.

He reached for Virginia and held her close. "So, what do you need to be careful about?" he asked.

"I guess asking God for something that I shouldn't be asking him about. I don't know. He seemed pretty frustrated with me. There was a boy there, someone stocking the shelves, and he seemed more concerned about him. Kind of left me standing there."

"Did he say anything else?"

"Nothing much. I was just reminded about the rocks; how I should remember them."

"Oh." Richard brushed at her hair but he didn't say anything. Still, his thoughts went to the stones again and what they represented. Listening to God, trusting in him, having optimism no matter your situation, being tenacious and never giving up and being constant with God through it all. Were they both doing that?

And then Richard thought of something else. Perhaps the cupcake with the ring in it had been a furtherance of learning so to speak. But what happened after a person was constant with God? He considered his talk with Virginia and went over the thoughts they'd spoken about.

The little girl had been helped by God, and he was committed to his wife in marriage. What did the two have in common?

Virginia was brushing away her tears and looking up at him. "So, where are you?" she asked.

"Sorry. I was just thinking about the cupcake with the ring in it."

Virginia laughed. It was more of a cough with a laugh at the end, but it was something. "Kind of reminds you of the stone thing," she said.

***

Later that night Virginia noticed that Richard was reading his Bible. He sat in the corner chair by the lamp and appeared pretty intent on the words. She was watching her favorite program along with popcorn and a soda.

After a while it was hard to focus on the program. It was just eating at her, kind of like the hole in the couch. What could possibly be more interesting than what she was doing? She wasn't sure that she could ask him, though her thoughts wandered in his direction during commercials. The buttery smell of the popcorn filled her nostrils and the soda sparkled, just egging her on to take another sip. She did and then turned her attention back to her husband. He was still reading that stupid book.

Finally, she couldn't help it. "So, what's so interesting?" she asked.

He looked up, smiled slightly, then put his nose back into the book. "Lots of things."

She was infuriated. "Like what?"

"Do you really want to know?"

She nodded her head, put another handful of popcorn into her waiting mouth, paused the show, and chewed.

"I've been wondering about the cupcake all day," he said, "especially after you returned." He paused for a moment, took his eyes from the Bible and looked directly at her.

"You know about constancy, but really, what do you think it means?"

"Being constant with God. It means you walk with him," she said.

"Right. But I think there's more."

She got a sudden chill up her arms and waited.

"Virginia, what do you think it means to be committed. I mean, really committed?"

She shrugged. "Why don't you tell me," she said.

"Walking with God is only part of it. God expects us to walk with him through good times and bad, right? And it's great when times are good. It's easier to walk with God."

Don't I know it, Virginia thought but didn't say?

"Listen to this: 'And they said, Go to. Let us build us a city and a tower, whose top may reach into heaven... (Genesis 11:4).' He looked up. "I've heard this story ever since I was a little boy but never really understood it. I knew that the people had built the tower to get into heaven; they thought they could climb it. But the only way to really get to heaven is to obey God."

"So?" Virginia's heart was beating quickly. *Why that scripture?*

"The people actually thought that if they put in some physical effort like building a tower, that nothing else would be required of them. They'd be in heaven and they wouldn't have to do anything else. Remember what happened next?"

"God came down from heaven," Virginia said, "and he created more than one language." She stopped. "That's right, isn't it?"

"Yes, but why?"

"Well, if the people couldn't speak to one another they wouldn't be able to finish the tower."

"And maybe," Richard added, his eyes piercing her own, "just maybe they'd have to communicate with God so that he could help them to get to heaven. It's really about keeping the commandments."

Virginia rolled her eyes. "You sound just like a Sunday school lesson," she said. "I think I'll go back to my movie." She reached for the remote.

"Wait. Just a minute. Can you do that for me, honey?"

He'd been using the pet name 'honey' a lot recently. And she'd noticed something else. He seemed more kind, more sensitive of her. He wasn't as critical. "Okay, but just a minute. I want to finish my show."

Instead of reading from the chair, he stood, bringing the Bible with him. At the couch he sat next to her, his body turned slightly to the right so that he could see her. "Do you think we've been trying too hard? I mean, we put together that nursery, did all of the doctor testing and stuff, and spoke to each other as if we were going to get a child within the week."

"And what's wrong with that. That's optimism." *There, right in his face. What could he do now?*

He hesitated. So, she had got him. "You're right," he said, surprising her. "And then we followed the

138

optimism with tenacity and constancy, and when nothing happened we stopped listening and trusting in God."

"That's right. We did what was required. We did what God wanted, and we were supposed to get the prize..." She stopped herself, for suddenly she was thinking about the precious gift that God had spoken to her about. Her heart seemed to stop. What was Richard saying?

"Don't you see, honey? We were building a tower to God. We thought if we did all of the right things we'd get to heaven."

"But shouldn't we, get there, I mean?"

"Not in the ways we were doing it. We were going through the motions, taking the steps, but we weren't drawing closer to God. We were building our own tower, thinking we could get there without him!"

Richard's face was flushed. He reached for her hand and squeezed her fingers. "God wants us to be committed to each other. We learned about that in our marriage vows. But he also wants us to be committed to him."

Richard stood, walked to the kitchen, and returned with the pink cupcake. He'd decided to save it against her wishes, and it was still pink but crusty from the outside air. He handed it to her.

"Commitments go two ways. We make a commitment to God and he makes a commitment to us. And though God always keeps his commitments we don't always keep them back."

"You're talking about me."

"And me."

"Well, I just don't see how we'll be able to keep all of the commandments. I mean, I had a hard-enough

139

time following the parable of the five stones, how in the world am I going to do more?"

"So that's it."

"What?" She handed him the cupcake and reached again for the remote.

"The stones. They became difficult because you were trying to use them on your own."

"I wasn't in the beginning."

"But later, what happened later?"

Virginia couldn't believe it. Her husband was right. She hadn't remembered. In her anger she'd forgotten God.

"You make is sound like the stones are a circular process, never ending. I guess I knew that."

"And forgot. We all forget." He wrapped her in his arms. "Why don't we start over?" he said, returning to his former position in front of her. "God gave us the cupcake lesson for a reason, and I'm bound and determined to find out what he wants for us."

The Feast: A Parable of the Ring

The Choice

The talk with his wife had gone well. He hadn't planned it, and yet the timing had been perfect. A sudden warmth reached up his back and filtered to his heart. Things would be alright now, now that he and Virginia were on track.

They'd decided to pray together, and last night he'd taken the first shift. He'd spoken to God about being thankful for what they had; their business, his wife, his home, and had ended the prayer with even more thanks. He really couldn't be thankful enough for what he had.

Tonight, was Virginia's turn. He wondered what she would say as they knelt beside their bed, clasped hands, and spoke with God. He wondered if she would do it.

But she was happy today; happier than he'd seen her in months; or had it been years? A new class was beginning the first week in February, a class for couples called, "Knowing Your Spouse's Heart," and Virginia seemed excited about teaching it, though she had enrolled him in the class as well.

"It will be good for us," she'd explained. "I'm going to use some positive stuff I've learned through the years."

"The stones?"

"The stones AND the cupcake."

"It's fitting that we are holding the class next to the bakery," he'd said.

"There are no accidents," she'd answered.

***

"Dear God," Virginia prayed. "Please help us to know thy will. Please help us to know what to do next in finding our child. We are thinking that maybe we'd like a girl. Yes, a girl, but she doesn't need to be a baby. She could be like the little girl at *Just Desserts*. You know the one."

She felt Richard shift at her side. Maybe the prayer was wrong. Maybe she was doing it all wrong...

"And... God? Keep us safe until that time comes. Amen."

The prayer ended, Virginia didn't dare look into her husband's eyes. It had been so long since she'd prayed, and never in her life had she prayed out loud. She felt suddenly silly and insecure.

***

Virginia was nervous. There were only seven in the class, two returns, but all she could think about was who was sitting near the back. Perhaps he only wanted to make sure that she kept on track, or that the class was interesting...or something, but God was silent and it appeared that no one else saw him but herself.

She handed out the bags of stones, a treat that she figured others would appreciate. They weren't the expensive kind, of course, (she'd written the words on them herself) but there was something about remembering what to do when you had physical objects to look at.

"So how do you know your spouse's heart?" she asked, following the stone presentation. It had occurred to her that the stones were really a representation of a person's personal relationship with God and that this relationship must be somewhat in order to have a close marriage relationship--or the symbol of the cupcake.

There were a few nods of the head.

"I think I get the stones bit," said a woman in her mid-thirties. "I mean, you have to have a relationship with God, don't you, before you can really have a great relationship with your husband. But I don't see how a wife can see into her husband's heart, especially if he doesn't talk and when he does it's all about sports."

There was laughter from the group, and the only man in the class raised his hand.

"At least we're not emotional. I mean, women can't handle anything. It's like they have to have us men to support them, both financially and emotionally."

The woman's face in the front row turned a burnished red. "So, you're saying that without men we wouldn't be able to go on in life."

The man smiled and winked at her, which only disturbed the woman more.

"I really want this to be a positive experience," said Virginia. "My question has to do with men *and* women. How does a husband better understand his wife and his wife better understand her husband?"

A young woman raised her hand. "I would like my husband to see me better, I mean--really see me. You know that movie, 'Avatar?' I want it to be like that...'I see you...'"

The man coughed. Briefly, Virginia looked at the back of the room. God was still there but, like usual, she couldn't tell what he was thinking.

"So why weren't our spouses invited to this event?" asked another woman. She was heavy set, wore a flowered dress and spoke loudly, as if she wanted to make sure that everyone heard. "I want my husband to know what is happening so that you can fix him."

Virginia giggled with the rest of the class. But the woman appeared serious. "He is the worst husband on the planet. Always telling me what to do; never respecting my opinion..."

"I know just what you mean," suggested the young woman. "It's like I'm 'his woman' and I could never have a thought of my own. So, what about inviting our spouse's next time? I would like that too. If he'll come, that is."

Virginia felt as if she was suddenly in an AA meeting; the class hadn't gone as she'd planned, and thoughts of having double the number next week disturbed her more than she wanted to let on. She looked towards the back of the room.

God was gone.

***

"What?" Richard was laughing, his sides breathing in and out like bagpipes. "So, did you finish the class, or what?"

"We...finished."

"Well?" He was sitting on the living room couch and they were sharing a bowl of popcorn. Dinner had been a bust. She'd been so worried about the class that she'd burnt the lasagna. At least the popcorn had turned out.

"I don't know if I can say it."

"What...what?" He stopped eating and touched her leg. "Whatever you say won't faze me, I promise."

"This will. The only man in the room got so fed up with the ladies that he walked out! Can you believe it? He said, 'This is the dumbest class I've ever attended,' and he walked out."

"What did you do?" He reached his hand into the bowl.

"What do you mean, what did I do? I didn't do anything, I just continued the class. It went much better after he left."

"Well, maybe the idea of having both spouses there is a good idea," he said. "It is a class on marriage."

"I know." She took another bite, feeling pretty stupid that she hadn't thought of that in the first place. But then again, life did nothing but show her what was working...and what wasn't on a continual basis.

***

Richard reached for the pink cupcake.

"The ring isn't like the last one," the little girl said, but she licked the frosting off of the top, working her tongue around the ring that was still planted there. "My mom won't like it."

"These are special cupcakes, too," said Richard, walking around the counter and bending so he could be at her eye level. The girl had green eyes, the color of deep satin, but her cheeks were ruddy and red. It was still cold out. She wore an old coat, torn at the sleeve. The coat was dirty almost everywhere else. Her blond hair was clean, as was her face before the licking of the cupcake. Richard noticed she had a pink oval around her tiny lips. She was licking the sides of it.

"So, there was a real diamond in the last cupcake."

"Must have been a mistake," the girl offered, licking another section of the cupcake.

"No mistake. So, the money has been spent already?"

"No, but I wanted to get prepared. Mom says that she wants to be prepared for the inevitable."

The ring came off the top of the cupcake, was licked and then placed on her forefinger like before.

"I think you mean inevitable," Richard said.

"Yeah, that."

"So where is your mom going?"

The little girl blinked over at him and in that moment, Richard took greater notice. "My name is Richard," he said.

"Joy," said the little girl, taking her first bite.

***

It was Saturday and Virginia was home working on the guest room. It felt sort of funny calling it that, but

Virginia knew that changing the room, including the yellow paint, would only help her to heal.

She'd decided on an eggshell white with lavender accents. They'd purchased a twin bed, new end tables, new drapes for the windows and plenty of pillows. These were placed lovingly on the bed and reminded Virginia of something from the Victorian era. The color was subtle, calming and reflective.

A chair with a lavender cushion stood in the corner of the room along with a small desk for writing and the closet had been decked out with the latest shelving.

Virginia couldn't help smiling. The room was beautiful after all, and she was doing much better. She walked to the window. All the clutter had been removed and disposed of weeks before but she could still see it there, clustered on the snow that would one day melt to make room for spring.

As she continued to look out the window, she saw a neighborhood child look up at her and wave. Virginia smiled and waved back. It made her heart fill with warmth and a little loneliness. Perhaps, after all, it was unfair of her to think she would never have children.

***

Richard was grinning from ear to ear. "Really? You really mean it?"

"I don't think it would hurt."

"I didn't think you wanted to adopt."

Virginia paced the living room. "I didn't think so either, but maybe this is the answer. If we can't have children, maybe the Lord wants us to adopt."

"Are you sure, I mean, what about the whole thing with carrying a baby and having it be our own..."

Virginia waved her hand. "Come see what I did today," she said.

Richard followed her into the guest room. It was beautifully done, all the way to the throw pillows. "Wow. It looks like something from a magazine."

"So, what do you think about bringing the little girl here?" she asked.

"A girl? You want to adopt a girl?"

"I think so," said Virginia. "No, I know so."

She walked to the bed, caressed the pillows and sat down. "I think this would be a perfect room for a little girl."

***

The choice wasn't an easy one, but Virginia was happier now than ever and Richard, well--he was beside himself with joy. Joy, that was her name, wasn't it?

He pictured the little girl with the golden hair and green eyes in the room and imagined her sleeping in her bed and cuddling her favorite stuffed animal. They didn't have any toys yet, but once they found out her age then the problem would be rectified.

Richard got on his knees with his wife and together they prayed for the little girl that would soon be theirs. Virginia prayed that all would go well, that the girl would come without trouble and that she would be happy with them.

"Dear God, we know this is the right thing, and we know you will support us in this worthy desire. Amen."

149

There was something about the prayer that disturbed him, but he shrugged it off. Virginia was glowing and Richard, well--he was beyond joy.

***

The terrible dream awoke her. She had been fitfully chasing a little girl with golden hair. Joy continued to climb the mountain away from Virginia's waiting hands.

"What is it?"

Richard sat up. "Have a bad dream?" he asked. Today was the day they were going to visit the Tucked in Tight Adoption Agency in Idaho Falls. Today was the day her dream was to be realized.

As she got ready, she watched Richard from the corner of her eye. He was as excited as she was.

"Ouch!"

"What did you do now?" she asked.

"Nicked myself again. Can you grab me a tissue?"

The tissue in hand, Richard stuck a small piece on his chin. "I don't know about you but I'm a nervous wreck."

She smiled, wrapping the colorful scarf around her neck. It would be good for their future child to see her in a bit of color. "Do you think it will be quick?" she asked.

He shrugged. "We can only hope. Anyway, we need some time to pick up those toys you talked about."

"Yeah, but not until we see her. We also will need to know her clothing sizes and what she enjoys doing."

"Have you thought about an age?"

"Six or seven? I'd like to get a girl that's young enough that we have some say in the matter."

He looked at her squarely. "What matter?"

"I've heard that some children are abused. I'm not sure I could take on a girl like that."

"Like what?" He wiped his face with a towel and watched her through the glass. "Whatever she's been through, we'll get her through it. How bad could it be?"

Virginia thought about her dream. "I don't know," she said. "Are you sure we're doing the right thing?"

"Oh, no, no, you're not going to back out now."

"I'm not...backing out as you say...it's just that..."

"What?"

"What if we don't know how to be parents? What if a baby would be better, then we wouldn't have to worry about so much stuff."

Richard touched her on the arm. "We'll be great parents. As for getting an older child we've already talked about that. It takes months, sometimes years to get a baby, but an older child will cut down the waiting time. Besides, you've changed over the room."

Virginia shrugged. "I know, but I'm just worried. What if they won't take us as parents?"

"You mean the agency?"

She nodded.

"Why wouldn't they take us? We're healthy, we make enough money to support a child...we..."

"We're old. At last look I'm 40 and you're a mere 42."

"So?"

"So maybe they don't want old people adopting children."

151

"I can't believe it. You don't actually think our ages will keep us from adopting our girl?"

She shrugged, brushing back her blond hair from her face. It had grown longer since she'd been married and curled naturally down her back. "I don't know, I'm just worried."

"You already said that."

***

"Remember, this is a great opportunity," he said.

The huge red brick house in front of them seemed to speak of times long gone but difficult to let go of. Virginia had thoughts she had no idea how to express. They'd said a prayer that morning about getting a girl and being good parents. They'd left the house with high hopes and a myriad of questions.

At least, that was the case with Virginia.

She wasn't sure that Richard was right but she believed he was, and as the doors of the old house loomed before them, Virginia considered how boxed in she'd been.

She'd been single for most of her life, had spent her time primarily indoors and now--now she was married and going places she'd never dreamed she would visit. Still, as Richard opened the door, they entered a warm visiting area that could only be thought of as a home away from home. She and Richard stepped inside, as ready as they'd ever be for what wonders would come next.

***

152

The woman before them smiled hesitantly. Her short, dark hair hit at chin level, and her wide face and glasses gave her that 'please don't disturb me' look. And yet, here she was interviewing them as if this was her talent in life. Her business tag revealed her name: Sandy. It seemed like an appropriate name for someone dealing with the grit of matching up families.

"I see from your paperwork that you are married and that you both have jobs, but are one of you ready to leave your career to be home with a child?"

"We've already discussed that," said Richard. "Virginia will be home with the child."

"No desires to pursue school?"

"Not at my age," said Virginia.

"As for your age..." The woman looked at Virginia. Richard pictured some sort of dinosaur before attack. "Are you concerned that your age will cause a problem in the future...with a baby..."

"Actually, we're wanting a girl, an older girl, so that should take a few years off and give us a better head start," Richard joked.

The woman didn't laugh. Richard could see distinct frown lines on either side of her face. Sure, she was probably sixty or so, but still..."

"It usually takes a year or so to get a baby, but since you are opting for a child and a girl, we may be able to fit you with a child sooner. You have already paid the application fee but we will need to set up a home study. Are you considering adopting internationally or domestically?"

Richard turned to Virginia. "We haven't talked about that," he said.

Sandy looked down at the paperwork. "Well, after you do, you'll have to finish this, but consider how an international child might be best for you because of your ages. Actually, an international child is usually harder to adopt. But please, please, don't decide that now. Get back to me in the next few days with your answer."

She handed them back their forms, including a couple of others she suggested they both look at. "These must be filled out completely before we can proceed."

Richard realized that they'd forgotten to check the appropriate box. No wonder the woman had been a bit, well, stiff. He looked over at Virginia and handed her the papers. "Then, we'll be back soon," he said, "after we've made our decision."

Sandy stood. "There are many children needing a home. Usually boys are adopted first, and girls, sadly, only about half as often. I am happy that you've made this decision." Sandy tried to smile, but like before it was restrained, though her handshake was firm.

**

It was just easier not to think about it. As Virginia paced the house she thought of the challenges they might have adopting a child outside of the U.S.

There was so much red tape! She gaped at the list Sandy had given her of laws, processes, home study information; even what to expect following the adoption. It made her head swirl.

Was this the right answer?

It was Saturday and Richard was at work. The pink cupcakes were selling marvelously, and many couples had discovered the find. Just yesterday one couple had given her an order for 250. "We're going to use these for the guests instead of a wedding cake."

The idea was cute and Virginia had smiled at the couple before telling them about her new class. It was going alright, but Virginia was missing something, though she wasn't sure what. She'd involved both spouses, but the arguing had continued. Richard continued to attend, breaking up minor squabbles as necessary, and getting the group back on task.

And then he'd come up with an idea.

"I think you need a booklet," he said. "Sort of a working guide. And what about writing love letters, sharing thoughts about what is working in the marriage; sort of a positive motivation project."

It was a good idea, though Virginia wondered why she hadn't thought of it first. She was a woman after all, and didn't women usually have the heart to think of all that mushy, close-knit stuff?

God was no longer attending her classes, but the thought that he was still there knowing what she was doing worried and comforted her at the same time.

Would he like what she was doing?

Though the five stones were beginning to gather power again within her mind and heart, Virginia was also thinking of the pink cupcake and diamond ring and how much the symbol was beginning to mean to her.

Had Richard been right? Was the cupcake more than a sweet treat--a way to understand the commitment they'd made to each other? Commitments came in all sorts and included the commitment a mother had to a child and God had to his children.

And then a new thought came to Virginia. It was about the tower, about climbing to heaven, and she felt ashamed. That was what she was doing, making a commitment to God and then doing it all on her own. Sure, she got his help sometimes, but only at the expense of the tower. That's why she had fixed up the room for the baby, gone through all of those tests, visited various doctors; she had been living and breathing optimism and tenacity, and wasn't that being constant with God?

Of course, she'd missed the first two steps, and was continually forgetting about listening and trust, but they were the hardest stones for her--the ones that took the most effort to be with God and to walk with him.

Walking to the kitchen Virginia grabbed the stale cupcake and tossed it into the garbage. It was turning a sickly white-pink anyway, and the ring was stuck in the cupcake for all time.

***

Richard reached for the newly frosted chocolate cake and handed it to God. "And what would you want with a chocolate cake?" he asked.

"As I told you before, sometimes chocolate is my favorite."

God paid for the purchase, which appeared strange to Richard; and God picked up the cake. "Before long it will be spring even in the mountains," he said. "And you know what spring brings."

It was more of a statement than a question but Richard got the gist. "I guess I should be watching for flowers," he said.

"And other things," said God. "But I don't want you to be too disappointed. Just have an open mind, keep praying and allowing me to be a part of your life. Can you do that?"

Richard nodded. A sudden lump had grown in his throat.

***

"So, what did he say?"

Richard plunked the bag of groceries on the counter. She reached inside and began pulling things out.

"Oh, you know--stuff that we're going to need to get us through this challenging time."

Virginia turned to him. "So, what specifically did he say?"

***

Virginia considered Richard's words as she cleaned up the house. It sounded as if things were going to be harder than they'd anticipated. Would the adoption take longer than expected? Once they'd been chosen, the waiting time would be roughly a year. Would they be waiting even longer? What if the child had a problem of some kind and they'd have to deal with physical or emotional issues? What if the child was a boy?

The sudden thought made her gasp. Just because they wanted a girl, that didn't mean that's what God wanted for them. What would they do with a boy? A chill raced up Virginia's back.

The mop stopped in the corner. Well, if it was a boy, then they'd just do the same things. Except boys liked different things and they played much rougher. But they weren't as catty as girls, so that had to be a plus. Still...

"What if we get a boy?"

"But we've asked for a girl." The words coming from the other end of the cell phone were just like she remembered of Richard, before he'd made some slight adjustments that had brought life and a renewed love into their home.

"I know that." The mop was propped now and she was sitting on the old couch with the hole in it. "What would you do if you knew God wanted you to adopt a boy instead of a girl."

There was a pause, far too long for the previous Ms. Virginia Bean.

"Well?"

"If that's what God wants us to have, then we'll get a boy. Right?"

Virginia sighed with relief. "That's what I thought. So, what if it's also a boy and he has, you know, problems."

"What kind of problems?"

"Maybe he is...I don't know, different."

"We're all different. Does that really matter?"

Virginia considered Richard's words. Did it matter? Did any of it really matter? They were going to have child, and healthy or not, they would be parents.

***

"So, you're saying you want to change the forms," asked Sandy. She had that straight face that Richard hated.

"My wife and I (and God, he thought to himself) have considered the importance of keeping things open. We'll take and love a boy or a girl; we've even considered adopting a child with difficulties."

"What sort of difficulties?" asked the case worker.

"Well," Richard looked toward his wife. They had discussed them all. Autism. Cerebral palsy. Aids. Down Syndrome...

"It says here that you don't have any other children. Usually families with biological children will choose to adopt a child with disabilities simply because they've had the experience of raising children and the adopted child will have older siblings to help him or her out. They feel as experienced parents they have something to offer a child with disabilities. Of course, no matter which child you receive, there will be adjustments. We talked about this before..."

Richard remembered. There was the issue of abuse and neglect, drug addiction by a mother passed on to the infant...the list went on and on...He turned to his wife: "I really thought we'd figured this one out," he said.

"Well, this isn't like buying a loaf of bread," Sandy interrupted, standing up. She paced the room as she spoke. "A child is a special gift, and what you want and know you can handle must be carefully discussed. You wouldn't want to make the wrong decision."

"Has that ever happened?" Richard asked.

The woman turned and replanted herself in the swivel chair. "Of course, it's happened, and it's quite disturbing I can tell you, but you need to know that we do all in our power to weed out the undesirables." She paused. Richard's heart thundered. Who was this

159

woman? And why was she working at an adoption agency?

"Of course, if you fill out all of the required forms appropriately, there should be only minor problems that every adoptive parent has to work through. I don't want you to worry about it." A rigid smile. "Just make those decisions and get back to me."

She stood again, ushering them out.

***

Weeks later they'd opened the door even further.

"So, you're considering a baby as well?" Sandy asked, pushing her glasses back on her nose. "Are you sure about that?"

Virginia felt the chills up her arms and knew it was the right decision. "I'm sorry," she said, "but we really need to be open to what God wants for us."

The woman smiled. It was the first real smile Virginia had seen.

"Well then. I'll open it up then as you say. Put together some letters and photos and I'll get these promptly in the binder. All the girls go through them when deciding on the parents for their baby."

She stood and walked to the window. "We'll keep things open, and see what happens, alright?"

When she turned, she was still smiling and Virginia couldn't help it. She was smiling too.

***

Virginia stood in the center of the kitchen. Well, it was the best she could do. The cupboards had been polished to a shine, the floor mopped, the counters wiped until they gleamed. She'd even done some deep cleaning to make sure everything was in order both visually and behind cupboard doors.

And she and Richard had had to pay for the home study visit from Sandy. $2,000 wasn't a mere pittance, and Virginia hoped that all the money forked out would be worth it. The bottom line?

She hoped she passed.

***

The moment God walked around the corner, Richard knew he was in trouble. "Virginia needs you," he said. "You haven't taken any of her calls."

Actually, Virginia hadn't called him. His phone hadn't rung once, had it? Richard's thoughts whirled. So, God knew his wife was in trouble and he wasn't going to lift a finger to help her?

"It's you that must help her."

Richard placed the newly baked cookies under the counter. He was suddenly more worried than he could explain. He looked up. "I'm sorry," he said. "I'll go right now."

***

The room was shuttered dark. The blinds were closed. Virginia sat on the bed, wiping at her eyes. She had done everything right, and now this. She blinked and a tear slid down her cheek. She thought of the child, the boy or girl that might never come. And she was afraid.

What if she'd blown everything?

161

They'd recently painted fluffy white clouds on the ceiling, and as Virginia watched them, she could imagine the wind ripping by and pushing them along. In time the clouds would be gone and she'd see blue sky again.

Was she making a big deal out of nothing?

"Virginia!" The call came from the front of the house. Richard.

"I'm back here!" she sobbed back, wiping at her tears. She'd called him numerous times on the phone without an answer, and now he was here. "In the baby's room!" She'd said it without thinking; as if she'd never torn down the crib, the drapes, or scattered the clothing. But the room was beautiful now, fit for a child, though probably not a boy.

"Virginia!" Richard raced into the room. "How are you?" He scanned her face and drew her to him. "What's going on?"

"The home study."

Richard sniffed. "Smells like the cleanest house on the planet," he said.

"I wish Sandy thought the same."

He pulled her from him and looked into her eyes. "It went alright, didn't it?"

A sudden sound like a branch scraping against the window, startled her. "Yes, I mean no..."

"No and yes?"

He was frustrated, she could tell.

"She was happy at first. Thought the place was spruced up nicely..."

"And?"

Virginia wiped at her nose. She didn't have a tissue. "She was angry about us not having a fire extinguisher. 'That was on the paper I gave you,' she said. And then she complained about us not having outlet covers...I don't even remember seeing that one on the list."

"Outlet covers?" Richard asked, aghast.

"Can you believe she wiped her hand over every piece of furniture to make sure that there were no sharp edges? I don't even want to speak about the hole in the sofa."

"Holy cow."

"Not only that, she asked about the parent training classes. I told her we hadn't been to any of them yet. The first one started last week. I guess I forgot."

"We haven't even been chosen yet. I thought the class came later. How many of them do we have to go to?"

Virginia looked at the paper by her side. She'd picked it up right after Sandy had left her. "Four."

"Then we'll go to the next four," said Richard. "Anything else?"

"Well, just this one thing."

Richard sat waiting. She fingered the comforter.

"The garage. Seems there's some hazardous stuff low enough for a child to reach."

"Oh. Well then, I'll need to get to it. I'll do it this Saturday."

"You work this Saturday."

"No, you work this Saturday."

***

Virginia had just finished cleaning the outsides of the counter when she saw him.

163

"So, how are you doing today?" he asked. This time he had a small girl at his right holding his hand. She looked just like the little girl she'd seen out the lavender window.

"Miss Joy here, she would like one of your pink cupcake's, please."

So, it was the little girl. Virginia tried not to stare, but the girl was beautiful. She had striking blond hair and green eyes. She was petite and her dress was a bit baggy for her small frame, but she was still captivating. She wore a pink sweater and scuffed, black shoes. No tights.

She reached for the cupcake and handed it to the child. "How old are you?" she asked.

"Ten."

A small girl for ten, Virginia thought but didn't say. "So, why do you like pink cupcakes so much?" she asked.

Joy looked up at God. Her eyes said everything.

God reached into his pocket and pulled out some change. He laid it on the counter. "Take what you need," he said, "the rest can go to Miss Joy here."

The girl smiled and hugged him, but not before mashing some of the frosting onto his shirt. The child didn't seem to notice and neither did God. Virginia took the few remaining coins and placed them in the front pocket of Joy's dress. God touched Virginia briefly on the arm and then he turned with the child.

"Thank you, Virginia," he said.

***

Richard coughed. The dust in the garage was thicker than fog. It bothered him in more ways than he could say. What did it matter if the garage wasn't sparkling clean? He'd lock the door or something--keep the child out. He'd bought shelving, brackets, bins to keep everything in, and his arms were beginning to cramp up from all of the lifting.

It was noon already and today he'd remembered to turn his cell phone on--the problem of a few days ago when Virginia hadn't been able to reach him. He couldn't forget that one ever again, especially after the child arrived.

The shelves up, he reached for the first bin. It slid nicely on the shelf. He reached for the second. Each bin was already full of tools, ropes or other supplies. He even had a bin for camping gear--actually he had three of them. He reached for the last bin. This one held memorabilia; his wife's. He was tempted to look inside but didn't. Instead, he placed the last bin on the shelf and turned back to his work.

When the same bin came crashing down seconds later, Richard was beyond patience. "What?" he screamed, though no one was there to hear him. "Why couldn't you stay on board like the others?" He bent down and reached for the various cards, letters and photos. Grabbing them by the fistful's he'd gathered most of it when he saw the photo.

It was Virginia alright, and next to her, Paul. They held each other in a warm embrace. Virginia was kissing him on the lips. The photo was small--a black and white, and like one of those taken at those instant photo places one might see at a carnival or mall.

Virginia had spoken about Paul like an old friend, but as Richard's eyes scanned the two letters he'd discovered within the memorabilia he realized

165

something else. Virginia had been in love with Paul and Paul had been in love with Virginia.

A sudden sadness filled his heart, though he knew that Paul was dead. He placed the photo and the letters inside the bin and sat it again on the high shelf.

***

"Wow! The place looks beautiful!" shrieked Virginia when she saw it. "You even got my memory box up there."

Richard's heart pounded. "Yeah, I was even able to manage that."

"You say it like it was heavy or something."

"No...it was just the last one and I was tired," Richard said. "Let's go inside and get something to eat."

***

Richard was jealous. No, he was angry. The poor guy was dead but he was still angry. The letters had been stunning, almost too perfect, and the two had obviously been in love.

There had been a "connection," a "bonding" that Paul had spoken about in the two letters Richard had found. And strangely enough, he'd discovered hearts on the edges of the letters. It was all he could do to eat dinner.

"So, the garage. How long did it take you?" Virginia asked.

Richard took a loaded bite of spaghetti. The noodles slid down his throat like unspoken lies. How could he tell her what he'd found and how he felt about what he'd found? She would think him stupid. Anyway, why would he find those letters and photo now, and why would he care about them?

"Well?"

Richard realized he hadn't answered. "About half the day," he said, though it had taken him longer. The reading of the letters had taken him about an hour. He'd read them over and over until he almost knew them by heart. He was embarrassed, but keenly aware that Virginia was staring at him.

"Something is wrong," she finally said. "Tell me. I have done plenty of crying and temper tantrums for the both of us. Did Sandy call or something?"

He shook his head.

"Then what?"

The idea of telling her revolted him. Jealousy was something that happened the first couple of years in marriage--if it happened at all. He could hardly believe he was thinking it.

"I dumped your box inside the garage."

Her fork with noodles and sauce rested in mid-air. "None of it got ruined, did it?"

He gulped. "No."

She took a bite. "I didn't see anything on the garage floor. Thanks for picking them up."

"You're welcome." He took another loaded bite of spaghetti and another. The garlic bread rested near his plate. He picked it up, dipped it in the sauce and took a bite. The bread was tasty, and the garlic perfect.

"You're awfully quiet."

He took another bite of spaghetti, and another until the plate was empty except for a bit of sauce. He finished the garlic bread.

"Wow, I've never seen you eat like that," she said, leaning in. "So, what is it?"

"I... I saw some stuff in that box."

"Naturally." She was grinning at him, but she didn't know his thoughts. He wondered how she'd respond if she knew.

"Well, there was a picture and some letters."

"I know. It is my box."

"You. And Paul."

"So that's it."

"What?" He wiped his mouth with the napkin.

"You're jealous. I didn't think you had a jealous bone in your body."

"Neither did I." He stood, taking his plate to the sink and washing it off.

"So?"

"So, I found it, and instead of putting them back I read them. I'm sorry."

"You what?"

He turned to see her fragile face staring up at him. She'd pulled her long blond hair back today and the style emphasized her eyes. They were even larger. He didn't answer her immediately and she was silent. All Richard could think about was taking every word back. That was until she said, "You know, that commitment stuff is really starting to sink in. Imagine, a man who I thought didn't have a sliver of jealousy in his body has some after all."

"It's embarrassing."

"No, it's not." She stood and walked to the sink with her own dish. "I like it that you have flaws other than leaving your clothes all over the place. But mostly,

I like that you are committed enough to me to tell me about them."

***

With the paperwork in and the additional items checked off of their list, she and Richard reached the doors. Today was the day of their first class.

Her heart was beating like a thunderstorm but she tried to maintain an exterior of calmness and courage, for she would need a lot of courage to get through this one. The class was full, not a chair remained, and as she and Richard stood at the back, Sandy motioned them over.

"There are more chairs in the next classroom. Do you mind getting a couple?"

Richard nodded and left the room, while Virginia stood waiting.

In the meantime, she surveyed the people in the room. Most were young; a couple had young children with them already, and one couple in particular looked about the ages of she and her husband. But they were sitting up at the front.

Richard returned with the folding chairs. He sat them up in the back.

"Let's begin then," said Sandy, as if on cue. "Most of you know me as one of the case workers here, but I also teach some pretty inspiring parenting classes."

The room was quiet.

Richard nudged her. "I can't believe she said that," he whispered, then turned his face toward the front. Virginia got the distinct impression that Sandy had heard him. But from way up front?

"As you probably know from the flyer, today I'll be speaking about beliefs and attitudes as they relate to adoption. The second part of today I will be focusing on mental preparation." She tried to smile. "If, during my presentation, you have any questions, please don't hesitate to ask."

Virginia thought of her marriage class and hoped she didn't sound as dry.

Richard nudged her again, but she pretended to ignore him.

"We will also cover diaper changing. For those of you already experienced in this skill, I expect you will help the others." She looked directly at Virginia as if she thought that somehow, she would be a likely candidate for either option.

Richard laughed. She nudged him back.

"We'll start with a short film." The room was darkened and Richard touched her leg in a romantic gesture. This was sure to be an enlightening experience.

***

The next few weeks were miserable. With the paperwork finished for the adoption agency, it was time for the waiting game, and that included saving a bit more money than they'd first expected.

Tonight, she was giving her last class and she was excited about the cupcakes she'd baked with the diamond rings on top. It was to be their last hurrah, and Virginia was excited about the prospect of letting go of the class and allowing God to take each couple forward.

The next day she got a call from Sandy. "Can you come in to the office right away?" she asked. She sounded excited.

"Sure."

"I'll be in the office until 6. Just make sure you make it in by then."

Virginia turned to Richard. They were both working at *Just Desserts*. "Sandy wants to see us," she said.

"Both of us?" Richard was busy with a customer. There was a line and Virginia had only just dashed in-between customers to pick up the phone. She eyed the woman who was next in line and turned back to her husband. "Why don't I help you for a bit and then I'll go when things die down." She walked to the counter. "What can I help you with?" she asked.

The woman smiled wearily. She wore a thin coat and a dirty, crocheted hat, but her smile was warm. "I just want to thank you," she said.

Virginia blinked.

"I mean, it isn't every day that someone gives you a ring."

Virginia was silent as she watched the woman stare at her. She had the most vivid blue eyes, but her face was lined with worry. "I want to thank you for the diamond ring in the cupcake."

"But it wasn't me," Virginia said.

"I know." The woman wiped at her brown hair, pulling a few strands away from her face. "That's what Joy said..."

"God has a way of helping his children," Virginia said.

171

"Through other people. Joy has such faith in God."

A warmth like sunlight caressed Virginia's back. "I know. You have a beautiful little girl."

"Thank you." She turned.

"Can I get something for you?" Virginia asked.

"Oh, no, no. But thank you again."

As Virginia watched the woman, she couldn't help noticing the young blond girl standing nearby. Her mother had evidently asked her to wait by the last cash register in order for her not to overhear the conversation. But there was something about the little girl's face that told Virginia she'd somehow heard.

***

Virginia sat across the desk. Sandy smiled that crooked smile she was fond of. She pushed a colorful sheet of paper across the counter. Virginia looked down. It was the photos and letters she and Richard had written a few weeks ago.

"You must need an edit," she said, feeling discouraged again and not up for any more paperwork.

"Not an edit. I just wanted you to know that your profile has been taken out of the binder."

"My profile? Why?"

"Because someone has chosen you."

The Feast

"Richard, Richard!" The scream seemed hollow in the large classroom, but as Virginia reached the counter her voice stopped at Richard's chest. The place was vacant for a change. Perfect, it would give them a moment to celebrate.

"We've been chosen!" Virginia shrieked.

"Chosen for what?"

"As parents, you dummy!" She didn't tell him that she'd been wandering in the same clueless darkness only an hour earlier.

"You mean, we're getting a child?"

Virginia smiled and hugged him. "Not just any child," she breathed, and the scent of Irish Spring filled her nostrils. "A baby girl."

***

"We need a crib, clothes, everything, everything I threw out the window."

"Yes, and what about bottles..."

"That's right bottles..." Virginia was making a list and her hands couldn't move fast enough.

"What about the girl. When do we meet her?"

"The girl? When she's born, of course."

He nudged her. "The girl who is having our baby," he said.

Virginia shrugged. "Oh, that girl. I think Sandy said next week or so. She's scheduling a meeting."

"Stop." He held out his hand so Virginia knew he was serious. He'd become much more serious the last few weeks as they'd prepared their minds for the child they wanted. "Can the girl change her mind after meeting us? What is her name anyway?"

"Gail Shepherd...I think."

"You think?" He stared at her incredulously. She felt her stomach turn. He was stressing her out. Suddenly she didn't feel very well.

"Well, I was so excited about being a mother that I didn't hear much of what the case worker said." She paused, looked up from the list, and smiled over at him. "Really, I'm sorry. I'll call her tomorrow, okay?"

He touched her hand. "You're not going to like what I'm going to say. I don't think we should make a list yet."

"Why not?"

"Because, honey, if she does change her mind we'll have a nursery once again without a child. You sure she said it was a girl?"

"Of course, I'm sure!" She threw the list at him and the pen whirled to the other side of the room.

***

Richard was worried. So, Virginia wasn't going to talk to him--again. So be it. He had plenty of work, plenty to do to keep his mind off of the situation...

He looked up.

"Hello."

"Hello, Richard. Heard the news about the baby."

"You too?"

God chuckled. "Well, actually..."

Richard felt suddenly stupid. "Sorry," he said. "I'm just worried about her, that's all."

"As well you should. She really wants to buy those clothes, and I think she's already picked out a crib."

"Is that so."

"Why are you so worried?"

"I'm not worried." In the very mention of worry Richard felt guilty. If anyone knew when he was feeling guilty it would be God. "Sorry," he said again.

"Stop saying sorry and do something about it," he said.

"I have no idea what to do. She thinks...I can't believe what she thinks."

"Tell me."

Richard looked into God's eyes for the very first time on this visit, and he liked what he saw there. Virginia was right. God did love him.

"She wants to buy everything and I'm afraid it's just not going to happen."

"What makes you say that?"

Richard looked past God but there wasn't anyone waiting for service. He turned his eyes back to him. "What if the girl changes her mind? It's been known to happen. I don't know if I can go through all of that again.

Wouldn't it be better to hold off, just until we knew for sure?"

"It would be easier," said God.

"So, you agree."

"It would be easier. Consider the path you have trod up until this point. Hasn't everything served as instruction?"

Richard thought about God's words. Well, sure. He'd married Virginia and they had spent years trying to have a child. He understood Virginia better now than he'd done when they'd first met. He understood marriage better. He'd learned about patience, the importance of really seeing his wife and doing for her; yes, he'd even learned a bit about jealousy--why it didn't work in a marriage. He'd also learned about God and the relationship he needed to have with him, and combined, the relationship he needed to have with God and his wife.

"Those are some good thoughts," God said, placing his large hands on the counter and clasping them together. "But there is more yet to learn."

"You mean that Virginia just doesn't get it? Here she is doing exactly what she did the first time for a baby that might not even come."

"Where is your faith?"

"Well, at least I'm being realistic. At least I know what end is up."

"And what end is up, Richard?"

Richard eyed God closely but all he could see in God's eyes was love.

***

"I'm sorry," said Richard, taking his wife's hand. "What do you want to buy first?"

Virginia couldn't believe it. "You mean you'll go with me to get the crib and all the other stuff?"

Richard nodded. "Anything you want. I love you, honey."

Virginia hugged him. "You're a good man," she said, breathing into his ear, "but I don't want to buy a crib."

"She'll need a crib..."

"Look, we can wait awhile. Let's meet with Gail; get to know her a bit. We have plenty of time to get everything. Remember, we did this once before so now we have some practice. Imagine how fast we can purchase things this time around."

"Are you sure? What changed your mind?"

Virginia smiled, and pulled him to her again. "Let's just say I had a little talk with God."

***

Gail was a bright girl. She sat across from them at the adoption agency and read again from Richard's letter:

"'...Children come from the Lord and I want to be a good father to one of God's children.'" Gail looked up, a small tear traveling down her left cheek. Her stomach was round, and her blond hair was brushed back from her eyes in a large ponytail. "I think that's what did it," she said. "It was the part about God."

Richard looked at her, smiled, and patted her hand. It was a sweet gesture.

"I mean, I didn't want to get pregnant but now that I am, I'm happy to be giving my baby girl to such spiritual minded people. You will make good parents."

"Thank you," said Virginia. "We'll do our best."

"And I don't want you to get worried. You know, I won't change my mind, and I won't decide to keep it or anything."

Virginia's heart pounded. She looked over at Richard. His face had suddenly gone pale.

"Really. I am planning on going to college. My boyfriend...well, that's another story, but I'm going to make something of myself. I'm going to learn stuff."

"What are you going to major in?"

Gail shrugged her slim shoulders. "I'm not sure yet, but I've always been interested in bugs. I used to collect them as a kid. Maybe there's a major for that."

Richard smiled.

"And you." She turned to Virginia. "I like that you have blond hair. The father has blond hair, too, so there's a pretty good chance..."

"I can hardly believe it," said Virginia. "I feel so honored."

"You don't need to cry. Besides, the baby will be beautiful and you can cry then, after I have it." A sudden crinkle in the girl's forehead made Virginia wince. She was only 15 and she was going to have a baby.

***

It was the fourth week of their classes, and he and Virginia had already learned about coping after the adoption. They'd learned about the adoption triad, a sort of triangle representing the birth parent, the adopted child and the adoptive parents; the rite of passage and life art of raising an adopted child, and the intertwined culture and positive imagery necessary when times got hard.

Richard considered what he had learned, and he counted his relationship with God as his greatest asset. For wasn't it God that had brought he and his wife together and wasn't it God who was now engineering this new life into their lives?

"Now, I don't want you to get discouraged," Sandy was saying. "There will be times when you will need a time out. You will need to leave the room and let the baby cry."

"I could never do that," whispered Virginia to Richard.

"It won't hurt the baby to cry a little. And if your spouse is at home with you, this is also a good time for him to do a bit of helping. Any questions?"

Virginia raised her hand. "I just don't think I could let my baby cry," she said.

"That's well and good but consider how much work you'll be doing on a daily basis and how tired you're going to be after a long day. Leaving the room is always better than picking up a baby when you are angry or tired."

"But I would never..."

Richard nudged her. "I think what's important here," said the case worker, "is that you know your limits for the protection of your new baby or child. It's important that you listen to the warning signs that we discussed. Any other questions?"

"Are we finished?" shouted someone in the back.

Sandy blushed. "Almost. I have brought some treats as a thank you for your participation. I know you will all make great parents. If you ever have any concerns, please don't hesitate to call me." She opened the boxes on the table and reached for the juice.

***

"So, what do you think?" Gail patted her round belly. She was eight months along and the time was nearing. "Do you think she will be a soccer player or a ballerina?"

"Soccer player...ballerina," she and Richard echoed in unison, making Gail laugh. They were out on a picnic of sorts, and Gail was telling them all about her likes and loves as well as those things she couldn't stand. She handed them a paper. On it she'd written everything: Her favorite foods, her least favorite sport; her favorite and least favorite colors.

Richard thanked her and handed the paper over to Virginia. Birds twittered in the trees and the grass smelled of new growth. Spring was almost here.

***

Virginia finished the last of the pink cupcakes and shelved them behind the case. It was amazing, how the flavor (a rich strawberry) had taken over almost every sale at *Just Desserts*. The classes long ended, she and Richard were preparing for the little one. The crib was finally in the lavender room; though much of the room itself hadn't changed. Still, the baby's outfits of pink, yellow and purple peeked from inside the shelving, and whispers of 'little girl' surrounded the room in the form of pillows, play things and tiny polka dots.

It was Saturday, just three weeks before Gail's due date and everything was ready. She was ready. It felt as if she was pregnant and would soon deliver. She breathed in the pink frosting and slid the glass shut.

From behind her, Richard was getting the sweet rolls out of the oven and displaying them on cooling racks. It was morning, near 7 a.m., and only a few shoppers were walking, shopping and visiting. She hadn't seen God for nearly two months, but somehow her visits with him through prayer and scripture study had fed her mind and heart. She knew he was there even if she couldn't see him.

Richard was looking good. He'd started a diet plan just six weeks ago, and she could already see some changes, mostly around his middle. He smiled at her now and placed the pan on the cooling rack.

"You're deep in thought," he said.

"It's too perfect," she said. "I can hardly believe we're going to have a baby."

"And you look so good," he said.

She smiled down at her stomach. "Almost as nice as yours."

"So, you think I'm getting buff?"

"Something like that."

He held her close. "Can't look chubby for that new baby."

She laughed. "She'll be chubby for you."

"But that's different. So, what are we going to name her?"

They'd discussed multiple names but none had really spoken to her until she'd brought up the name, Joy.

"I still think, Joy," she said.

"But that's that little orphan girl's name."

"She has a mother."

"Right, but I don't know. Shouldn't we pick something inspiring?" he asked.

"Joy is inspiring. Her mother is inspiring. I'm grateful for both of them. Maybe...we can give this little girl a better life than either of them has likely had."

Richard smiled down at her. His eyes were warm. "Hmmm, I'll have to think about that."

***

A week later, Virginia wasn't feeling well, so Richard went to work without her. She spent the day in bed and nursed her flu with fluids and lots of television. By afternoon she was bored so she pulled out her Bible and began to read.

She'd discovered the verse that Richard had found a few months ago and thought of it again as she pondered God's words: "And they said, Go to. Let us build us a city and a tower, whose top may reach into heaven... (Genesis 11:4)."

Was she reaching heaven?

Doing all of the right things was an interesting thought, but Virginia knew that it was much more about repentance than it was about being perfect. Life with God was about giving herself over to him; it was seeing his will for her more than the desires she had for herself. It was about trusting him; he would help her get into heaven.

She placed the stones before her like a map. One led to another until she reached the stone of constancy that led to the pink cupcake, commitment. Yes, she even had a pink cupcake with a ring in it. Tears welled then, though she wasn't sure why, but she was happy for the new commitment she'd made with Richard as well as with God. She was glad that they were a part of her life.

Reaching for the cupcake, she pulled out the ring. It glittered, though not gold. But it didn't have to be gold, it could be anything now, anything that drew her closer to God. Placing the ring on the coffee table she reached for the pink wrapping, and slowly pulled the pink paper away. Once off, she sat the wrinkled mess next to the ring and took a bite of cake.

It was yummy. The taste of strawberry melted and filled her mouth. With another bite came even more taste, and so she continued to bite and chew and swallow until the cupcake was finished and she could lick her fingers.

Boy, she made a heavenly cupcake!

When the phone rang moments later, she didn't hear it at first. Enjoying the last taste of strawberry leaving her lips, she finally stood and walked to the kitchen where her cell phone was sitting. It was Richard.

"Hello, lover!" she answered.

But he didn't reply.

"How are you feeling?" he finally managed.

"Much better. I just ate a cupcake."

"Well, you'll want to get over here as quickly as you can. There's been an accident."

"What? Where?"

"Now I don't want you to worry. I don't..."

"What is it?"

"It's Gail."

"What about Gail. Is she alright?"

183

"She's had the baby."

"The baby?"

"She's had the baby." Richard sounded so sad. She couldn't imagine what was wrong.

"Get to the hospital as soon as you can."

"What's wrong? What's wrong with the baby?"

"Do you want me to come and get you?"

"You mean you're already there?"

"They called. You were sick, but now..."

"What?"

"Virginia. Calm down. I'll come and get you."

"No, no." Virginia took a deep breath. Something was wrong with the baby but she had to get there. "I'll do it," she said, and then hung up before saying good-bye.

Racing into the baby's room she gathered her favorite little outfit, some booties, a blanket and a bottle. What else, what else? Yes, she remembered now. Everything else was packed in the diaper bag. She picked it up, stuffed the little things she'd gathered inside, and slung the bag over her shoulder.

***

She'd forgotten her jacket and it was cold. As the doors swung open, Virginia raced inside. She ran to the first booth she could see someone standing behind. She didn't look at the sign above or the people sitting near her. All she could think about was the baby.

"Labor and delivery!" she yelled.

A nurse stood, looked toward Virginia's feet, and then back at Virginia. "You don't..."

"It's not me, I'm...I'm the adoptive mother. I need to get to my baby!"

"Your name, please."

"Ah...Virginia. Virginia Bean I mean Virginia Green."

The woman looked down.

"Hurry, hurry!"

"The wife of Richard Green?"

"That's me!"

"Follow me."

Virginia followed behind the well-endowed woman. She walked slowly, and her legs were too short like a child's. Virginia was breathing heavy, she knew, but she also knew she needed to get to her husband and to her new baby. What was wrong? Why had Richard sounded so quiet? Was something wrong with the mother? She'd never considered that. Was something wrong with Gail? And all she could think about was the baby! *Please forgive me, Father!* she prayed. *And bless me, that no matter what happens that I will remember Thy great love for me. Thy will be done.*

At the end of her prayer they'd reached a room. She could see Richard inside and Gail lying on a bed, and she could see Gail's parents; she'd met them only once, when Gail had invited them to dinner at their home. But now they all looked solemn. It took all she had within her to walk inside.

Gail was crying, and so were her parents. Richard reached for her. The little baby carrier on wheels was empty.

***

Baby Joy was dead.

Gail had fallen down the stairs at her parent's home and they had raced her here, but not in time. The baby was gone.

"My baby!" Gail screamed, and in that instant Virginia wondered if the baby had ever been hers. Virginia took the petite girl in her arms and held her close. Gail shook and the cold returned to Virginia's arms. "I killed her, I killed my...baby."

Fresh tears creased Virginia's cheeks. She held the girl as she sobbed but the words wouldn't come. And then she felt a hand. She didn't turn but she knew instinctively that it wasn't Richard's. Still, the warmth that filled her was immeasurable.

"Do you forgive me?" the young girl asked.

As she felt the hand burn love within her there was only one thing she could say. "Yes, yes, I forgive you. It was an accident, a terrible accident."

The girl sobbed again, holding Virginia close.

Virginia heard Richard's voice. This time she turned to see him standing by the window. "Are you alright?"

She left Gail and raced to him. The top of his shirt was already wet and he cried along with her as even more tears came to his eyes. "I'm so sorry, Virginia, so sorry."

She felt so weary.

"How long have you been here?" she asked. She looked up then to see Gail's parents standing at either side of their daughter's bed.

"About two hours. I didn't want to worry you...until I knew."

"So where..."

"Do you want to see her? She's beautiful, just like we always wanted." He touched her face and wiped away the tears.

"How is Gail?"

"She'll be alright. She's young and strong. So, do you want to see the baby?"

***

She was surprised at how peaceful she looked. How still. But she was gone. There was no light and the 7 lb. 2 oz little girl was perfect.

***

"How are you doing?"

He was worried about her, although she'd told him otherwise. "I'm at peace," she said, holding him and crying. "It's God's will, and I will be alright."

He'd watched her in forthcoming weeks, when the due date arrived and the nursery remained empty. He'd watched her rock in the rocker in the baby's room. He'd watch as she handled the itty-bitty clothes. He'd watched as she read her favorite children's books aloud in the lavender room. And he'd watch her as she cried.

But she didn't throw anything out. Not the crib, not the blankets, not the books. And after three weeks she was joining him again at work.

She looked pale, and she wasn't eating like he was used to seeing, but she was smiling and talking about starting up some new marriage classes. "Now, we have an even deeper element to share about children," she'd say. "Now that we have experienced it for ourselves."

And he would nod and hug her and pretend that he was doing as well as she was. "If it wasn't for him..."

When the day drew closer for their anniversary, he'd explained about the trip up the hill. It would be a remembrance of sorts, for their wedding day, now six years past. When she'd remained quiet and thoughtful, he'd put the matter aside for another day.

And now it was here.

***

The walk wasn't an easy one. In early spring the hill a few miles behind their Idaho cabin was as covered with snow as icing on one of her favorite cupcakes. She thought of the cupcake now, pink and ready.

Her boots stepped through the thick snow. The air was crisp and as Richard held her gloved hand, she thought of the last time they'd traversed this area. She couldn't help it. All the feelings came back, though this time the wilderness was covered in snow.

"So, where are we going?" she asked.

"My surprise," he said. But the way he said it, she knew.

The walk was a good 30 minutes on a summer day, and Richard was silent as she followed him from behind. They'd brought along plenty of water, some mixed nuts and dried fruit, and a couple of green apples--his favorite.

Her breath was floating through the air like ice skaters on wings. The trees were covered in white powder, and the top of the hill, that almost resembled a mountain, stood before them like a tower--her tower. How well she knew the changes that would need to be made. How well she knew where she had been and what it would mean to move forward, not only on this snow-covered trail, but in her life.

***

Richard's thoughts couldn't be restrained. He tried to remember the ceremony like it was yesterday...

"And do you, Richard, take Virginia as your lawfully wedded wife, to have and to hold, from this day forward, as long as you both shall live?"

"I do."

The eyes of the preacher had turned then to his future wife. She was resplendent in white satin and pearls; her blond hair was drawn up in wildflowers, unexpected strands of hair curled around her face. She wore no veil, and her smile took him in and carried him away.

"And do you, Virginia, take this man to be your lawfully wedded husband, to have and to hold, from this day forward, as long as you both shall live?"

There was a pause, and for a brief moment Richard wondered if she had changed her mind. And then he'd looked deeply into her eyes. Warmth was there, and love. "Yes," she'd said, although the appropriate words were to be, 'I do.' She looked at him, warmth filling her face, the feel of her hands in his connecting them both. And now?

As he held her hand, they walked. The snow was deep, and his love for her had increased. Six years later he loved her more than he could express.

"We're almost there," he breathed, a small fog coming from his mouth and filling the sky. "Are you ready?"

"For what?"

He thought again of the day he'd kissed her, long and lingering, on this very hill--wildflowers and a few friends and loved ones as their only backdrop. It was all he could do to remain patient as they took the last few steps to the top. "To marry me again."

***

She wasn't sure how he had done it, but the table was spread, a small table with lit candles and her best dishes. She would have killed him if she hadn't been so touched. And then there was the red heart tablecloth made of material, not one of those plastic kinds that you can find at the local dollar store. But that's not all. Somehow, he'd managed some violinists. They must have been shaking in their boots. They were playing music, what was it? She didn't know, but the soothing tune just made her cry. He took her hand.

"You know the first time we were here..." He wasn't looking at her but off into the distance as if reflecting on the first time. "...there were friends, some food, but not nearly the privacy afforded us now."

She blinked over at the violinists. The tone was slow in movement, almost like the day air that curled around her face.

"Except for them," she said.

He walked her to the table. "I think you should know that I've made some very fine plans, and not all of them have to do with food."

She giggled and sat down. There was nothing on the table other than the linens and dishes. She wondered what they were going to eat. Snow? The thought of it made her even more cold.

And then, in the distance she heard it, sort of like her car's wiper blades, but louder. In moments she could hear the helicopter as it reached the hill's peek. A metal bird, its blades whirred until the beast landed, the tablecloth fluttering slightly at its approach. The whirring continued and then slowed and stopped.

In seconds someone was getting out. Actually, there were two of them, including a boy who looked like the boy she'd seen that day stocking shelves at Wholesale Max's. The women who came out were familiar too. How had he roped *them* into this?

It was two of the ladies from her class! The young woman named Brianne and the middle-aged woman named Tracy whose husband had a huge thing for sports. They were carrying huge plastic tubs, walking through the snow like the troupers she had no idea they were. As they approached they opened the tubs. A sweet and memorable scent entered Virginia's nostrils. Why it smelled just like turkey with all of the trimmings!

"You're right, of course," said her husband as if he'd heard her. "We are having Thanksgiving early this year."

Virginia sat stunned as the women dished them up. Both were wearing red heart aprons over their coats. As expected they wore boots as well and handed them some hand warmers--something they'd forgotten to pack in Richard's eagerness to get up the hill.

"Now, you're going to have to eat sort of fast," Tracy said. "It's sort of like the Winter Olympics up here,

191

though I know it's spring down there. The helicopter pilot assures me that he will be back for you in a short time to take you down."

Richard smiled over at her and then looked down at his steaming plate of turkey, potatoes, yams, rolls and pumpkin pie. "I'll have you know," he said clearly for all to hear, "that this is by far the coldest Thanksgiving meal I've ever experienced."

"We'll leave you then," said Brianne, waving to the other woman. They took the containers and walked to the helicopter. The violinists were still playing. It was as soothing, but the cold was feeling its way through her pores. The downdraft from the helicopter blades rushed near them again and in a few moments the helicopter lifted into the sky and was gone.

Richard smiled. "Now, they'll be back in about 20 minutes or so. By that time, we should be halfway through with our meal and I can do what I came here to do."

"Surely, not *that*..." Virginia said, taking a bite of potatoes.

"No, *that* is reserved for later. The *extra dessert* if you will."

Virginia giggled, she couldn't help it. Fortunately, the chairs were padded with a red cushion. She couldn't imagine sitting on frigid wood. Still, the seat was not heated. She'd already placed the warmers down her boots and those in her hands were heating up nicely.

A few minutes into the meal Richard stood, motioned to the violinists, and dropped next to her on one knee. She could imagine the chill quickly traveling up his leg as it met the snow. The song was their wedding song, and all Virginia could think about was the glorious warmth and happiness of that day. It was cold, but not as cold as today. Spring had come much earlier that year and Virginia could still smell the new buds peeking out from green in some places and from snow in others.

Richard reached inside his coat pocket and pulled out a ring. At first, she imagined it as one of those nasty ones, the old cheap things she used in the cupcakes, but then...

"Now, I know exactly what you're thinking," he said, "but I want you to know I had it sized perfectly for your *right* hand."

"My right hand?" Virginia turned from the sweet smell that was quickly growing cold.

"Hold it out."

Virginia put down her fork and held out her hand. "If you will remove the glove, please." He grinned mischievously up at her.

Against her better judgment, but captivated by his smile, Virginia removed the glove along with the hand warmer. He slid the ring on. It was warm and it was real.

"Why..."

"Now I want you to know that I spent a lot of money on this," Richard said, surprising her more. "But that's not why I bought it."

"Okay?"

"Well, it spoke to me. It said, 'This is the ring for your wife. She needs to know how much you love her. She needs to know that the baby will come.'"

"It really said that?" Hearing the voice of God was one thing, but hearing the voice of a ring? Okay, so it was like hearing a voice from the stones. She could believe anything.

193

"You'd better switch knees. This one's going to freeze off."

"Not until you tell me you'll marry me again."

"Sure. Now get off that knee."

He switched knees.

"Now that you've said yes, I'd like a kiss." He pursed his lips.

She leaned over, her Thanksgiving meal in May forgotten. The kiss was long and sweet and reminded her of the one shared just a few short years ago.

"I want you to remember this cold day with the lovely Thanksgiving meal, and I want you to remember how much I love you."

"I love you, too," she squeaked, for suddenly the cold was gone and all she could think about was how much she loved him. And something else. She'd waited and waited and waited for the right moment, and of all things, her sweet husband had given it to her.

"Thank you for the beautiful ring," she said, "but I'm getting cold."

***

Virginia pulled off the glove and fingered the ring on her right hand. "You're a pretty strange man," she said. "Why didn't you have the helicopter pick us up in the first place?"

"And miss the great hike? I don't think so." He laughed.

He turned from the helicopter window. Fresh tears were falling down his cheeks. "This ring's our new commitment, to each other and to God."

"I love it. But what about my commitment to you. I don't have a ring for you."

"You don't need one."

"But I do."

"Just count the ring I gave you as a commitment for us both."

"But it doesn't work that way. When we land, let's go shopping for a new ring. I have something to tell you anyway."

His eyebrows raised. The helicopter was landing. It appeared to be stopping at some helicopter port near a mansion.

"The boy and his father," he answered.

She could barely see the top of the boy's head from where she was sitting, but there was definitely two of them sitting up front.

Richard reached for her hand. The metal blades whirred to a stop and the man and his son got out. Again, she noticed the striking resemblance to the boy that God had gone to help at Wholesale Max's.

The older man shook each of their hands and Richard thanked him for the free flight.

But it was the younger one who spoke.

"Hi," he said. "Have a good time?"

"We did." She couldn't help thinking of the day that God had left her standing alone in favor of going to the boy who stocked the shelves. The boy in front of her now appeared to be the same young man. Hadn't God called him Trevor? She had stood quite a distance from him then...still...

"How has your work been going at Wholesale Max's?" she decided to ask.

He seemed momentarily surprised. He looked at her closely for the first time and appeared to consider her words as well as her face.

And then a surprising thought struck Virginia. Could Trevor be the father of Gail's child?

"Good, much better, thank you," he said.

Trevor walked away with his father, and then quite unexpectedly he turned, allowing his father to walk ahead. Virginia's car was parked in front of the mammoth house, ready for their return to their humble abode, but something had struck the boy, and he was grasping for the right words.

She watched as the cool air brushed against his hair, the way he stood in that thoughtful position, hands to his side, his eyes looking slightly up. He shifted his feet.

A chord had definitely been struck.

"And you, are you feeling better since losing your baby?" he asked.

Her heart thundered in her chest. Her baby. He had called the baby, hers. "You know...Gail?" she asked.

He colored slightly. "I love her, you know. I want you to know that."

Virginia imagined God then, walking up to Trevor, the boy standing before her now, the same boy she'd been *put out* about at Wholesale Max's. She imagined him taking the chocolate cake to the boy and telling him something about cakes and how it's the frosting that takes the cake or something like that. She imagined him spilling the beans about commitment; and she imagined that the boy felt love and joy within his soul.

The Feast: A Parable of the Ring

***

Their shopping finished, Virginia placed the newly purchased ring on the frosted pink cupcake and walked to the living room. It was the same routine every night. Leave your shoes on the floor by the bed and your clothing next to it. Put on pajamas. Go into the bathroom, take off rings. Wash face. Brush teeth. Go into the living room. Watch T.V.

As she watched the silver ring glitter on the top of the cupcake, Virginia thought about how much she loved Richard and how much she loved God. After everything they had been through, she had begun to really listen to God. Her trust in him consumed her. It really was about doing her best and trusting in God's will for her. And if she listened, she could do that, even if she didn't like it.

Optimism wasn't something she carried around simply for the sake of carrying it. She carried it always, whether her life was turning out the way she expected it to, or not. She just kept going. Kept going. Not on her own, but with God. Always with God. The constancy with God was a consistent walk, through thorns as well as roses.

Would it be tough?

She touched her belly. Like a glittering ring on a pink cupcake, surprises came when you least expected them. After continuing to feel sick for weeks, she'd decided to go in for a checkup. Her tiredness, her queasiness actually meant something. She laughed to herself as she remembered jumping off the examination table buck naked.

Would it continue to be tough?

Yes. But with God and Richard at her side, she knew she would make it.

The Feast
A Spiritual Guide

The Ring

- Marriage means helping each other.
- Trials are necessary.
- Humility helps you to hear God.
- Miracles happen every day. They often come in small packages.
- Communication takes work and patience.
- Sometimes you have to try again.
- Sometimes you don't get what you want when you want it.
- When miracles happen, you don't always see them.
- Sometimes you get too comfortable with life.
- Sometimes you avoid the one you love instead of facing the problem head on.
- Sarcasm rarely helps an already tender situation.
- When God speaks peace to your heart, that's a message, too.

The Vow

- You cannot force your way into heaven.
- Pray even when you're angry. Especially when you're angry.
- You create the distance between you and God.
- Optimism has its boundaries--without God.
- Jealousy can creep in when you least expect it.
- God provides in mysterious ways.
- A gesture of service can open both windows and doors.
- Prayer opens the heart to hearing answers.
- God's will for you is not always the same as your will for yourself.

The Choice

- Yes, the timing of God is everything.
- Commitment travels three ways.
- Pay attention to life. It might just tell you something.
- Answers take work.
- Sometimes our spouse will surprise us for the better.
- An open mind does wonders for disappointment.
- God may speak to you unexpectedly, be ready to respond quickly.
- Again, jealousy creeps in when you least expect it.
- Forgiveness is key.

The Feast

- Waiting takes patience but it helps with understanding.
- Everything you go through in life lends instruction.
- Have faith.

The Feast: A Parable of the Ring

- Repent.
- Forgive.
- Perfection comes in the next life.
- See God's will for you and have the courage to follow it.
- Learn through experience.
- Commitment to God is key to success.

KATHRYN ELIZABETH JONES

Notes

Notes

KATHRYN ELIZABETH JONES

Notes

THE GIFT

DEDICATION

A big thank you to my beta readers:

Joan Tolman
Tricia Leslie
Carolyn Tolman
Bethany Wursten
And, as always, to my husband and number one
cheerleader, Doug

Preface

In The Feast: A Parable of the Ring, Virginia sought for what she wanted most, a child, and got her. She strengthened her marriage with Richard, and learned even more about Listening, Trust, Optimism, Tenacity and Constancy through the trials and joys of bringing a new life into the world. But life isn't always what you expect. And the stones, well-meaning as they are, can't begin to create the person you want to be (especially a person like Virginia is) if you no longer have the courage to really live their teachings.

Like now, for example.

The Beginning

Beatrice was 9 months old when the key turned for Virginia. The summer leaves were just beginning to dry, preparing themselves for yet another fall and heavy winter in Idaho Falls, Idaho, and the little babe Virginia had finally managed to bring into this world had left it too soon.

No real cause. No real solution. But crib death was like that. "Don't turn her on her belly." "Don't put stuffed animals in her bed." "Don't smoke."

Well, she hadn't done any of those things and the baby girl that she'd waited for, for so long, was under the cold earth, never again to reach out her tiny little hands.

God was cruel.

No, that was the wrong thing to say.

God was...

She didn't know what God was. And she didn't know if she'd truly ever believe him again.

Richard was smart. He went to work. Struggled with the doughnuts and cupcakes that she still made for the tiny shop they'd finally managed to purchase away from the grocery store. He was smart because he kept himself busy, like a tall elf in Santa's shop, doing the busy stuff so the doughnuts could be delivered on time to the smiles of every heavy, needy customer.

All of her thoughts were negative now - the size of the customers, the way the air blew through the bottom of the front door in a sort of chilled whirr, the remembrance of icicles that would soon be dangling from the rooftop of their tiny home, like sharp knives penetrating her heart.

***

It would soon be Christmas.

And it wasn't fair. In spite of all she knew about God, all that he'd taught her, all that he'd shown her in the birth of their baby Beatrice, he had taken her daughter home. With so many children already, probably catering to his every need, he had taken her baby home. He had taken her home!

She sat, as she did most days since Beatrice's death two months ago. She hadn't put away any of the baby things, or taken down the crib. She couldn't touch the crib. She was lonely, sad and angry. She didn't know what to do with her pain, except cry.

Beatrice. What a beautiful little girl she'd been. She liked music, and when Richard danced with her, she'd smile, her first tooth protruding through her gums, like a tiny jack-o-lantern with a light inside.

It wasn't like Beatrice to cry. She was more likely to smile and giggle and drool.

She wore pink, of course. And Virginia had put her in fluffy dresses with pink bows and matching booties. She'd read her stories about princesses and queens and handsome strangers. Nights were filled with feedings and cuddling, and playing "This Little Piggy..." but that night...

Tears spilled down Virginia's cheeks. They'd replaced the couch that had sported the hole from the rock of trust. But now, even though their newfangled red couch was perfect in form and stability, she needed that hole; yes, somehow that hole would have soothed her soul.

She still had the stones; had kept the stones for these few years since she'd first walked with God. They were still with her, even now, as she sat on the couch and looked up at them on the mantel.

Listening...Trust...Optimism...Tenacity...Constancy... So close and yet so far away.

She couldn't even think, let alone stand to take the first one in her hands and listen to God. She wondered what he would say...

"I needed her..." "She's a sweet girl..." "You'll have another child..."

But she couldn't think about having another child, and she couldn't think about herself, and she couldn't think about Richard. Or God.

Richard...

***

"Virginia?"

Virginia was still sitting on the red couch when he approached. It was 7:30 p.m. and she still hadn't made lunch for herself or dinner for her husband.

"Yes?" She looked up at him and tried to smile.

He sat beside her. "How are you doing?" he asked, stroking her blonde hair though it was matted.

"Fair, I guess. You?"

"We had a big sale today. Sold almost all of the pink cupcakes." His arm reached around her back. "Would you like to go out to eat tonight?" he asked. "There's a great restaurant that's just opened up."

"Where?"

"Practically up the street." He forced a smile. "Italian."

She forced her own smile. "I guess it wouldn't hurt," she said.

"Tell you what. You get ready and I'll clean up a bit of the dishes..."

"Thanks." She stood and retreated to the bedroom, trying not to look at her daughter's old room across the hall. But she felt it nonetheless, would always feel her daughter within the room across from her own as if her she was still with them.

Changing from her pajamas, she slipped into a pair of jeans and a gray t-shirt, reached for a sweater, some socks, and finally a pair of tennis shoes, hoping but not really caring, that the place was casual.

Richard smiled over at her when he saw her. He'd almost finished loading the dishes in the dishwasher - only a pan remained. "What about your hair?" he asked, turning back to the sink.

She ran her fingers through the tangled strands. "I'll be back in a minute." She turned down the hall to the bathroom. Per his request, she brushed through her hair, and pulled the long strands into a ponytail, trying to avoid her reflection. But it was no use. Her eyes looked like giant red balls, puffy and swollen like the back end of a baboon. She looked sickly, and it pained her to see what she'd become.

Was it ever going to be different? Would she ever feel happy again? Or would this sadness drag on, hanging onto her every limb as she went about her day?

"Ready?" Richard had been standing at the bathroom doorway. She had no idea how long, just that he looked at her with loving eyes, like the way he'd always looked at their daughter, except with her there was this sexy blink that always happened when he was trying to see inside her. Like now.

"Don't."

"You mean I can't look at my beautiful wife?" he offered.

"Not now. I'm not much to look at."

"I wouldn't say that." He breathed next to her and wrapped his arms around her waist. She watched him from the large mirror. "I think we make a terrific couple," he said.

"Without a child," she added.

The smile faded. "Let's go to dinner."

***

"I don't think it's supposed to be easy," he said.

She smiled, this time for real. He'd brought her to a pizzeria. The place was decked out in red and white checkered tablecloths, waiters that looked as if their smiles were painted on, and plenty of water in clear, plastic pitchers.

"Welcome to The Pizzeria," the waiter touted.

Virginia blinked over at him. The boy was in white except for the green apron he had tied around his neck and waist. He was a tall boy, and sported gangly arms and some fine chin hairs - probably his first.

213

"Do you have Canadian bacon and pineapple?" she asked.

The boy moved his narrow hips back and forth in a Hawaiian sway. "Of course," he said, and Virginia held her tongue. It wouldn't have been polite to tease the boy, especially if he thought he was truly funny.

"We'll get a medium Canadian bacon as well as a pepperoni with extra cheese."

"Right. And to drink?"

Richard looked over at Virginia. He winked. "What would you like?"

"Just grab me a Coke and some water, please."

"Ditto for me."

"Anything else?" The boy swayed in the nonexistent wind, his narrow hips moving back and forth in the same Hawaiian dance.

"That should do it."

"Except when dessert comes. You'll not want to miss our cookies and cream."

"What's that?" Virginia asked.

The boy blinked over at her. "A large, warmed chocolate chip cookie with a scoop of vanilla ice-cream on top."

Virginia was suddenly hungry. "I think I'll have that first," she said.

Richard laughed. "Me, too," he said, his eyes watching the waiter as he left the table.

"So what do you think?" she asked.

"About what?"

"That kid?"

Richard brushed back his hair. It had grown longer since Beatrice's death, and she wondered why he hadn't cut it yet. Soon his hair would be long enough to put into a ponytail.

"Seemed kind of strange to me. Did you notice the hips swaying?"

"Couldn't miss it."

Richard took a sip of Coke. The water and Coke had been delivered moments before and Virginia had already downed half of her glass.

"So, what do you want to do this weekend?" Richard asked. At the first of the week they'd discussed going to the cemetery where Beatrice was buried, but Virginia had said she wasn't sure she was ready for that yet. He'd suggested the park. Didn't she love the swings, and wasn't it always her idea to take a load off by sitting amongst the trees? "What about the mountains?"

"Too cold, besides..." she smirked wearily at him, "you'll probably propose to me again."

He held up his right hand, palm forward. "Will not. I don't want to be turned down."

She forced a smile. "You know, maybe we should go to the mountains. There are good memories there. I can pack all the food you like and we can sit amongst the snow drifts like we used to."

"You really mean it?"

"Sure, why not."

***

It was with some reluctance that Virginia packed the food and prepared for their trip. She'd had a few days to think about the cold as well as the walk and wondered how she might convince Richard to do something else.

What she really wanted to do was sleep. And eat. And sleep. And maybe he could hold her in the darkness.

"Ready?" he asked. Richard was standing at the kitchen doorway this time, and all she could think about was God standing in Paul's kitchen before Paul had died. How he'd smiled at her, how he'd prepared all of those doughnuts..."Virginia?"

"Sorry, honey. I was just thinking about God."

"Oh?" He gave her a little smile.

"It's not what you think."

"What?"

"About God. I was just remembering him in Paul's kitchen."

"I bet you miss him."

"Paul or God?"

It was a wicked question, but it made Virginia think about her friend and about God. Her friend because he'd practically died in her arms, and God, because he'd died for her, so very, very long ago.

The Change

"Richard?" She banged on the door to the bathroom but there was no response. The shower had stopped at least 10 minutes prior to her banging and now the room was silent. No shaving. No toilet flush. Nothing. "Richard!" She tried the door. It was locked.

Leaning her head against the door she couldn't hear a thing, but he had to be in there. Their non-existent hike up the mountains for a picnic replayed itself in her mind.

"You don't want to go? I thought..."

"I've changed my mind."

"Figures."

"I'm sorry, I just can't help myself."

He'd looked at her strangely and brushed passed her.

Her mind returned to the present. "Richard!"

"What?" he hollered.

"Oh, good. I was worried."

"About what?"

"You, silly." He was silent. "What are you doing?" she asked.

"Nothing. I'll be out in a second."

She waited at the door. A few minutes later the door opened. Richard's eyes were as red as her satin pajamas. She thought briefly of the baboon. "Are you okay?" she asked, touching him on the arm and feeling his skin. He hadn't yet put his shirt on.

"No. You?"

She watched him walk to the bedroom, reach inside the closet for one of his blue dress shirts, and put it on. He turned to her. "I don't think I'm going to go to work today," he said.

She laughed. "So why the dress shirt?"

He picked at it strangely. "I don't know. I guess I'm just used to wearing it. Can you go in my place?"

"You can't be serious."

"You used to work," he said. "I need a day off."

"Oh."

"Is that all you have to say?"

"Well, I suppose I can go. What will you do?"

He looked down at the floor. "I don't know, probably the stuff you've been doing lately."

"What's that supposed to mean?"

"Nothing."

She frowned over at him. "Well, okay, I'll go to work, open the shop. Is there anything specific you'd like me to do?"

He shrugged. "Oh, I don't know, sell some stuff."

***

It was the strangest thing she'd ever done. Work at *Just Desserts* without him. But it was sort of freeing, too, like standing on a mountaintop with a kite. There was no one hovering over her, no one to ask how she was

218

doing, no one to wonder if she was going to make it through the day.

She opened the blinds, checked the register, and busied herself in the back room. There were a few spaces to fill in the front displays, and the *sale* sign, tucked in one of the small paned windows, had to be removed. The sale had obviously ended last week.

It was 9 a.m. She unlocked the door and invited the small group of waiting people inside.

A girl peered over at her. She was with her mother. "Joy?" she asked.

At least a year had gone by since she'd seen the girl, and she had grown taller, but still wore clothes much too large for her. Today it was a green dress with some sort of stain on the collar, though Virginia had to admit that the green emphasized her eyes.

"What will you have today?" Virginia asked.

The mother peered inside the display case. Her hair was a matted wad of black. Her eyes looked tired, and her smile was invisible. "She always wants the pink ones."

Virginia reached inside.

"With a ring on it," the woman, added blandly.

Virginia searched. "Looks like we're completely out of rings," she said.

"Figures." The woman looked over at her daughter. She and Richard had been married almost seven years, so the girl was at least 16. Joy had caught up with her mother some in height. She touched her mother's arm and smiled over at Virginia. "That's okay. One of the plain ones is fine," she said.

Virginia reached for a pink frosted cupcake. "Do you want it in a box?" she asked. "There is plenty of seating, if you'd like to eat here," she added, hoping that the two would stay for awhile longer. She wanted to take in the sweet growth of the girl, and remember everything, including how God had been a part of their first meeting when she was only ten. But it wasn't to be.

"Just put it in one of those white boxes like your husband does," the mother said.

Virginia reached for a box and placed the cupcake inside. "On the house," she said, though the mother had reached her hand inside her raggedy coat pocket.

"I always pay," grumbled the woman. "And I will pay now."

The change was splattered on the glass counter. With dirty fingernails the woman counted out the money. "That should do it," she said, and grabbing the box, handed it to her silent daughter.

"Thanks, Mom."

"Is there anything else I can get you?" Virginia asked.

"Some sanity," the woman answered.

Virginia watched Joy's eyes as they looked into hers. She tried to read the volumes of pain stored there. But the girl said nothing. "Thank you," she offered.

***

The smell of spruce filled the room. The soap Richard always used turned her mind for a moment to other things...He was sitting on the red couch watching some movie. "So, how was your day?" he asked, dipping his hand into a bowl of popcorn.

"Good. Yours?"

"Fine, as you can see."

Virginia took off her coat and hung it in the closet. She walked down the hall to remove her shoes. Passing Beatrice's bedroom, she stopped. "Richard!" she yelled, looking into the emptiness. "Where's all of the furniture?"

"Away, in the basement!" he hollered back, "and I've boxed the clothing and stuff and put it down there, too."

"All of it?" Suddenly Richard was standing there, his right arm carrying the popcorn bowl, his left hand dipping to retrieve yet another handful.

"All of it. I hope you don't mind."

"Mind? Of course I mind!" The words sprang from her aching throat, like an anxious cat. How could he do it? How could he clean up the room as if Beatrice had never been there?

Richard shrugged. "It was time, and I knew you wouldn't be cleaning it up anytime..."

"And that's as it should be. I respect her memory!"

"Then go to her graveside, don't keep all of this junk in the room, hoping that she'll return!"

"So that's it. You think I believe she'll come back!"

"Well, what else could it be?"

"I... don't know..." Her heart ached. She wanted to scream, but nothing came. For the next two hours Virginia sat in the lavender room and wept. Richard did not join her.

***

The following day Virginia returned to work. Richard had not spoken to her since the incident in Beatrice's room and she hadn't volunteered anything.

It was just two weeks before Christmas.

She wasn't sure why she hadn't thought to ask Richard about a tree. She'd wondered about gift giving this year, but hadn't even considered buying anything. Perhaps that wasn't right. Perhaps Beatrice would want them to celebrate the holiday. She would discuss it with Richard when she returned home.

But he was asleep after her day at the bakery and she hadn't wanted to wake him, so she'd pulled the *listening* stone from off of the mantel instead and held it within her hands. She stood gazing at the stones lined up on the mantel and realized how much she needed them now.

"So, you've come at last," she felt the stone of *listening*, say.

"Yes, God."

"And you're angry with me."

"Yes." She gulped and took the rock into the bedroom.

"You must trust me," he said.

"I know, but I miss her..."

"I know. She is well and happy."

"I'm glad."

"Trust that I know what's best. Think about your many blessings. You do have them, you know."

"You've read my mind," she said, "as usual."

"So trust that I know what's best for you."

She wiped at her eyes and dropped the rock of listening in her right coat pocket, just so she could remember it in the morning before work. She reached for the Bible.

She wasn't sure what was happening within the mind of her husband, but she also wasn't sure what to do next. Another week went by, and they spoke little; just short conversations at dinner (when they had them) and moments in the morning before she returned to work.

Richard had said nothing about her sacrifice, but then again, the house was clean when she returned home and the household chores seemed to be getting done, so she tried not to worry.

Tried was the key phrase.

Though she journeyed to *Just Desserts*, and her presence in the little bakery for the day soothed her mind and cleared her head, her return home would gather in the stress and make her feel as if her day away from home was not really worth the effort.

Still, she went. It was all she could do.

A week before Christmas she went out shopping for a Christmas tree without him and found a straggly one lying against the fence. It had been marked down to half price. She dragged the tree to the lot attendant, and in the freezing cold, paid for it. The man, who had a striking resemblance to God in the fisherman's cap, loaded the tree on top of her car, tying it down for her. She thanked him and drove home.

The driveway had already been cleared by her husband. That, and something was cooking on the stove when she dragged the tree in. He looked at her in amazement. "Pine needles are going to go everywhere," he said, and she had to smile. Hadn't that *once upon a time* been her line?

But she continued to drag the thing in as he watched, found the stand in the basement, and got busy trying to saw the bottom off the tree with the old hand saw. That's when he reached for her. "Let me help you," he said. "The least I can do is to help you saw the piece off."

The grinding of saw on wood came next, followed by a spattering clunk as the piece broke off. She reached for the broken trunk and stood. "Now put it in the tree stand. I'll get some water."

He smirked over at her and stood the tree up. Truly it was an awful, naked thing, but it was the best they could get this late in the season. She poured the water. "I've got to get the lights."

"No worries." He sat on the floor by the tree and looked up. She paused only once at the top of the stairs, taking him in, feeling the rock of *listening,* now in her pant pocket. Then, flicking on the light, she returned to the basement.

Life Patterns

The girl was wise beyond her years. "I might be able to help you with that," she said. Her mother looked sick, her skin yellow; she sat on the only vacant chair left in *Just Desserts*, her eyes staring into nothing, or so it seemed to Virginia. "We had a tree once."

"You don't have a tree?"

"Would be hard to cart around," said the girl, "since we're homeless."

"You're homeless?"

Joy yanked on her dirty shirt. It was orange and had small holes near the hem. Her short jeans barely touched her ankles. She wore dirty, black shoes. No socks.

"So what did you think, that mom and me, we were some stylish rock band?"

Virginia laughed. "Sorry," she said. "I had no..."

"Christmas was great for me once," she returned, avoiding Virginia's eyes. She breathed into the air as if somehow, even in this warm space, she could still see it, her breath flowing in and out like a thousand fluttering angels. "When dad was with us, and before mom..." She looked behind her to see her mother's head on the table. "Sorry."

She wasn't the only person who was sorry. Strange looks occupied the eyes of the visitors already eating or drinking. Before long, they'd be finding excuses to leave before they'd even have to, and Virginia wasn't even sure if she cared. She touched the stone of *trust* in her apron pocket and thought of how renewed she'd felt...renewed, since returning to her study of the Bible. Her daughter was gone, but, perhaps, it would be alright if she read about God.

"A pink one, please?" Joy asked, breaking Virginia away from her thoughts.

"Of course." She reached inside the case. Recently purchased, the glittering ring yet captivated the green eyes of her young friend. "Maybe one day I'll get married," she said.

So that was it.

"I'm sure you will," Virginia offered, placing the pink cupcake inside the small box, closing the sides, and handing the gift over the counter.

"Thank you." She turned, and nudging her mother, reached for the front door. Her mother looked up.

"What do you want?" she moaned.

"I have the cupcake, let's go."

Her mother stood. Every eye was on her, but the woman, stooped over like she was eighty, reached for her daughter's shoulder. "Help me up," she said.

The girl reached out a slender hand, and with the pink cupcake held within her right, led her mother out the door.

***

Richard didn't look well. Besides the redness of his nose and eyes, he looked as if all energy had been drained from his body. Lying in the bed, his head propped up with his pillow as well as hers, Virginia tried not to think about all of the unseen germs crawling around on it.

Instead she smiled over at him. "Had a hard day?" she asked.

"Sure."

"Eaten?"

"No."

"How long?"

"I don't know."

"Want something?"

He turned from her. "Just sleep. Maybe later."

The room smelled like a mixture of cough medicine and liquor. But Richard didn't drink and she couldn't see any bottles. Plenty of tissues had been strewn around and plenty of cough drops, so maybe that was it. Richard had a cold.

Moments later, as she sat in the chair opposite the bed watching him sleep, she remembered their life together, with and without Beatrice. She touched the stone of *trust*, now within the palm of her hand. It was no longer black, but the gray mists within it only reminded her of where she was spiritually - where she was without him. While Richard appeared to be wallowing in his loneliness, she wasn't doing much better away from him.

***

It was Christmas.

They sat near the tree and she was stunned at the beauty of it. No gifts this year. Nothing but bright lights, sparkling ornaments, and a tree that reflected where they were together. She, beginning to fill with light, he, still sorrowful, still remote. A thin, naked tree, just waiting...for what? She hadn't been able to find him, even now.

"So, what should we do first?" he asked.

"I made plum pudding," she offered. "Don't you smell it?"

He sniffed, but his cold was hanging on like a pearl in an oyster shell not wanting to be found. If only they could find that oyster. If only...

"Wow. I think I smell it."

She stood, releasing his hand, and walked to the kitchen. Smells of cinnamon, nutmeg, and cloves filled her nostrils like a dream. It was ready.

***

She wasn't sure when the idea had come to her, maybe in the moment between sleep and that first moment when her eyes opened, but there it was. If nothing else the girl would have a little money to take care of her mother, and in working at *Just Desserts*, Joy would develop some well-needed confidence.

But Richard didn't agree. "You can't hire a homeless girl to work in the bakery," he said. It was morning, and the sky, a pale blue, a striking contrast to the workings of her heart.

"Why not? They need the money."

228

"Then donate something."

"That's not the same."

Richard stretched on the bed, begging her to return to it, but she was already at the window.

"I guess you're worried about the customers, all of the gawking customers..." Virginia said.

"I guess you could say that." He sat up and adjusted his pillow. He was no longer using hers, and she had since washed the pillow case.

"But I need to do something."

"Why?" he asked.

"I just feel it in my gut." She'd since forgiven him of the lavender room fiasco, and his cold had healed up nicely, but he was still spending much of his time at home and she, within the walls of *Just Desserts*.

"Well, your gut should tell you that you can't hire a girl just because you think she needs the money." He stood from the bed, and in the same moment, reached for her, pulling her into his arms. "You've changed," he said.

"I know." She brushed her cheek lightly against his. "We need some warmth here."

He kissed her neck, the first ounce of love he'd expressed in some time. She allowed it to continue, the soft yet prickly sensation of lips and chin traveling against her skin, making her smile. And then she thought of Joy.

***

Nearly two months later, Joy came in with her mother. It was February, and the chill of the air made Virginia want to curl into a small ball and sip hot chocolate for the entire day, though she realized a

229

sedentary life was a pipedream, and not a very healthy one.

Someone had to work.

Richard kept house, and fairly nicely too, but Virginia just couldn't connect with him, at least where moving forward in life was concerned.

But she had the bakery. And she had Joy.

"So how are you today?" she asked Virginia.

"Very well," Virginia answered, reaching for a pink cupcake. Joy stood next her, an old coat draping her tiny frame. She wore the same black shoes without socks.

Weeks prior, she and Richard had gathered in the winter clothing. Two hats, two pairs of red gloves, a couple of scarves, socks, new coats and boots. They sat even now in the back room, and she hoped she'd managed the sizes correctly.

Walking into the back room, she returned with a medium-sized box in her arms. She sat it on the floor.

"What's this?" Joy asked, reaching to touch a hat that lay near the top.

"A hat," Virginia offered simply. "I also have a scarf for each of you, some gloves and..."

"We'll not be wanting charity," the mother said.

Virginia was stunned. Would she rather walk around cold?

"But Mom, this is good stuff," the girl said, lifting a hat and placing it on her head. It was perfect.

"We'll not be accepting charity." She reached for the woolen hat and pulled it off her daughter's head.

Virginia breathed slowly. Why was the woman so stubborn? Could she live in rags and refuse something that was offered freely? And then Virginia thought of

God. God offered his gifts freely; in fact they were the very key to happiness, but sometimes she did not listen. Sometimes she didn't want the gifts. Sometimes, it just felt better to remain in her misery.

"The key to receiving these gifts might be of interest to you then," said Virginia. "I am positive you will take these gifts after what I tell you."

The woman blinked over at her and for the first time Virginia noticed her eyes, green like her daughter's. "What's your name?" she asked.

The woman hesitated. "Grace," she said, "but your husband knew that."

The comment had been said to prick her conscience, but Virginia was beyond the hurt. She just had to help them. "Grace," she repeated, looking into the woman's eyes. "I am in need of some help here. Dish washing, sweeping up, attending to the customers - baking. Are you and your daughter up for the task?"

The woman blanched. "You're kidding," she stammered, touching her coat and wiping her grimy hands against the worn fabric.

But Joy's eyes lit up like a Christmas tree. "Oh, Mom!" she sang, "it's an answer to our prayers!

Fortunately, at that particular time, no other customers were at *Just Desserts*, but perhaps having other customers there to see what transpired that early February morning, would have been a life-changing experience, just as it was beginning to be a life-altering experience for Virginia.

KATHRYN ELIZABETH JONES

Just Desserts

Maybe it was the way she told him, the sort of sly way she spoke about the new workers at *Just Desserts,* or maybe it was merely that she'd hired Grace and Joy *period* that had created such a frenzy within her husband's mind. Or maybe the frenzy had more to do with Virginia allowing the two to stay in the now vacant lavender bedroom.

"You what?"

"I've hired Grace and her daughter to work for us."

He stood up, the entire bowl of popcorn tumbling to the ground.

"Why would you do that?"

"Well, I told you...I said that I couldn't allow the daughter and her mother to be hungry anymore, and I couldn't allow them to be cold and without shelter, and so..."

"You didn't say any of that. You just...just wanted to hire them! Where are they now?" he asked hotly, reaching for the bowl.

There wasn't much time. "They'll be at the door in a second. I want you to be nice."

He scowled over at her. "Nice...nice? What do you think I am, some ogre?"

She winked at him.

"I can't believe you did this!"

"I hear them. Now, do as you promised." She smiled over at him but he didn't smile back.

***

"Hello, Virginia." The man in the fisherman's cap peered over at her from the opposite side of the counter. "How are you doing?"

Virginia grinned widely. She'd just shown Joy how to use the mixer for the latest batch of cupcakes, and her mother, Grace, was doing swimmingly. Virginia even wondered if the skill of baking had been part of her daily life before the woman and her daughter had left their home.

She realized there was a lot that she didn't know. Had Grace been married? Had they *ever* had a home? What had caused them to leave their previous life? And Richard? You could say that his heart was softening; albeit slowly. Their daughter's room had a new bed, two chairs and a table (so the girl and her mother could eat alone at times) and plenty of closet space for the clothing they were quickly earning.

At *Just Desserts*, while Grace worked, her daughter took some time away to read, but she was always eager to welcome customers with her winning smile. She was clean, beautiful, and charming, and no one seemed the wiser. For all they knew she was a new girl they'd hired, not the young girl who'd stood in rags months before, wanting a pink cupcake.

As for God, he was gazing at her, his eyes twinkling. "So what have you been up to?" he asked, peering down at the pink cupcakes once more filling the case.

"As if you didn't know."

He looked up at her again, this time more seriously. "Be careful," he began. "You are doing a good thing but it's important to be wise." She felt the stone of *optimism* in her apron pocket and smiled over at him.

Virginia's heart pounded. "What do you mean?" she asked, whispering this time, hoping Grace or Joy wouldn't see who she was talking with and that Joy would remain intent on her nature book.

"Just as I said," replied God. "Perhaps it's time to sit down with Grace and discuss her future plans."

Virginia tried to remain optimistic. Hadn't God once said that if she trusted him and listened to his voice, she would know what to do in her life; that she would know that it was by him that she was led? But of course. She was hearing him now, and he was telling her to be careful.

She decided to listen. "What should I say?" she asked, fearful now that she might brooch the subject awkwardly, making Grace mad.

"That is entirely up to you," God answered, and Virginia felt somehow deflated. Why wouldn't God tell her what to do; it would be so much easier that way.

But God only smiled. "I would like one of those pink cupcakes," he said, waving his hand in their general direction.

"Boxed?" Virginia asked.

"No, just plate it," said God.

Virginia reached for the cupcake, and, carrying it to the back table, placed it on a small white plate. She turned and offered it to God. "On the house," she said, making God smile. He took the cupcake and plate and walked over to where Joy was sitting.

***

As the weeks went by, Virginia found herself getting more and more frustrated with her house-guests. The room, if you could call it that, was such a mess she wondered if they'd soon be harboring other guests.

Mice had never been welcome in her home, whether they'd been purchased or otherwise, and she was not about to welcome them now.

Still, for days on end, the door would be shut - the two doing *who knows what*, and some of the meals she offered had been met with distance. "Wouldn't it be better if we had our meals alone?" Joy's mother would ask at least three times a week, though she'd never offered to cook one of them herself.

Both mother and daughter did better at work, but if the truth be known, it was the daughter, not the mother, who had a knack for baking and almost everything else in the kitchen. Just recently, her mother had even feigned sickness and had stayed in her home while everyone else worked.

The situation made Virginia crazy. What was the woman doing while they were away? Would she even have a home to return to?

At night she'd whine at her husband, only to be met by steely eyes. She knew what he was thinking; more important she knew what she had done.

One day she couldn't take it any longer. The two had spent the evening alone, as usual, and when the door finally opened, a smell like death reeked from the very walls of the lavender room.

"What have you been doing in here?" Virginia shouted at her guests, as her husband looked on. She peered inside only to be shoved back. The place was a terror.

"So you don't trust me!" Grace wailed.

"No, I don't! Look at this mess! Do you believe in cleaning - at all?"

The woman blinked at her. She didn't look right. No, her eyes didn't look right.

Joy peered behind her mother like a small child. But she wasn't a small child. What was the woman doing to her only daughter? Whatever it was, she wouldn't stand for it.

"We have a right to our privacy!" the woman screamed, taking her daughter by the hair and pulling her in front of her.

"I'm so..." Joy began.

"Don't you go apologizing!"

"We're... in... their...house," Joy stammered.

Grace glared at Virginia. "It doesn't matter," she wheezed, letting go of her daughter's hair and taking her daughter by the hand. "I suppose you want us to leave."

Virginia was dumb struck. What could she possibly say to this woman? Do? And then the words came:

"We will not allow drugs in this house! I don't care if it's booze or needles!"

Joy blinked her large green eyes. "I told you, I told you they'd find out!"

237

Grace scowled. "I told *you* to be quiet."

Joy laughed. But it was a sickly laugh, almost as if she couldn't believe what her mother had told her to do.

"Look. We really appreciate the place, but we have to get along in this life the same as you," Grace said, pulling at her daughter's arm, and, at the same time, trying to get around Virginia and Richard.

"What about our things?" Joy asked, peering behind her.

"Oh, yeah. We'll just get our things, and then we'll be out of your way."

"Sounds good to me." Even as she said the words Virginia knew that part of what she'd just said was a lie. What was good was having the mother vanish from off the planet. Perhaps there was still time to save the daughter.

"Excuse us," Joy said, following her mother into the lavender room.

Richard blinked over at her. "I'm sorry," he said, taking Virginia's hand. "We should have done this weeks ago. This is our house, we should feel safe."

They left the two to pack up. At the end of the hall they waited. Moments later Joy and her mother rejoined them. But something wasn't right.

It was a feeling more than anything else, an aching feeling of loneliness that suddenly enveloped Virginia's heart. How could she do it? How could she let Joy go? She was...she was...And then the words were there, as if they'd always existed, and only needed the right moment for release.

"Don't go. I...I mean we'll get it to work out."

Richard looked at her numbly, but said nothing.

Virginia touched Joy on the arm. Her skin was clean and her beautiful blond hair was brushed and styled. Everything from her head to her feet was shined up. No one would have ever known she'd once been homeless.

And then a new thought struck her, like a glowing wind, a breeze...

Changing the outside of both Grace and Joy was all that she and Richard had managed to do. Both mother and daughter were cleaner, surely, but after only a few weeks, their old life appeared to be seeping through their otherwise clean exterior. How could she have been so wrong? Merely changing the outside had not really changed how mother and daughter thought about life.

Virginia thought about cupcake making, about her focus on making the experience for Joy and Grace a positive one, and she'd seen some changes in behavior, an inner light surely; and yet, were mother and daughter still anchored to the life they'd been living for how-many-years now?

Yes, it was God who'd come into the bakery and told her that trouble was coming, but what had he said exactly? What was it that she'd been counseled to do?

"Perhaps it's time to sit down with Grace and discuss her future plans," God had said. But how could she do that, now that mother and daughter were leaving?

"I bet you have dreams," prompted Virginia, thinking of God's words.

Grace was already outside. As the girl stood waiting, a tear dripped down her left cheek. "I did once," she said, turning from Virginia.

A small breeze like breath, blew in through the door of their three-bedroom home.

239

"Maybe if we sat down and talked about it," she offered.

But the girl only continued to cry. "Thank you for the nice meals, and the clothes, and this...this beautiful home, but I have to go."

Virginia looked out at the snow. She felt the bitter air against her cheeks. It would be a month or two yet before the weather warmed up. She nodded at the girl and watched her go, for the words would no longer come.

***

They hadn't eaten dinner; in fact, the entire evening had been spent trying to figure out ways to get them back. With the entire list in front of her, from taking a walk and dragging them back, to finding another home and paying for them to live in it, what kept coming back to Virginia's mind was how the inside of both Joy and her mother, had not yet caught up with the outside.

Could new clothes, a daily shower, and plenty of food change what had been growing in both of their hearts for years? And what about the inside? What desolation and bad habits held mother and daughter captive? What would finally release them both?

A sudden light entered Virginia's own heart. What had God said about making the inside of the cup clean *first*? She'd read about it, probably not recently, but the thought of cleaning the inside of the cup before the outside revealed itself again and made her walk to the bookshelf for the Bible. She reached for the black Bible with the gold lettering and returning to her husband, read: "Woe unto you...for ye make clean the outside of the cup and of the platter, but within [you] are full of extortion and excess. Thou blind...cleanse first that which is within the cup and platter, that the outside of them may be clean also" (Matthew 23:25-26, KJV).

She placed the book on the table. "So what do you think?" she asked.

Richard smiled and touched her hair. "I think," he said, smiling widely, "that perhaps we have been doing it all wrong."

He'd said *we*, but she knew what he meant and his words were the last thing she needed. "Okay, so I'm human," she offered. "String me up."

"Anywhere?" he asked.

"Anywhere, what?"

"Strung up." He laughed.

"I'm serious."

"So am I."

"I mean, about the cup. Do you think we need to take them to church?"

"What?" He laughed again, but this time it sounded more like a choke.

"I'm serious. It's been a long time since *we've* been to church."

"We've *never* been to church," Richard offered.

"Yes, but..."

He touched her hair again and looked easily into her eyes. "I think..." he said, "that it's time for dinner. Do you want to cook or shall I?"

***

It was late winter before Virginia saw Joy again. This time she was without her mother. "I bet you thought you'd never see me again," she said.

Virginia nodded, remembering the angry words, the separation that had been caused by the drugs and alcohol in the lavender room.

The girl pressed her grimy hands against the glass countertop and looked in. "I don't know what it is about those pink cupcakes, but they make me feel better...somehow..."

"Want one?"

The girl held her hand up. Dark lines of dirt followed the lines of her fragile palm. Somehow, she looked even smaller than when she'd last seen her. Virginia noticed the coat she had given her and the gloves and hat, but the colors had changed; they appeared as muted and withdrawn as the girl wearing them.

"I don't have any money," Joy said, raising her face to Virginia. Her eyes looked tired. "But I didn't come to mooch off of you anyway," the girl continued. "I was hoping you had a job for me."

"Of course..."

"Mother is dead."

Virginia's heart stopped. She looked past the girl. Two tables were already filled, and along with them, inquisitive eyes.

"Mother...drugs...I told her not to take them but..."

"Where is she?"

"Who knows? She wasn't at the shelter, under the freeway, at the park, nowhere..."

"So you came here?"

The girl's eyes swam with tears. "Does that surprise you? What would they have done with me, huh?" She wiped her eyes. The tears had started with the telling of her mother's death, and now, the dirt was mixed in and the girl's eyes appeared irritated.

"How old are you now?"

"Funny you should ask," Joy said. "I just had a birthday. I think I'm seventeen." The girl smiled but it was about as long-lasting as a hiccup. "I wanted to come in, get a cupcake, steal a candle, you know, sing. But Mother would have none of that. Told me that you'd force us to come back. But I wanted to come back..."

"You did?" She touched the girl's hands then, still planted on her glass counter. But the girl didn't jump and she didn't move her hands. Slowly, Virginia curved her hands around her slim ones. What could she possibly say?

She looked over at the customers. One of the group, a girl and her boyfriend were getting up; the second, a family of four, continued to peer over at her as if waiting for what she might do next. But she had no idea what to do, no idea at all.

"I'm sorry," Joy finally offered, and Virginia smiled.

"I'm sorry, too. I'm sorry about your mother." She released the girl's hands and continued to the front of the counter. "What would you say to a home-cooked meal tonight?"

Joy's eyes lit up. "Food?"

She heard some negative talk in the corner but ignored it.

"What's your favorite?"

"Favorite?"

But the girl had probably not eaten in days and suddenly Virginia felt particularly stupid. Joy wouldn't care about a favorite food, she would just like to eat. But the girl's next words surprised her: "I like fish," she said.

***

Richard took a bite of fish stick. So, it wasn't the fish Virginia had first considered when Joy had told them what she wanted for dinner, but in a somewhat roundabout way, it still was fish.

She laughed to herself.

Joy had washed her hair and she smelled as fresh and clean as a newborn babe. New clothing, clothing that Virginia had saved for the few months after she and her mother had left them, still fit the young girl, albeit loosely around her arms and legs. Joy was growing up, but she still appeared smaller than the average 17-year-old.

"These are good," she said. "I never liked salad though, but now, it doesn't really matter what I eat."

Richard blushed. "I'm glad you'll eat it," he said. "You can't eat fish sticks all of your life."

The girl blinked. They sat around a square table and Joy's face was to the window. Virginia and her husband sat on either side of the table, their typical places.

"Thank you for the rolls," Joy said, adding butter. "We always had rolls at dinner. I remember once when my dad started choking on one," she began, chewing on the roll in between portions of the story. "He was choking and my mom got up and slammed him on the back, trying to dislodge it, you know..." She looked up. Virginia was silent, so was Richard. There was no way on God's green earth that she was going to say anything...now.

"Well, father yelled, so the thing had been dislodged. After that, Mother never made rolls." The girl grew silent. "So it's nice to have them now."

Virginia wasn't sure what to say. What a strange story, and what, truly, had she gotten herself into?

When the meal ended, Joy helped her gather and rinse the dishes so that she could put them in the dishwasher, all the while whistling some tune that Virginia didn't know. Once finished, they gathered in the living room to have a chat.

It was awkward at first - sort of the feeling you get when going into a job interview, or meeting with God, but Virginia knew one thing; if she and Richard were going to take the girl in, they would have to know something about her past. They would have to do this legally, and if that meant some prying was called for, then so be it.

Having been told that Grace was dead, and no way to find out who the girl really was, it was the only thing they could do anyway. So while the girl sat, playing with the white tassel on the pillow nearest her, Richard and Virginia looked at each other, hoping that the other one would begin first.

The silence got to Richard. "So, have you been to school?" he asked.

Joy smiled wearily. "Used to," she said, "before mother pulled me out."

"How old were you?"

"Eight." The girl peered over at him from behind the pillow. "What are all those rocks on your mantel for?" she asked.

245

Virginia's heart stopped. "We'll talk about that later," she said hastily.

"What school did you attend?"

The girl hesitated. "Kennedy." She stood, taking the pillow with her, and found her way to the mantel. "These are pretty cool," she said. "Can I have one?" With a deftness only a teen could manage, the stone of trust was quickly swept into her hand. "It's smooth," she said, her eyes opening wide. "Hey, it's changing color!"

Virginia's greatest fears realized, she stood from the couch. "Hand me the stone," she said, holding her hand out.

But the girl only peered into the cup of her hand. "Really!" she sang. "The stone is turning white!"

"Figures," Richard mumbled.

Virginia turned. "What's that supposed to mean?" she said, her heart pounding.

Joy suddenly released the stone into Virginia's hand. The stone, once white, had turned gray.

"That's cool. What do the other stones do?"

"Nothing," said Richard.

The girl sat. "This is one strange place," she said. "I mean, you guys are great and everything..." A sudden tear welled up in the girl's left eye. She brushed it with her hand. "I guess I just miss Mom. And I can't even visit her, you know? I have no idea where she's been buried."

Virginia didn't want to think about that. Where did they bury the homeless anyway? And had she even been found? If not, she didn't want to consider the condition of her body, or where she was lying.

"So where have you been living?" Virginia asked.

The girl hugged the pillow even tighter. "Oh, wherever we could. The park. Under bridges. In the winter we had to find our way to the shelter."

"Which one?"

"*Safe Haven*."

***

The girl was asleep in the lavender room; Virginia couldn't sleep.

"So?" Virginia asked.

"I don't think we should bring the girl there. I'll stop by tomorrow."

"But what about the store?"

"Take Joy with you tomorrow. I'll figure it out."

***

Richard returned but he wasn't smiling. "You'd think they'd be organized, what with all of the transients and such in that crusty building." Richard was as white as a sheet. Evidently his trip to *Safe Haven* hadn't gone well.

"Did you find her?"

"In a manner of speaking, yes." He reached for a cupcake. Joy was looking through a teen magazine and chewing slowly on a cupcake.

"Keep your voice down. Let's go in here." The room that housed their cooking and baking supplies was about as organized as their garage, and that wasn't saying much. Maybe she could get Joy to help her straighten it up a bit.

247

Richard ran a hand through his hair. "She had no ID on her, but after checking around the local shelters her body was discovered in an alley by the freeway. Looks like she had no family other than her daughter. Her husband is nowhere to be found. He could be alive or dead, they don't know."

"What of other relatives?"

Richard shrugged. "It's sad, I know. But I guess the good news is that she doesn't have to legally be shipped off to some crazy uncle." He picked up a bowl with pink frosting and plunged a finger into it.

"Richard!"

"Sorry." He sat the bowl down and licked the pink icing off of his finger. "But it was so weird. I felt as if I was the criminal, as if I had killed that woman. They wanted to know where the daughter was now. I lied. I told them I didn't know."

"Joy was already in the missing person's file," he continued, looking straight into Virginia's eyes. "They seemed quite excited to see me. I've got a bill for the burial costs." He handed her a white sheet of paper. "Evidently, any way the city can be relieved of this financial expense, is a burden off their backs."

Virginia looked down at the paper. The bill was paid in full, a mere $695 for cremation services.

"Oh, Richard. Cremation?"

"It's the cheapest route when relatives can't be found."

"Yeah, but..."

"They couldn't find Joy, and there was no other living relatives that they knew about; the county took the cheapest route, though I was told she had a brief funeral supplied by the coroners."

"So where are the ashes?"

"At the downtown cemetery. They've put her remains in the garden mausoleum there."

"That's only a few minutes' drive. Maybe we should take Joy..."

"It might be better if we don't..."

"Why?"

"There's no marker with her name; basically, she's buried with the others. They told me that the county doesn't pay for the extra expense of an individual marker. Just a number. She's 34."

Virginia didn't know what to think. But Joy had to know where her mother was, didn't she? She watched her from a short distance just finishing off of the pink cupcake. "We need to tell her anyway," she said. "The girl needs to know."

***

Telling Joy about her mother wasn't Virginia's only worry. As she made her way through the day, making cupcakes, doughnuts, and whatever else needed to be done, she thought about the secret. They harbored a homeless teen.

She knew in some states this was breaking the law.

But what choice did she have?

The girl needed them, and they couldn't put her back in a shelter. She and Richard knew her as 'best' as they could, not really knowing her. She hadn't told them much, and Richard had received few of Grace's 'valuables' even though he had footed the bill for her cremation; "We knew the mother and daughter," he'd offered.

"So my mother is really gone?" she asked. The girl had changed into another outfit - her third for the day. She was wearing her favorite color - red, and the stripes across her belly and chest reminded Virginia of something in nature, although she couldn't quite place what it was.

"She's gone." Richard touched her hand but she didn't react. "But you have this."

With a gentle hand Richard reached for the necklace in his shirt pocket, a necklace Virginia hadn't even seen, until now. It was a simple thing, a small, ornately carved key, half the size of her index finger, hung on a silver chain; but it made the girl smile. A tear ran down her cheek until she brushed it away. With a dainty hand she reached for it, and then, asking for assistance, had Richard place the chain around her neck. It fell just below her collar bone.

She touched it. "Thank you," she said.

"They wanted you to have it," Richard said.

"They?"

"Those at *Safe Haven*."

"So you went."

Richard shrugged. Virginia looked deeply into Joy's face, but the girl didn't meet her gaze. She looked down at the key.

"Mother always loved this," she said. "Told me that it was the key to her heart and that one day it would be opened and I could see it."

Joy's mother must have been speaking metaphorically, but her daughter seemed to understand.

So, she had the key to her mother's heart, a heart that had never really been opened. Or had it?

"You're probably wondering where I should go next?" Joy offered, touching the key and then looking at them both, alternately, like she was at court and they were two of those who had come to the trial, sitting way beyond the witness stand.

"We should probably take you back to the shelter."

"What?" She gaped at them, her green eyes large and searching.

"What we mean to say is," Virginia began, though the words tightened inside her throat, "perhaps you would like to go to a teen facility, or...something..."

"You don't like me, is that it?"

The girl's face had suddenly gone pale, almost as if the very thought of being alone again in a strange place was beyond her coping skills.

"That's not it." Richard's face was soft. He touched her hand again. This time she withdrew.

"My mom wanted me to be with you. She told me that if she ever left this earth I was to find you."

Richard and Virginia were silent. Actually, Virginia had thought about taking the girl in numerous times, and had discussed it with Richard.

"Would you like to live here?" Virginia asked.

"Oh, please!"

Richard coughed. "You would really like to live with us?" he asked. He didn't touch her this time but looked at her, as if trying to read all of the emotions the girl could not put into words.

251

Safe Haven

"I had a feeling you had her," the woman behind the counter said. "I mean, it was written all over your face."

"Why didn't you..."

The woman brushed a thick hand through her thinning black hair. "I guess I had a choice, and you seemed nice enough." She blinked over at Richard. "I hope my instincts were right." She reached below the counter and retrieved a cardboard box without a lid. "I've been saving this for you," she said.

Richard looked down. In the box was a red hat, some mittens, and a torn yellow notebook. No pen.

"How is Joy doing?" the woman asked.

"Fine," Richard answered. "But..."

"No worries. Are you considering foster care and possibly...adoption?"

Joy was at home with Virginia; it would have been difficult for the girl to return to a place filled with cockroaches or rats. To the naked eye, the family shelter that also served as a foster care and adoption facility, wasn't the worst he'd seen; the white paint looked fairly fresh, and the place was picked up, but one could never tell.

He looked behind her. A family of four stood behind her, though he really hadn't needed to look. The smell of dirt and sweat penetrated his nostrils and funneled its way through his skin. He tried not to cough.

"Isn't there a lot of paperwork?" he asked.

"Plenty." The woman smiled. "But worth it for a girl like Joy. You need to return her," she added lazily. "I mean, we need to know she is with you, and we really need to do this whole thing legally..."

"What do you know about her?"

"With her mother dead, she has no living relatives that I know of. Not even a father." She paused for a moment, and looked searchingly into his eyes. "Evidently, the girl and her mother have been on their own for about eight years. Before that, Joy's father was in the picture. His death brought some pain to Joy's mother. But I've said enough. Why don't I give you this?" The woman reached for a piece of paper. "Then I can take care of these folks, here. You don't mind, do you?"

Richard turned briefly. "No of course not," he said, smiling at the couple.

With the paper and yellow notebook before him, he briefly scanned the "First Contact" paper. The form was written in basic 'check the correct box' answer format asking for his particular interest in *Safe Haven*, how he'd heard about it, and included blanks for his name, address, phone number, and email address. He quickly filled out the form and returned it to the woman at the front desk who smiled at him.

"Good. Let's set up your orientation. Can you meet next week, say Wednesday, at 9?"

Richard had no idea. He'd have to talk to Virginia. "Can I call you?" he asked.

The woman blinked. "Sure, but Joy needs to be here by tomorrow morning."

Richard touched the yellow notebook now under his left arm. Why had the woman given him such a prize when she had no clue who he was? And the key? Why give him these items if he was not legally entitled to them?

Once inside the car he sat behind the wheel, took a deep breath, and looked down at the yellow front cover. It revealed a cover page with stark black letters that read:

**Property of: Grace Sorenson,
mother of Joy Sorenson,
in search of a better life this day,
February 1.**

***

Joy scowled up at the woman. "Why can't I live with Virginia and Richard?" she asked.

Richard took her arm. Fortunately, all of the beginning paperwork had been filled out; unfortunately, there was still some red tape before he could actually bring her home.

"It's what my mother wanted," Joy added.

"We know that."

Joy smiled over at Richard. "You haven't read all of my mother's book yet," she said. "It's in there."

So that was it.

"You'll see your new parents on Wednesday. You remember this place..." the social worker began.

"Sure."

"We'll take care of you until then."

"And then I can go home?"

"Not quite. There is some training for your new parents, a home study..."

Joy rolled her large green eyes. "I'll be 18 by the time you figure this stuff out! Legal and on my own!"

"When is your birthday?"

"December 24."

"Oh, yes, I remember now. The Christmas child."

"I am NOT a child," said Joy.

"Well, taking care of the paperwork, the classes, all of the..."

Joy leaned in. "You'd better do it quick. I don't think I can wait a year."

The woman smiled, and looked over at Richard. "Do you think you can manage it?" she asked.

"Leaving Joy, you mean?" he answered.

"No, taking care of her as a teenager."

Joy blinked, and squeezed his arm. "We'll see you soon," Richard said.

"I guess."

"And before too long we will be a true family."

***

"Listen to this:

'February 20. Went to the doctor today. Probably my last appointment. Living in a small apartment, but the money doesn't stretch as much as I want it to. Joy seems depressed. She is young and doesn't understand. It has taken me years to do this, and Joy need never know.'

That's the end of that entry. The next one starts:

'Joy is sick and the money is gone. I have just a few days to find the rent before March. I should have

255

planned better...Jobs are scarce and I haven't held one in years. Even with all of the drinking there was still money somehow...but Tom is no longer with us...'"

Virginia paced the bedroom floor and it was all she could do to keep calm. "This sounds serious."

"It might be. Maybe we can read more later." Richard slid into bed and patted the sheet. "Why don't you come to bed? It's late."

Virginia looked at the clock. "Okay, so it's late, but I need to get this journal read."

"All in one night?" He smiled. "Besides, there are other things to do around here."

"Oh, is that so?" She shut the book and placed it on the nightstand before slipping into bed. The old routine had returned. Richard had returned, body and soul.

***

"I can't believe you're here!" The scream of Joy filled *Safe Haven* and eyes peered over at them briefly. "I mean, I thought I was going to die not seeing you two!" Joy plopped in the adjoining chair and stared at them. "You wouldn't believe the terrible...food." She turned to check her surroundings. "And the boys, all they want to do is try to kiss me."

"What?" The remark, though apparently sincere, had shocked Virginia. "Well, what are you going to do about it?"

"What boys?" Richard asked.

She peered behind her. "That one over there with the dark shirt and white hair. Don't you think he looks like an albino? And him-" She pointed her slim finger on the other side of the room. "He's short."

Richard coughed. "So, you like them, huh?" he asked.

"Like them? I'm trying to tell you..."

"Ah, Mr. and Mrs. Stone. Glad you could make it."

Virginia stumbled to her feet. A tall, stout woman in her 50's peered down at her. Richard stood. "Well, hello again," he said. They shook hands.

"The meeting will begin in a moment."

Virginia searched for a name badge. There was none. "So, who was that?" she asked, when the woman had retreated to the front of the room.

"The woman behind the counter. The one I've been working with."

"I suppose she has a name."

"I suppose you're right. Funny thing is, I've never heard it."

"It's Jean. Jean Rasmussen. She's not really the boss here, but she really likes to tell people what to do."

Richard smiled and took Joy by the arm. "And what, pray tell, have you been doing the last couple of days...besides, kissing boys?"

Joy blushed. "I told you," she whispered. "They tried to kiss me but I wouldn't let them. And besides, they have crummy books over here. I like yours better."

Virginia thought about Joy's love of nature and wished she'd thought to bring the book along. As it was, it was enough to remember to bring herself. She was so nervous she could hardly breathe.

After an initial introduction by a few of the teens living at the facility, they were sent away, and she and

Richard had to listen without Joy. It was just as well. Virginia got to the point where she wanted to block out the worse case scenarios and just take in the good stuff.

Two lengthy speakers and many forms later, they were able to leave - without Joy.

***

Three weeks later, on a calm Sunday in March, Joy was gone from *Safe Haven*. And although it didn't take a rocket scientist to figure out why she'd gone, it was where she'd gone that worried Virginia and Richard the most.

"She is a great escape artist," said Jean. Her bulky form leaned against the counter as she spoke. "I guess I should have told you about that. But she...when she was with her mother, was always coming and going. Are you sure she's not at your place?"

"Why would we be here if she was?" Richard said. He looked angry.

"Right...Right. She took everything with her. Pillow, blanket, toiletries, and of course her coat and the other items you gave her. She practically slept with them. I'm so sorry..."

"How long has she been gone?" Virginia asked.

"Must have left last night. Learned of her escape this morning when her bed was empty."

"So, no one checks on these kids?"

"Well, sure. But...you must know that Joy has been in and out of shelters her entire life. If things aren't going her way..."

"What wasn't going her way?" Richard asked.

"Being here, without you two. It's practically all she talked about. Being in your home. Are you sure she isn't there?"

"We're sure," said Virginia. "So where do you think she went?"

"Wish I could tell you. She slept under viaducts sometimes, at other times in the park. But it's cold now, as you know; she would want to find some better shelter."

It occurred to Virginia in that moment that there was only one place she knew of, other than their home, that the girl would go. Or maybe two. But it wasn't until they'd left the facility that she felt free to tell Richard about either of them.

The Key

"That book of Grace's is more cryptic than Egyptian hieroglyphics," said Virginia, facing her husband. "But I think I know where the girl is."

"And that would be?"

"We need to start where her mother is buried, or entombed, or whatever you call it when a person is cremated. Or we can start at *Just Desserts*. She doesn't have a key to the place but that girl could probably break in if she wanted to; and not having an alarm on the premises would make it that much easier."

"Let's start there," said Richard. "If she isn't at the bakery, we'll work our way downtown."

***

Just Desserts was closed every Sunday - Virginia's idea - but they were both disappointed to find that Joy was not there. Not in the back room. Not sitting at one of the tables. Not hiding in a closet, though both Richard and Virginia doubted that a 17-year-old would do such a thing.

Still, they would be safe and look.

Without customers, the place breathed of vacancy and loneliness, and after fifteen minutes of looking, it was time to venture out.

The streets were clear, but it was early March. Bundling was still necessary, including hats, scarves, coats, boots, and often, thick tights for women. Virginia was glad of one thing: At least the roads weren't icy.

She prayed in that moment that Joy was warm, wherever she was, and that their journey to find her and bring her home was a short one.

But some dreams weren't meant to be realities.

At the cemetery, they looked for the spot, what Sunset Cemetery called, "Garden Abbey." Trudging through snow and past tombstones draped with lacy ice crystals, they finally found the spot on the northwest side. Here they stopped.

"This is interesting," said Virginia. She looked down to find a large slab of cement engraved with dates, but without names, lined up in rows like soldiers waiting for a command.

"What day did you say Grace died?" she asked.

"The coroner recorded it as December 28."

"Here it is. The last one." She pointed. The carving appeared fresh; the black engraving had not yet grayed like the others. She bent to touch it. The stone was cold.

The cloudy sky was darkening. Joy wasn't anywhere that she could see.

***

Back inside the car, Virginia rubbed her hands in front of the heater vent. Though gloved, they had still managed to absorb the chill. "So, what do you think?" she asked. "I mean, if Joy isn't here, where else would she go?"

Richard turned out of the parking spot and began to drive. "You said you knew of another place, I thought."

"Oh, that." Virginia was more than slightly embarrassed that the idea had even come to her at all. I mean, how would they know where to look? All she had was a memory of a key around Joy's slim neck, and that journal at home. Maybe it held a secret. She'd started the journal but hadn't finished it.

"Do you remember how excited Joy got when we gave her that key and chain?"

Richard smiled. "It was like the sun suddenly lit up in her eyes. Who could forget?"

Virginia's heart pumped. There was silence in the car, and although Virginia's body was warming, there was something disturbing about the silence between them, almost as if he knew something she didn't. Finally she asked, "Grace's journal - have you read all of it?"

He nodded.

"When?"

"When, what?"

"When did you read it?"

Richard colored. "That same night," he said, "when I got you into bed instead of allowing you to read it. I waited until you were asleep..."

"Why? I mean, why didn't you tell me?"

Richard's face softened. Now, it was a pleasing pink tone. "I'm sorry, honey. I was curious at first, but once I got reading I felt as if maybe I needed to think on what I'd read a bit before discussing it with you."

Virginia couldn't be angry. She felt the same way about the yellow journal; it should have been important to both of them. So what had her husband found? "Stop the car," she said, "there, over at that park. We need to talk."

The place was bare of people, and all of the leaves had drifted to the earth, where they'd glued themselves. He grinned over at her. "I can't remember the last time we *parked*." He paused before continuing. "Virginia, before I say anything, you've got to promise me not to get angry."

"Okay, I promise. So?"

"Promise?"

She breathed in and out. "Okay! Enough already. Tell me."

"Grace was having an affair. Her husband found out. The drinking began."

"What?"

"I said..."

"I know what you said. But I thought the journal started after they'd left him, not before."

Richard turned to face her. His eyes looked sad and reflective. "The journal starts out with their first few months away from home. Grace talks about trying to find food to eat, a place to sleep, meeting you and me...and then, about midway through the book she shares some stuff...I wonder if Joy knew."

"Knew about what?" Her heart pounded.

"About the affair, about the abuse."

"What abuse?"

"When Joy's father got drunk, he also got violent."

"Oh." She was thoughtful for a moment trying to take it all in. "Well, Joy must have seen that. I can't imagine someone getting violent without a child knowing about it."

"That's what I thought."

"What else?"

"Well, there's the bit about the key."

Virginia nodded.

"Seems the key really does hold some special meaning. It was Grace's key. She got it from her mother after her death. Evidently, it was left to her."

"Wow."

"But that's not all. I guess the key opens an old box." Her husband reached for her hand. It had warmed some and she took it easily remembering the first time he'd looked at her this way and the second time he'd proposed. "I think Joy has gone to her old house. She has gone with the key to retrieve whatever is inside that old jewelry box."

***

Virginia stumbled to the bedroom and picked up the yellow notebook. Sure enough, on the back inside cover, was a thick piece of tape that must have been partially removed by her husband.

Joy, it read, *here is the key. The jewelry box is yours. The old man promised me he'd take very good care of it, though some secrets are best left buried. Let this key be a reminder, and remember my love for you. RWYA.*

"So it's buried. But that could be anywhere! And with an old man, no less! No name. Nothing. We don't even know where Joy and her mother lived; Joy never got that far in telling us. And we've received all of the paperwork. Everything."

"I know." Richard sat on the bed and patted a place for her beside him. "Look, that child is almost an adult and she's used to being out in the cold. She's old enough to get a job, and perhaps in time, get a place for herself. Maybe it's okay..."

"Okay? The child, as you say, is only 17! What were you doing at age 17? Surely not shopping around for a place to live!"

"No, but I was working, and you need to remember that Joy knows the streets..."

A dark thought entered Virginia's mind. Anything, but that.

He held her close. "We'll keep looking. And we'll look until we find her."

***

By April, Joy still hadn't returned to *Safe Haven*. And she hadn't shown up for a cupcake at *Just Desserts*. The paperwork, for a girl they would probably never see again, had halted. In its place were long nights of searching and reading, and days when Virginia could hardly focus on the task at hand. She and Richard grew closer in love and companionship than ever before, but life just wasn't the same without Joy.

Jean Rasmussen, the social worker, had almost given up hope that the girl would ever return. "It's to be expected," she'd said on their last visit in late March. "We lose many teens around her age, some even earlier.

That's why foster care and eventual adoption are so important early on."

Virginia's face burned but she didn't say a word. If they'd been able to take Joy in early on, take care of her, even before the foster parenting stuff was finished, the girl wouldn't be gone.

Her body ached as she got into the car, and her anger couldn't be removed.

Once home, Richard placed an arm around her shoulders. "We'll find her, like I said." His breath smelled of recently chewed gum, his skin like Irish Spring.

"But how?"

"We just will." He smiled over at her and kissed her on the cheek.

The Gift: A Parable of the Key

The Journal

March 15.

Joy and I have found a safe place, actually it's more of a place for her than for me. There are times only a drink will satisfy me and besides, Joy deserves a nice, warm meal every once in a while...

As she read, Virginia couldn't help but think about the woman and the terrible things she had done to her daughter. She was upset, and again wondered how much Joy knew about her mother. As she grew up surely she must have discovered her mother's journal at one time or another and read it when Grace was too overcome with the liquor to do anything but sleep. Then Virginia remembered the needles in the lavender room...

"It's amazing to me that Joy has lived as long as she has," she said, placing the journal on her lap.

Richard appeared reflective. His eyes traveled past her own and to somewhere far beyond them both. "I hope Joy isn't drinking," he said, "and taking drugs. Do you think she stayed clean in order to help her mother?"

Virginia didn't know. She hoped so, but she continued to read:

March 21.

See the picture in the corner? Joy's own artwork. We found a fairly warm place in the park and decided to have some lunch. It will get warm soon, and I hope, by then, I will have found a place for her...

Richard stopped her. "Do you think they were thinking of us even then?" he asked.

"Probably not. We weren't even together." She thought of Paul and God then, and wondered at the stones she sometimes carried in her coat pocket. Listening, Trust, Optimism, Tenacity...She'd reached for the white stone only the other day, after her prayers. She hadn't seen God in quite some time, and she missed him, though she still felt his presence whenever she prayed and read His holy word. It was enough. She knew God was helping her.

April 22.

I'm done. Joy cries all the time. I can't keep her warm enough. I can't keep her fed enough. I can't keep her happy enough. I've left her at Safe Haven. It's been a week. Tom would never have allowed it. "You are a terrible mother, always passing the responsibility. You're no good."

I'd better stop crying or this page will be unreadable, as if that were really a problem. I don't know why I'm keeping this thing. Joy will never read it, I won't allow it. But I have to talk to someone.

Tom, how I miss him, but he is gone and it's my fault.

April.

I think it's still April. The buds are on the trees and I see a hint of new growth in the park where I am currently staying. There are friendly people here to offer a person whatever they need. Even what they don't. I won't speak of what I do to get what I want. I cannot speak of it.

May 10.

I need to see my daughter. When I went back for her yesterday, she cried. 'I missed you, Mommy!' And when I took her in my arms I knew I could never leave her again. The lady there, Jean Rasmussen, expects to see me and my daughter once a week. She says she expects that I'll allow my daughter a warm bath and a place to sleep.

Her words made me angry. The key is the only thing that kept me from screaming out at her. The key. How could such a simple thing keep a person going? But mother was always thinking of everyone, even me, even in death. She said, 'This key is yours,' in her last breath. 'Take it and remember who you are.' I'd already forgotten, but I knew my mother loved me, and that the treasure would be held in my heart forever...

"That's it for now," Virginia said. "So, what sort of jewelry box does the key fit?" She paused, and when Richard was silent she continued, "Why couldn't Grace have said 'the treasure is in the upstairs attic,' or something? Then we would have the box *and* Joy."

Richard laughed. "Oh, come on, Virginia. Even if she had, would we know any more than we know now? How many thousands of homes have attics?"

Virginia was embarrassed. Okay, so the clue would have to be more specific than that, so why didn't Grace give it? But maybe she had! "Remember who you are," she said out loud. Why do you think those words were so important?"

"She had a mother who wanted the best for her children."

"Right! But maybe there's a clue hidden in the words somewhere."

"You've got to be kidding." This time Richard rolled his eyes.

"I'm dead, I mean serious."

"Maybe the jewelry box is somewhere near a church. Perhaps, 'Remember who you are,' is something Grace heard every Sunday."

"Now you're really stretching," said Richard.

Virginia looked down at the worn, yellow cover. Then she looked again. With the front and back covers lying flat, the silver spiral circling down the center, she could see what had only appeared to be only random letters before. She wondered if Richard could see it.

Property of: Grace Sorenson,
mother of Joy Sorenson,
in search of a better life this day,
February 1.

and on the back:

R W Y A

Richard reached for the journal, and at the same time a small piece of paper, that had been shoved inside the spiral section of the notebook, fluttered to the floor.

Virginia picked it up. *Right Way Youth Academy,* it read.

Virginia showed the scrap to Richard.

"I guess you were wrong," he said, reaching for the piece and spreading it out on his leg. His eyes glowed. "Don't you think it's funny that *Remember Who You Are* and *Right Way Youth Academy* have the same first letters?"

***

Work at *Just Desserts* seemed to be calling for her, and they hadn't, as yet, discovered the meaning of the small note. Looking in the old phone directory had produced no results; neither had searching the name on the internet. But it had to be a place, or, at the very least, a clue to something.

March had rained some, and in its place new growth was springing forth in the city of Idaho Falls, Idaho, though it would be some time yet before the sun spent more than a few scattered moments warming her face.

Every time Virginia thought of Joy, she thought of Grace, and then her thoughts turned once again to the journal she and her husband had finished just last week. Sure enough, she and Richard had been spoken about in glowing terms, (and sometimes, not), but nothing else was said about the key or where the box had been buried.

It was too bad they couldn't speak to Joy about the jewelry box. Perhaps she knew who the old man was, though maybe not. The girl had been wearing the key for awhile, and she had never seen the box amongst Joy's valuables - such as they were.

Virginia had begun to ask those who frequented *Just Desserts* if they'd heard of *Right Way Youth Academy*, and so far, had received only no's for answers.

And then it happened.

Virginia was serving God one April morning near Easter. That morning he said he needed at least a dozen pink cupcakes.

She'd smiled over at him, reached for the box, folded the corners up, and had begun to put the tasty treats inside when God added, "And you never know what one cupcake will mean over another."

"What?" Virginia gasped, stopping for a moment and peering at him through the glass. "What did you say?" She had meant it to come out kindly, though something else entirely had occurred.

"Cupcakes may even look the same on the outside, but often, it's the inside that gives us the real clue."

Now Virginia stood, six cupcakes filling the half empty box, and stared over at him. "If you have something to say, just say it," she said.

His blue eyes blinked. "Really, Virginia. All I need is another six cupcakes, and then I'll pay you for the order."

"But what did you mean about the insides?"

Richard peered at her from the back room. "Oh, hello," he said, walking into the room. Standing behind the counter he said, "I'd finish God's order if I were you."

God touched his fisherman's hat. "I have a lot of fishing to do today," he said. "And these cupcakes will come in handy."

Virginia gazed over at him and reached for the final six cupcakes. Placing them in the box, she creased the lid, shut it, and placed the box on the counter. "$20.50," she said.

"Your prices have gone up," God answered, handing Virginia the money.

"Sorry. New place. More bills."

God smiled, his eyes piercing her own. "Do you know what, Virginia? You get prettier by the day."

Virginia must have blushed. Richard stood near her and took her hand.

"Now I must go," said God. "See you soon?"

Virginia nodded.

***

"So, what do you think 'it's the inside that gives us the real clue' means?"

"God is a tricky one," Richard said.

They were standing in the lavender room. It was bare now of anything baby or child. A small couch sat in one corner and an end table held the yellow journal which had both wowed and confused them. And now this.

"Why do you think God wouldn't just tell me straight out where Joy is?"

"As I remember, you didn't even ask him," Richard said, taking her hand.

"That's right. All he could talk about was cupcakes. How one of them will be different from another one. He's so funny. He bought all pink cupcakes, with the same insides, and he...he just makes me crazy."

Richard laughed. "I think you're right about it being a clue. But you do know God. He wants you to search things out for yourself. Perhaps he figures it will mean more to you then, though I have no idea where he's going with this one."

"Remember that cake he brought to Trevor?"

"Sure. The stock boy ended up being Gail's boyfriend."

"Isn't it interesting that God always appears to use our shop to help someone else?"

"I never thought of that before," said Richard. "But maybe he doesn't - always. I mean, perhaps he uses our shop because that's what we do; that's how he teaches *us*."

Virginia looked out the large window where she'd long ago tossed the clothing and other baby items in anger. "Do you think," Virginia asked now, "that God is really saying that he has at least a dozen people that he's helping?"

"Well, at least that's what was going on today," said Richard. "But I can't help thinking there are more. You know, others that are shown the way back to him in different ways."

Virginia blinked. "What different ways?" she asked.

"Oh, I don't know. Oh, okay, suppose you're a doctor. How would God show a doctor what to do in life?"

"He might use a scalpel," Virginia prodded.

Richard frowned. "Seriously. How would God talk to a doctor?"

275

"Oh!" Suddenly Virginia was thinking of Paul. He was always getting sunflowers - sunflowers that grew taller than his house. And then a new thought entered her mind. "Sometimes they say it's a miracle when a certain patient lives. Have you ever wondered if there are times God directs the hands of a doctor?"

"Sure. Of course. But if you had to pick an object, what would it be?"

"I don't know, I guess I would just have to know the doctor. But I would probably use something meaningful, something that the doctor could see on a daily basis as a way of remembering Him. For us it's the stones, for Paul it was the sunflowers."

"Exactly!"

"So we are back to the start. What did God mean when he said, 'It's the inside that gives us the real clue?'"

"The inside. Perhaps we'll find *Right Way Youth Academy* within some other establishment."

***

Twenty-plus phone calls later, Virginia had a lead. Unfortunately, Richard was at *Just Desserts* and couldn't close up shop until 8:00. "So, why don't you check it out yourself," he said. "When I get home, we can discuss it together."

Virginia frowned on her side of the line but she knew that Richard was right. They had already closed up shop too many times the last few months to go in search of clues for Joy. It was time to settle down a little and make some profit.

And so, she relented.

The church was just outside Idaho Falls. The journey was only a half hour drive south on I-15. Arriving in the city, Virginia stopped at Stockman's to get a bite to eat. The place was pleasing, though not fancy, and the waiter seemed too young to work there, though Virginia guessed he looked young because she was obviously getting older.

She smiled at herself and ordered a rib-eye. It was already 5:30, and the place would be closing in just half hour more, which seemed early to Virginia. After dinner, she'd venture to the Baptist church. Virginia hadn't stepped foot inside a church for years, but Pastor Rest seemed nice enough when she spoke with him on the phone.

A few minutes following her meal she was at the church. She spotted the cross on the small, white building, even before she discovered where to park. Soon enough she reached the doors and was knocking.

With a click of the handle the door opened, and a man wearing a regular white shirt and slacks asked, "Virginia?" His beard was filled with splotches of grey and his smile reminded Virginia of God's - warm and inviting.

"Yes. Thank you."

He instructed her to come inside.

The place was clean and orderly. She followed the pastor down one hall; then at the beginning of another. He led her inside a small room and asked her to sit down. The room looked like an office - probably his own. Pictures of Christ graced the walls, and a large wood cross hung on the wall behind the pastor's chair.

In moments he was asking her questions, and it wasn't easy to answer them, but she did. Answers about where she lived and what she did for a living were easy. The hard ones came after that. What church she attended and how God had helped her in her life. Virginia didn't want him to ask too many more of those, and when he didn't bring up the reason for her visit, she decided to speak up.

"Uh, Pastor. Could you tell me a little bit more about your program for teens?"

"Oh, yes." He stroked his beard. "That is the reason you came. But I need to tell you first off, it might have been better if you'd made an appointment with the pastor in Idaho Falls where you live - a shorter journey."

"I know, it's just...Well...I am in search of a missing girl."

Pastor Rest stroked his beard. "Who are you looking for?" he asked.

"A girl, 17 now, who may have attended *Right Way Youth Academy*. Joy...Joy Sorenson.

"Joy?" Now the man's face turned a striking white. "What do you need to know?" he asked. "Are you a family member?"

"No...a..."

"I can't give out any information unless you're a family member."

"I soon will be," Virginia said, trying to keep her voice calm though her heart was thundering in her chest. She hadn't considered this segment of the interview. "You see, we, my husband and I, have been trying to adopt Joy. Her mother died just a few months ago..."

"Her mother's, dead?" The pastor's voice echoed off the ceiling. "When?"

"In December."

"And the child is alone?"

"Somewhere. She was at *Safe Haven* for some time, and then one evening she went missing."

"I see. And Joy, how was she before she left the facility?"

"Fine, I guess. We wanted to bring her home but we were still in the paperwork process, the finalization of her foster care."

Pastor Rest was silent. He looked at her as if considering what his next words should be. Finally, he said, "Well, Virginia, Miss Joy did take my class; a sort of camping experience where kids learn the art of the outdoors and the wonders of God. Unfortunately, after she graduated from the Academy, I didn't see her or her mother again. Of course, when the father left them..." The pastor frowned. "So, how can I help you now?" he asked, searching her eyes.

"A key was left with Joy upon the passing of her mother. My husband and I think the key is more than just a trinket handed down. Where the key is..."

"There will Joy be also," the pastor said, and Virginia instinctively thought of the scripture more than likely that had inspired the comment.

"I'm sure you know where they lived," Virginia said.

"Yes, but their home has since been demolished. Too many problems to fix, said the city. The place was, shall we say, brought down to nothing but wood and cement about two years ago."

"Oh." The news brought a shudder through Virginia. How would she find the girl now? And then the initials her mother had left on the outside of the journal as they related to the words inside came to her mind. "Do you know the meaning of 'remember who you are?'"

"Of course." The pastor laughed. "It was what we said during *Right Way Youth Academy* every morning the entire two weeks we were together. Why do you ask?"

"Well, we've learned some things about that slogan," Virginia began, trying to keep her voice calm and even. But the feat was difficult. When would she find Joy? Just talking to this pastor was taking precious time; and yet, she needed answers, and he appeared to be ready to send them her way.

Pastor Rest waited, and as Virginia gathered up renewed courage she said, "*Remember Who You Are*, is written in Grace's journal, an old yellow notebook we picked up from the center where they were occasionally staying. Inside the cover we found the place where we imagine the key was taped, and the words, '*Right Way Youth Academy*' on a small piece of paper within the spiral spine of the same journal. Important, don't you think?"

"I know they've been important to every teen and their parent going through the program," answered the pastor. "But I know for Joy and her mother, the words took on special significance. Seems Grace's own mother sort of passed the saying down from her mother."

"So what would the saying have to do with a key?"

"Grace was a collector of sorts, if I'm remembering correctly," he wiped his beard, "she was the one who always initiated the craft days here, though she wasn't one to take on the cooking. So how were Joy and her mother getting along the last time you saw them?"

"Homeless. Grace was into drinking and drugs. I don't know about Joy."

"Probably the same. But you never know, she and her mother made some pretty firm commitments while in the Academy - commitments they weren't supposed to take on lightly, though I know how the world is."

"So, they attended together?"

"It was a mother and daughter event in the summer. During early fall we did the same thing with fathers and sons. The program is still going famously, though I have stepped back a little since then." He rubbed his beard.

***

"So, the pastor knew her?"

"Yes. And he knew about the program and he knew about the saying between Joy and her mother. And of course he knew their address."

"Did you drive by?"

"Yes, but it was too dark and I couldn't see anything but rubble. Let's go tomorrow. *Just Desserts* will be closed and we can spend some time together in daylight searching the area.

***

Virginia had been right. The place was only rubble. One couldn't even tell if a house had been there before. And yet, there were still homes across the street - old, decrepit dwellings that Virginia could only imagine also housed rodents and bed bugs, which did little to assuage her fears.

Still, perhaps in the rubble they would find the jewelry box. Highly un-likely, but one had to check out these things. Joy wasn't in sight, and thoughts of her all alone somewhere, or maybe hooked up with some 'loser' drifted in and out of Virginia's mind like a dark cloud. Even if they found the box, they didn't have the key to open it; and they didn't have Joy.

The place where the house once stood was a mess. Plenty of 'someones' had already scrounged the area for trinkets, and mostly what was left was old rusted house parts, twisted metal and broken-down fencing. A shiny piece of paper caught her eye. Only a gum wrapper. Another piece a bit larger. Someone's castaway homework.

"Find anything?" she yelled to her husband, who was looking through something near the front sidewalk.

"Just junk," he yelled back. "Maybe the neighbors know something." He looked across the street, just as she had done when they'd first entered the neighborhood, only to see someone in a long overcoat approach them.

"So, what 'cha be a 'wanting?" the old man asked, shuffling to a stop. He wore old loafers and a battered hat. Virginia had already joined her husband when she'd seen the man coming.

"Know the woman who lived here?" he asked, pointing to the rugged spot.

"Everyone knew Grace," he said. "Everyone." He planted his worn hands in his threadbare pant pockets. "So, what 'cha be a wanting?" he asked again.

"Information," chimed in Virginia. The man visibly jumped. He must not have seen her.

"You together?" he asked.

Virginia nodded. "What would a couple of young folks want to know about a woman and her daughter? You know he left them."

"The husband."

"Yep. Never liked the fool. Never took enough care of his wife and child. I told him so on more than one occasion. You a relative or something?"

"Hope to be, for Joy," Richard said before she could stop him. It probably wasn't wise to share everything, especially those things that might not come to fruition anyway, and especially if they never found her.

"Then you must be related to the mother." He scuffed his old shoe against the cement and looked deeply into her eyes as if trying to figure out what she was trying not to tell him.

"We're not related," said Virginia.

"But you said..."

Virginia nudged Richard but he must not have gotten the hint. "We'll be adopting Joy. The mother was found dead this winter."

"Dead?" The old man's mouth suddenly crumbled. A small tear escaped his right eye. "When they left, I thought for sure they'd come back and visit but they never did. The place was finally torn down. I haven't seen the husband in years - good riddance; but the wife and child, well, I took right kindly to both of them. The girl must be, what now?"

"Seventeen."

The man whistled and removed his hands from his trousers. Rubbing them together he said, "You know, it's right cold out here. Want to come in for some tea?"

Virginia smiled.

283

***

The old man opened the heavy apricot colored curtains hanging in the kitchen and began to prepare some tea. "My wife, Dove, was with me for some years and she was right fond of that little girl. When Joy would visit they would have milk and cookies in the dining room (he pointed to a small room with a table just opposite the kitchen) and talk about life. "But I have forgotten myself, my name is John."

"Nice to meet you, John," Richard said, extending his hand, which John shook vigorously. Virginia reached forth her own hand, but this time John took it gently, lifted it to his wrinkly lips, and kissed it.

Virginia must have blushed because Richard was giggling.

"Now I've forgotten myself once again," John continued, releasing her hand and returning to the stove. "A man in my days was always quite respectful when a lady was in the room."

"So, what did you think about Grace?" Virginia asked.

"Oh, she was high class, even with that retch of a husband. Had a drinking problem, that one, and when things got even more impossible, my wife told Grace to leave him. But she wouldn't. She was of the religious persuasion and said she was going to work things out. Of course that never happened. The man left her before much could be worked out."

The old man brought the tea kettle over. The tea bags already sat in a small bowl in front of her. He returned to the stove and reached for the cups hanging on little hooks above him. "He more than likely left because of his drinking."

Virginia looked at her husband. She poured the hot liquid in her cup and reached for a bag. Placing it in the heated water, she watched as John sat down beside her husband at the table. "I'm glad you folks stopped by," the man said, pouring the hot water into his own cup and reaching for a tea bag.

It was funny, though it shouldn't have been. The man was kind, though they hadn't come to visit him at all.

Richard filled his cup and placed another tea bag. "So, is that why Grace left the house? Because her husband left her?"

"Mostly," the man answered, swirling the tea bag with his spoon. "She couldn't afford the place. Said she'd gotten a small apartment for her and the child. So where are they now?"

Virginia took out her tea bag and placed it on a small plate that was already on the table. "Like we told you, the mother is dead."

"Grace is dead?" John's mouth crumbled once more and another tear escaped his eye. "And the little girl, how old is she now?"

"Seventeen."

"Seventeen. And where is she living?" He removed the bag, added it to Virginia's plate, and took a sip. "I love this herbal stuff," he said. "We couldn't feed it to Joy, just milk. But she sure loved cookies."

Richard took his own sip and looked intently at Virginia. What he couldn't say in words, Virginia already knew.

"We are hoping to adopt Joy," she said now, placing her cup back on the table and smiling over at the old man. "But she has run away."

"What have you done?" the man hollered, dropping his cup. The liquid splattered on the table in front of them.

"Please, please," Richard said. "We didn't do anything. The girl ran away from the shelter."

"What shelter?" the man asked, slowly maneuvering his body to the kitchen sink and grabbing a paper towel. "I have to watch things, really watch things." He returned, towel in hand and bent to mop the spill.

"Let me help," Richard said, but the man was already waving him away. "Since my dear Dove's death, I have had to do many *womanly* things." He smiled. "So what about this shelter. Are you telling me that Grace and her daughter were homeless?"

He walked back to the stove and opened a cabinet where he deposited the paper towel. "Now," he continued, returning to the same spot at the table and refilling his cup, "tell me what is happening to Grace and her daughter."

Virginia took a deep breath and started from the beginning, relaying to the old man all their concerns about where Joy was, now that she had run away, where they had looked so far, and who might know where she was today. But John was quiet.

"If I'd only known," he said. "Dove and I... we...when she was here..." Another tear glistened in his eye. "We would have taken them in. But Grace, she was a proud woman, a very proud woman."

"A key was left for Joy by her mother. Do you know anything about that?" It was a sudden move, but John was likely to forget again and they'd have to clue him in, beginning all over again.

"A key? Why, yes, I remember a key. Grace wore it around her neck; would let no one touch it, not even that horrible husband of hers. I asked her about it once and she said it was...it was...oh yes, the *key to her heart*. I asked her what it fit. She said, 'Oh, you don't want to know about that.' But I did want to know and so did Dove. We both wanted to know."

"So what did the key fit?"

"She had a saying about the key. She was to remember something."

"Remember who you are?" Virginia prodded.

"That's it!" hollered the man, placing his cup down and standing. "I have something to show you," he said.

Ten minutes later the man hadn't returned. "Do you think we should go after him?" Virginia asked.

"Either that or have the man forget why he went down the hall in the first place," Richard answered.

They stood and together traveled down the long hall, past one pink bathroom and what appeared to be a guest room on the left. Near the end of the hall they found John, sitting on his bed, an antique bronze jewelry box sitting on his lap. He looked up. "Oh, it's you," he said.

Virginia sighed with relief.

The man caressed the old box. It was exquisite. The lid and sides appeared to be decorated with interesting scenes of life.

"It's French Nouveau," said the man. "Quite expensive. For years I wondered why Grace left the box

287

to me and my wife, but now, now I wonder if it had something to do with her daughter. You have the key, I hope."

"Joy has the key."

The man touched the engravings on the box, slowly, as if trying to remember something. "We can't damage it. It must have the key."

"Are you sure you haven't seen Joy? She hasn't come by for a visit?" Even as she said the words Virginia knew it was highly possible that Joy *had* come by but the man might not be able to remember.

"Joy hasn't visited me in years," John said, laying the box on the back side and looking at the key hole. "I always wondered why I'd get such a box if Grace was always going to have the key, but she told me to keep it safe, that she couldn't bring it with her. Had a fear of it getting lost or stolen."

John lifted it slowly and returned it to its place by the side of the bed. "I'm sorry."

The words sounded so final, and Virginia couldn't stand it. "Do you have any idea where Joy may have gone?"

"I wish she'd come here," he said, standing, and directing them to the door. "I wish she'd come here."

Back in the kitchen, Virginia helped John clear the cups and place them in the sink. "I'll wash them out later," he said.

Virginia and her husband turned to leave. No, they didn't have Joy, but they knew where the jewelry box was and that was something. "Did Joy know her mother gave you the jewelry box?" she asked.

"I'm not sure," the man answered. "Do you really have to leave? I can get you something else."

"Thank you for the tea," Virginia offered, "but we really need to know if Joy knew her mother left the jewelry box with you."

"I said I'm not sure." Suddenly, the man looked angry. "Why would you want to know about that old box?" he asked just as quickly. "Who are you, and how did you get inside my house?"

Richard reached for the old doorknob and opened the door. Taking Virginia's hand he ushered her out.

Virginia didn't know what to think, and Richard, well, he was beyond words.

***

"Some kind of memory loss, I guess," said Virginia.

"Definitely. The man shouldn't be living alone. I wonder where his family is?"

As they traveled home Virginia couldn't help but think of the two puzzle pieces that had finally led them to the French box. It was a beautiful thing, not easy to get one's hands on, especially in Idaho, and yet, hadn't the box come from Grace's mother?

"Grace's mother must have had some money," Virginia said now, watching the whiteness of covered trees as they sped past.

"I thought the same thing. It's too bad we don't know where Grace's mother lived."

"Why?"

"Perhaps we could track down Joy that way. Her mother is dead, but perhaps the current occupants of her childhood home would know about her."

"If her place isn't torn down as well."

Richard's eyes turned to her briefly and then back to the road. "I don't think so. If the box is any indication of the interests of Grace's mother, it may be safe to say she lived in some classical rendition."

Virginia laughed. "Rendition?"

"Why sure." Virginia watched the ends of Richard's mouth curl up into a smile. "And consider this. If not Grace's mother, then her mother. The woman may have even come from France."

"Like that's going to help."

"It might. Every little clue helps, Virginia. In time we'll have enough to find Joy and bring her home."

Virginia imagined, just for a moment, traipsing around France. Well, that was highly unlikely. They might find the long-lost house, but Joy would have never been able to afford the trip.

***

It was May when a phone message arrived from *Safe Haven*. It was short and sweet. "We've found Joy," said Jean. Virginia had been so busy at work, she hadn't checked the phone until now. She was teaching another marriage class and it had just ended, the final stragglers leaving and giving her a moment's breath. It was 2:15 and the message had been left around noon.

"We've got to go, now!" she screamed to Richard. He was in the back room, and something tumbled to the ground.

"What fell?"

"Just a canister. What's up?" He was wiping his hands against a *Just Desserts* apron as he entered the room.

"Joy. They've found her!"

If she lived to be a hundred years old, she would remember the day she and her husband closed down the store early and raced to *Safe Haven*. Stop lights that hadn't been there before appeared out of nowhere, and once, only once mind you, they'd been followed by a police officer. Virginia had forced herself to slow down. "We'll never get there!" she finally screeched, only to have her husband reply: "We won't if you aren't careful."

Her brow furrowed, they continued to *Safe Haven*, and once there, raced into the building. Her anxious face must have looked like a giant red apple, but she didn't care. Breathing in and out like an accordion on steroids she raced to the front desk.

Jean smiled over at her. "Finally," she said, "the girl has been driving me crazy!"

In their attempt to get inside quickly they'd completely missed Joy, standing by the door.

Seeing Joy for the first time she raced over. But Richard was quicker. In no more time than it would take a lap dog to reach its owner, Richard had scooped her up in his arms and was spinning her around. "Oh, Joy!" he screamed again and again. He was laughing and crying. Virginia was laughing and crying. Joy was silent.

"Stop," she said. "Put me down. I'm not...two."

It was like an electric bolt had entered Richard's heart. "Sorry," he said, pulling her back away from him.

Joy brushed at her torn sweatshirt, muddied and worn. She looked up at them. "Yes, as you can see, I'm back." She tried to smile. "I've never seen you so excited."

Virginia looked down at Joy's pants and shoes and the mud that had accumulated underneath her fingernails.

"I've been waiting here too long," she said. "I almost went to get a shower, but I didn't want to miss you," she said.

"See what I mean?" said Jean, approaching them. "This...girl seems to think that a shower could wait. I'm not so sure."

"So you waited all this time to see us?"

"Sure. What else was I supposed to do? You're my parents, right?"

Virginia could hardly think. Her heart was melting into a thousand pieces and she wasn't sure how she would ever be able to gather them up again.

Joy

"Why did you leave?" The question was abrupt, Virginia knew it, but it had to be asked. As the girl squirmed in her chair at *Safe Haven*, Virginia tried to be patient. Richard sat beside her and Joy across from them, lightly touching each of their hands at different times as she spoke.

"I missed my mother," she said. "I missed her so much!"

Joy's hands reached up to her eyes and she sobbed, rivulets of dirt and grime making their way down her cheeks. "I went to see her, the place where she was buried. I even stole some flowers from someone's yard, they were practically dead, but I..." She sobbed some more, and then wiping at her eyes, looked into the faces of Virginia and Richard.

"I had to do it," she said. "I had to find out." Another short sob escaped her throat before she continued. "You wouldn't understand."

Virginia wondered if she would. The child, a teen now, was obviously upset that her mother was gone, and she'd gone out in search of...something. Some healing, perhaps. A way back.

Richard reached for the girl. "We probably wouldn't understand," he said, "so why don't you tell us."

Joy blinked, the last of the muddy tears drying on her cheeks. "You promise not to get angry?"

Virginia swallowed. Richard was silent. "We promise," he said.

"I was only going to find the grave at first, but things got cold, so I made my way over to *Just Desserts.* It was Sunday, and I knew you wouldn't be there. Sorry," she added lamely.

Virginia couldn't help but think about how accurate they'd been in looking for her. It was almost as if someone had spoken in their ears, and she'd known what to do, albeit a little too late.

"When I couldn't get in I got angry. I almost came back here, but I couldn't. The waiting for you was just too hard! I thought...I could get a good job, or something, and that it would be easier for you to take me in, especially when I turned eighteen and should really be on my own." She paused, took a breath, and continued: "I know you would have taken care of me, but I'm not a baby, and...and I wanted to be sure I was doing the right thing in having you adopt me."

So that was it.

"I didn't want you to take me in just because my mom wanted it. I wanted to do it because it was the right thing. My mother always said, 'Remember who you are,' and I was trying to remember who I really was!"

Virginia covered her mouth, quickly. She felt a sob coming on and wanted the girl to continue. Richard was still silent.

Joy reached for the necklace. She pulled it from underneath her sweatshirt and looked down at the key on the strand. "This was my mother's," she said, "but it was also my grandmother's. My grandmother kept a beautiful box of secret things; I've never been told what she kept, and when she was close...to death, she gave the box to my mother. I don't know what she was supposed to do with it, but I wondered if she'd put some secret things in it, too. And now it's mine," she said, placing the necklace back behind the old sweatshirt. "Only I have no idea where the box is. I've read her journal over and over and all I know is that it was given to some old geezer. Why would my mother do that?"

"Maybe she had a reason," Virginia offered.

"I wish I had it," the girl breathed. "I mean, there's got to be some treasure inside, right?"

Virginia swallowed.

But Joy was standing. "I think it's about time I had a shower," she said, picking at her soiled shirt. "I probably stink, too. Can you wait for me?"

"Sure. Get your shower. We have something to share with you as well," Richard said, touching Virginia lightly on the arm.

***

Joy wore a clean blue shirt and new jeans and on her feet, toe socks. Each toe was a different color, and as she wiggled them, sitting on the same chair she'd left just twenty minutes prior, Virginia and Richard couldn't help but laugh. So this was part of tenacity...Responding to the fun as well as the turmoil and pain. Virginia's eyes canvassed the girl's green eyes. Her blond hair was wet, and lying at her shoulders in thick rivulets. For the first time she noticed that the slight girl was becoming a woman, too. How could she have missed it?

"So, what were you going to tell me?" she asked, placing her hands in front of her and looking eagerly at them both.

"We have some good news," said Richard, reaching for her. "We know where the jewelry box is."

In all of her life, Virginia could not have prepared herself for the response that came next. It was almost like a piece of sunlight had shot between them, as if in hearing the words, 'jewelry box', Joy, was finally able to reveal her true self.

"I don't believe it!" she sang, standing up and hugging them both. They still sat in their chairs. "You really have the box? Where did you find it? Is it still in one piece? Is it dirty, or ruined or anything?"

She sat, her breath coming out quickly, her legs trembling like a reed.

"We don't have it, exactly," said Virginia, remembering the cold departure from John. "But I think we can get it." Even as she said the words, Virginia hoped that she was right. She hoped in the deepest part of her soul that she and Richard's previous visit to see John would be remembered.

***

"And what would you be a' wanting?" John asked. Amazingly, the man wore the same clothes, though his partially bald head of hair seemed combed. He peered over at Joy. "And who are you?" he asked.

"Joy, you remember me, Mr. ah Franklin."

The man didn't smile. He glared.

On the drive over they had discussed John as the old man in the journal, though Joy had surprisingly admitted that she'd never thought of him as the *old man*. She'd told them how strange it had been to be in his house, how warm and unreal it had always been - like going to heaven without really going there. "Perhaps that's why I never thought of him as the *old man*. He was more like God," she'd told them.

And now they were here. And the man wasn't sounding anything like God.

He opened the screen. "What are you selling?" he hollered.

"Surely you remember us," Richard prodded. Virginia squirmed.

"What are you selling?" the man asked again. "I don't need a vacuum and I don't need any of that orange cleaner. Besides, you were here last week trying to sell me that stuff. So how much is it? I might just pay you for it so's you'll get out of my hair."

Virginia thought again of the man's hair and his messy wardrobe, and then tried to focus on his eyes. They weren't getting anywhere.

"You remember, John, you showed us the jewelry box the last time we were here," Virginia said.

"And look!" said Joy, releasing the key from underneath her shirt. "Here is the key!"

The man blinked and then he sputtered. "Where did you get that?!" he yelled. "Grace wouldn't have let that out of her sight. Where is Grace?" He looked around the screen door as if expecting to see her. The man's lips trembled, and as they stood on the porch, waiting for John's reply, she knew that his words could go either way. Either he would finally see or they would be brushed off the porch like the last time.

"Grace, my mother, is gone, Mr. Franklin."

"Gone, gone where?" was the answer.

Joy reached for the screen door, and, holding it with her left hand, reached out with her right to John. "She's dead. I'm Joy, her daughter."

If she lived to be a hundred years old, Virginia would never forget what happened next. The old man looked into Joy's eyes and it was as if a cloud had moved from his eyes. He smiled. "Joy? But you have grown, child!"

He took her hand, and looking into her eyes, kissed her sweetly on the cheek. "I have waited for you," he said.

A small tear found its way down Joy's cheek. "And I have been looking for you," she said. "Can we come in?"

"Why, sure, sure!" John sang, opening the inner door for all of them. "Richard! Virginia! When did you get here?" he asked.

They stood in the living room and all was the same, the same as they'd left it just a few weeks previous; except for two things. Joy was with them and she had the key.

***

In John's room, Virginia's and Richard's eyes turned to the place where the box had sat, but it was no longer there. "I almost forgot," said the man, turning to face them, his lips turned down at the corners. "Tom, he was here. He demanded to see the box." The man's voice shook. "I'm s... sorry."

"What man?" Virginia asked. "Who is Tom?"

John looked squarely into Joy's eyes and the girl was silent. Still, there appeared to be some recognition in her large green eyes. "He was here?" she asked.

"I had to give it to him," John said, sitting on the bed, and patting a place next to him. But Joy didn't move. "I told him he couldn't have it, that it wasn't his. I should have never let him in. He was going to tell me where Grace was, and you." He looked up at the girl who was standing like solid rock before him. "He...promised."

"He lied," Joy sobbed.

The man patted the spot next to him. This time Joy relented. She sat with her head bowed, tears streaming down her cheeks.

"Who is Tom?" Virginia asked again.

"Yes, who is he?" Richard offered.

The room was as still as night, without a cloud, without a star.

"Joy's father," said John. "He was here."

Joy looked up. The happiness that had once shined from her eyes was gone. Tears wetted her cheeks. "Everyone hated my dad, including me."

"His parents?"

"No, they didn't hate him. Thought he was perfect, I'm sure. Dead now."

"Other family?"

"I don't know. If he had them he never spoke about them."

Virginia was silent. What could she possibly say? How could this girl go on knowing her father held the secret to her mother's heart?

***

"We'll find it, that's all there is to it," said Virginia, her arm wrapped lovingly around the girl's shoulders. They sat in the back of the car as Richard drove. As the girl cried, Virginia's thoughts whirled. They had spoken with most of the neighbors after leaving John. Nothing. This time John remembered them all the way to the door, but he was sad, and Virginia knew, lonely.

"My father kept pretty much to himself," Joy said now, looking down at the blue and white tennis shoes covering her colorful toe socks. "When he left, no one cared."

The roads cleared as the day wore on to afternoon, and by evening, as the air grew chill, Richard, Virginia and Joy returned to *Safe Haven*, only to have to leave her again.

The Box

The following few weeks blew by like spring, and neither she nor Richard had learned anything about Joy's father, Tom. "Maybe we should forget about the whole thing," Richard said one evening after they'd returned Joy to the shelter. "Maybe..."

"Maybe, nothing," said Virginia, looking at the stones still gracing the mantel of their living room. "What do you think constancy means anyway? God has shown us the way, all this time. Do you think he's going to stop helping us now?"

Richard moaned. "Really, Virginia. Maybe we're not supposed to get that old box. Maybe having Joy with us is enough. The paperwork is almost finished as well as the visits here. And the classes..."

"Without that box, it will never be enough for Joy, can't you see that?"

Richard placed the Bible on the end table. Just the week previous they had decided to attend church. The experience had been refreshing, but without Joy, who said she felt 'funny' about church, things were strained and more than a bit difficult. Still, there would have been lots of questions from those attending services, so perhaps it was just as well.

"I don't know where we're going to look," said Richard. "We have less to go on with him than we ever had to go on when it came to Joy."

"What about that preacher? The one we met just outside Idaho Falls?"

"You mean, you met," Richard corrected.

Virginia thought back. "Right. He said something about Joy's father in the mix. Right as I was leaving the pastor said something that really didn't matter much to me then. But now... He said Joy's father had driven them to and from the Academy. They hadn't come themselves. Why he said he remembered the incident was because Tom was huffing and puffing about having to drive them over on a Thursday night - his night."

"That's interesting. Perhaps it was his drinking night..."

"And maybe they only had one car," Virginia offered. "Or maybe Grace didn't have a driver's license. She didn't have one with her when she died."

"You're right. Perhaps we can learn more from this preacher, uh...Pastor Rest. Up for a visit?"

Half an hour later they'd reached the small church, but Virginia hadn't called ahead. It was Monday and the place appeared empty. They'd decided to close up shop at *Just Desserts*, and hoped the already slow business they usually received on Mondays would be the standard fare today; in other words, not too many disappointed customers.

"Now what?" Virginia asked her husband, who was a few feet away from her and checking doors. "I don't think you should be doing that. Besides," she looked around the parking lot, "no cars."

"Maybe he lives close and can walk." He walked around the church. A few minutes later Richard hadn't returned, so she went after him. The door at the back was unlocked. She entered and made her way around the long hall until she heard voices. Yes, her husband was inside and so was someone else.

"Been talking to your husband," said an old gent, twice the age of the pastor. He wore gray overalls and a fisherman's cap. "God?" she stumbled.

"Well, hello, Virginia. How have you been?"

"You're cleaning a church?" she couldn't help asking. A broom was against one wall, and it looked like God was gathering up the large bucket for mopping. "Why, sure. Looking for Pastor Rest?" he asked.

Virginia was dumbfounded. Okay, sure, she'd seen God in her kitchen and at the grocery store and at *Just Desserts* but at a church? And then she couldn't help laughing at herself. Of course, God was at a church; where else would God be?

"Sorry, Virginia. I got so busy talking that I forgot to tell you I'd found my way in." Richard looked at her and offered his arm. She took it. It was much easier to stand with support. "I've been talking to God about Joy and her father, and he's given me..."

"Why didn't you tell me that Joy's father was still alive?" Virginia interrupted. She shouldn't have interrupted, but there it was.

"You didn't ask me," God answered. "Besides, haven't you had some fun learning on your own, with just a nudge here and there?"

303

"I would hardly call it...fun," Virginia said, her voice croaking a bit. "But we did meet John."

"Oh yes, John," God said, reaching within the closet and turning on the low faucet inside to fill the bucket. The water splashed and whirled, and the bucket, once filled, was rolled out the door. "John is one of my best servants." He smiled.

Virginia's breath left her for a moment as she looked at God and God looked at her. God loved her, she knew that without question, but did she love God as he loved her?

"I'm interested to know how you've been faring with the five stones," asked God, placing the mop in the bucket and leaning the handle against the wall.

She almost began, "Well, you know..." but checked herself. The reason she talked with God wasn't because he didn't know what was going on in her life; she prayed to him so that she might connect with him. "I've been using the five stones, religiously," she said, grinning a bit because of the pun that had managed to break forth from her lips.

"I'm glad to hear that," God answered, "but your listening could improve some. Remember, I always like to hear questions. Trust me, I know all of the answers."

Now God was getting into the act.

"I'm optimistic about that," said Virginia, trying not to laugh, but it was true. She was optimistic about all God had to offer her. She was glad that she hadn't given up on him or on Joy or her husband. The tenacity had paid off in all accounts and she was glad that her life was a constant (or practically constant) life with God. "So what have you been telling Richard?"

God reached for the bucket. "I've got a lot of mopping to do," he said. "Maybe your husband can relay the message."

For the first time since she'd entered the room, Virginia really looked at it. The room was large, and was probably used for family events. There was no carpet to speak of, just a shiny yellow floor with scuff marks in places that God would obviously be cleaning up.

Virginia smiled over at God, thanked him, and turned to Richard. "So, what did God tell you?" she asked. She watched from the corner of her eye as God squeezed the mop-head into the bucket and went about cleaning the first section of the dirty floor.

"I've been praying for days that we'd get an answer," Richard said. "But I never expected to find God here."

"I've been praying, too, but nothing came."

"I don't know what did it, but it might have been the question I asked."

"What question?"

"Well, I was reading in the Bible that passage, 'Behold, I stand at the door and knock...'"

"I know that one."

"Well, I was reading and suddenly it came to me like a burst of light. God wants to talk with us - even have a conversation, but first we must be willing to open the door! He reminded me of the experience today."

"And?"

"Don't you get it?"

Virginia didn't have a clue.

"Joy's father was here, at this very church with the old jewelry box, looking for the key that Joy has!"

"God told you that?"

305

"Not exactly. He said Joy's father had visited with the pastor just two days ago, and I thought to myself, what sort of questions would Tom ask?'

The answer was easy. "About the key, of course. But why would Joy's father need the key? He could have just destroyed the box to get what's inside."

"I wondered the same thing. God said to trust him."

Trust? Virginia felt suddenly frustrated. "So where is Joy's father?"

Richard frowned. "I think he was just about to tell me when you walked in."

Virginia could feel the warmth rise in her cheeks. She looked over toward the corner where God had begun his mopping, but he was gone. She surveyed the floor. It was clean.

***

"So, what was the question you asked God?"

In the kitchen, Richard was fixing dinner. She loved it when he fixed dinner. It always reminded her of how handy men could be in the kitchen when they wanted to be.

"Oh, I asked him how I could best help you, and he told me that I needed to always be open to your suggestions."

"Why that question?" Virginia asked. Richard stirred the chili - his own recipe - that was never the same each time he cooked it.

"I don't know. I guess I was thinking about what kind of conversation I would like to have with God and

I thought of the conversations I have with you. I wanted it to be like that."

A sweet warmth traveled up her back and arms but she didn't speak.

"You know, Virginia, the relationship we have with God can be a lot like the one *we* have. I don't know why it has taken me so long to figure it out, but I'm glad I'm finally getting it. We don't have to climb a tower to reach God, we don't even have to go up into the mountains. All we need to do is ask, wherever we are."

Virginia watched as he brought the bowls and cups to the table and then the large hot pad where the chili rested, still in the pot. A large green spoon poked out from the top. Richard had also brought to the table grated cheese and a pitcher of water. "Would you like to say the prayer?" he asked.

Virginia bowed her head. "Dear God," Virginia prayed. "Can you help us know thy will concerning Joy? Help us to know where to look for the box. Help us to love each other. Bless Joy. And bless this food. Amen."

***

Joy giggled. "I've figured it out," she said. "Yesterday, after you left I sat down and wrote a list of all of the places my father went. I thought of all the places he took me, and then a new thought came to me. I was eating dinner when all of a sudden the answer came."

Virginia's skin prickled.

"The first Thursday of the month when I was little my father wouldn't come home until very late. It was his 'bar' night, he said, and so mother and I watched

307

one of my favorite shows on television or rented a movie. Dad wasn't home when I went to bed but I remember hearing him about 2 a.m., as he slipped through the front door.

"One night, when I was a little older, I worked it out with mom to follow him. She didn't like the idea, but I'd been pestering her for weeks. 'I don't want you near a bar,' she said, and I'd promised we would only sit in the car and watch him go in. I think in the back of my mind I knew there was something else going on besides the bar and so did my mother, and so one Thursday she relented and we followed him. But dad didn't go to the bar, at least not that night. We followed him all the way to the city cemetery, can you believe it?"

Virginia swallowed. "So why the cemetery?" she asked.

"My grandfather and grandmother, the ones who gave my mother the antique jewelry box and key, are buried there."

"But aren't they your mother's mother and father?"

"Yes, and we thought that was a bit strange, and so we watched him. He walked to their graves and placed flowers on each one and stood there for just a little while before heading back to the car. After that he went to the bar. We went home after that but the following month we followed him out again. He did the same thing."

"Perhaps he missed your mother's parents."

"That's the strange part," said Joy, brushing her thin fingers through her wet hair. "He hated them. Don't you think it's funny that he'd want to visit their graves?"

"Funny doesn't begin to cover it," said Richard. "Unless there was something at the gravesite that Tom wanted to get an answer to."

"Like what?"

"Yeah, like what?" Virginia echoed.

"Before your father left you and your mother, what kind of interest did he have in the jewelry box?"

"I don't know," Joy shrugged. "I mean, it sat in my parent's bedroom on the dresser; but as far as I knew, mom always wore the key around her neck so he couldn't have even peeked inside. Do you think he heard about mother's death?"

"Well, that would be the only reason to search for the box now," said Richard. "And the key." He stood, waving them to sit in their chairs while he spoke with Jean.

She was all smiles today. "The paperwork is about ready," she said now as he approached.

"Good," said Richard, almost shrugging off her comment for what he was about to ask her. "Jean, has an older gentleman been around here lately asking about Joy?"

"An older man, no, I don't think so."

He turned to Joy and waved her over. "What does the man look like?" he asked.

"The man?" Joy hesitated for only a moment. "Dark hair the last time I saw him. He wasn't fat or anything, just big, you know. Brown eyes."

Jean frowned. "Sorry," she said. "Who is it you're looking for?"

"My...a ... this man who has been following me around."

"That's pretty scary," said Jean.

309

Virginia could hear the conversation from where she was sitting and was glad Joy had received the hint about keeping her father's name a secret. Still, Jean and those working at *Safe Haven* would have to know that the father was alive at some point, and Virginia just didn't want to think about that.

***

The cemetery they entered at dusk was not as well kept up as the one that Joy's mother had been buried in; still, it was good to know that Joy remembered the spot where her grandparents had been buried, having visited a few times with her mother.

The graves were nestled under a wide-spread tree on top of a fairly large hill. Unfortunately, however, there was nothing to block the quick winds or the darkness that would soon be enveloping them. Fortunately, there was a bench close by where they sat.

Permission had been granted from *Safe Haven* for a one-night sleep over, though Virginia wondered now if keeping the girl up all hours of the night had been the best choice. But Joy seemed happy enough. They'd brought along hot chocolate and doughnuts, and there was always the car if things got too cold outside.

They talked about Joy's early days with her parents, when life was happy - before the drinking had begun with both of her parents and before her father had left them. It was easy to see that Joy had loved her father once, loved their vacations together, the sweet way he lifted her up into his arms to piggy back her around the yard, their meals together.

And then, something had happened. Her mother had found someone else. Joy thought her father had gotten ill, but now that she was older and could think back on it, Joy knew that her father had become an alcoholic. If it hadn't been for her mother taking to the habit after him, and not handling the liquor as he had, he might even today be with her; but her mother's uncontrollable drinking had been the last straw.

"I can't believe he left mother for the same thing he was doing," Joy said now, "but he did, and maybe it's the best thing he could have ever done. I was drinking then, too."

"And drugs?" Virginia asked now as the night grew even more chill.

"Drugs? I never tried the needle," said Joy. "My mother was too protective. Even at your house..." Her voice droned on, and she looked away from the flashlight that Richard had just snapped on. "I'm so sorry. I told mother that she should have thrown them out before coming to your place, but she liked it too much by that time."

"As long as you didn't try them, that's all that matters," said Richard, flicking off the light suddenly and staring out into the distance where they'd parked the car. "I think someone's coming," he said, though Virginia hadn't heard anything.

They stood in unison, and taking their cups of chocolate with them, walked behind the large tree. It couldn't shelter them, at least not completely, but it was dark after all. And then Virginia noticed a faint light flashing, bouncing, until finally it stopped.

Joy gasped. "It's got to be him," she whispered. "What do we do now?"

Richard was silent. So was Virginia. They watched, as what appeared to be a man, knelt down and began whispering to the grave. They were too far away to hear it, but he was definitely speaking. Virginia's arms suddenly chilled and she wondered how much longer they would be able to stay out in this late, wintery night, if it wasn't him.

"What if it's not him?" Virginia asked, wrapping her coat tightly around her body.

"It's got to be him. Who else would want to visit my grandparents' grave this late at night? I'll go." Joy left them suddenly and began her walk to the graves just a few feet away. Virginia and Richard followed closely behind.

The large form was still pressing his hands on the grave where Joy's grandparents were buried, when Joy approached. Something was placed on the stone. A shudder like the beginnings of a storm creased the air.

"I'm so sorry," said the man to no one. "I have lost it. I have lost *her*."

"Father?" Joy's voice was small in the large space, and the air grew suddenly quiet.

"Who's there?" The man stumbled to his feet. Virginia wondered if he was drunk or if the surprise had momentarily startled him.

"Father. I'm here."

The man turned his flashlight to the girl's face. She winced.

"Joy?" he offered. "What are you doing here?"

"Same as you. Visiting."

"It's near 1 a.m. Where are you staying?"

"The shelter."

"I knew it. So, your mother is truly gone."

312

"Yes."

"And you are alone."

"Not completely, Father."

"The shelter. You shouldn't be staying there."

"I know, but it won't be for long. I will be eighteen soon."

The flashlight's beam traveled the length of the girl's body and rested at her feet. "I can't believe it. Pastor Rest said..."

"Father, why are you in search of mother's box?" The question was abrupt, and Virginia's heart pounded waiting for Tom's response.

"What box?"

"The jewelry box you swiped. Where is it?"

"It's not the old man's."

"Where is it?"

"Safe. Why do you care?"

"It was left to me."

"I thought I needed it."

"Why?"

"I thought..."

Virginia started to step forward, but Richard's hand was quicker. "Not yet," he whispered.

"Why did you need it? Are you drinking again?"

The man stumbled forward, reaching for Joy, but she'd already backed away from him. "I've read these tombstones over and over again," he said, stopping again in front of her, "and prayed over them, hoping something would come to me about the jewelry box; anything. And then one day I thought to check the old neighborhood. I went inside that house and he had it. It didn't belong to him but he had it. Didn't have the key."

"And so, you broke it open."

313

Once again, the flashlight traveled up and down the girl's form. "Yes."

"You destroyed it!"

"Destroyed what? Just some old..."

"Whatever you found in there was my mother's heart, and grandmother's heart, and I can't believe it! I hate you! I hate you!"

The girl reached for her father's coat and Virginia and Richard moved forward. Virginia could feel the wetness of the snow. She'd worn her tennis shoes and the water had finally traveled beyond the fabric and past her socks. She could feel Richard's breath behind her.

Suddenly, a blast of light hit her eyes. She covered them quickly but the beam remained.

"What are you doing here? Who are you?" Tom demanded.

"Friends, friends of Joy!"

Joy still held her father's coat sleeve. He wrenched it away. "I knew she couldn't be alone!" he hollered, stumbling away from her. "Leave me alone! It was just a book, an old book your mother kept when she was young, a journal she kept when she was dating me. And another, one of your grandmother's. I read them both. I didn't find the money."

"What money?" Joy asked.

"The money I thought your mother had kept from me," he mumbled. "All those years...And when I needed it she wouldn't give it to me, and so I finally left her. 'Deal with life on your own,' I said to her. I chucked the jewelry box hoping the spring would loosen the lid, but it didn't. It hit the floor and flew under the couch. I looked at your mother. She was in pain but I didn't care. I needed that money."

Virginia could smell the alcohol on his breath. The man's coat was worn and his clothes torn, showing exposed flesh on his knees. He was unshaven, his dark beard with a hint of gray covering most of his face. She clicked off her flashlight. "Where are you staying?" Virginia asked.

"None of your concern," Tom replied, kneeling at the graves.

"Where are MY journals?" Joy asked hotly.

"In my car, over there." He pointed a dirty coat sleeve.

"Your car..."

"Since I don't have a home to speak of, or a place to sleep..." He buried his head nearer the tombstones and allowed the tears to flow. "All this time..."

"I can't believe you, Father. I can't believe that you'd do this to Mother." Joy was like a scared deer, her eyes large, her voice suddenly small. It was if she was waiting...for something.

The man stood. "I did nothing to your mother. And it's just too bad you can't ask her to tell you what she did to me. You were just a child, believed everything she said."

"You...left us," the girl squeaked. "Just left us at the house. Mom went crazy for days, drinking, passing out on the couch. I was all alone."

"Serves you right," Tom muttered as he stood to look at her. Virginia held the girl close, and Richard was suddenly standing next to Joy on the other side; or had he been there all along?

"That's no way to speak to your daughter," he said.

315

"Perhaps not." The man swallowed. "Let me get the diaries." He hobbled from them and as Virginia watched she felt the girl relax. The tension increased as he returned.

"So where is your mother buried?" he asked, handing the girl two worn books. One had a blue cover, the other a silver-white.

"Thank you," Joy muttered, holding the books close to her heart. "Mother is at another cemetery."

"I figured that part out, but could never understand it."

"Why?" The girl was visibly shaking now but she stood her ground. Virginia's heart pounded.

"Why wasn't she buried by her parents? I looked everywhere for her, in every cemetery. Nothing."

"*Safe Haven* was our home, Father. We had no other relatives. We didn't even have *you*! Mother...she died alone because of you. She was all alone, and they couldn't find me, and they put her in a grave with only a number on it, and it's all your fault, your fault!"

The man blinked. "All alone? Where?"

"By the freeway near the park."

"Away from you?"

"She...she wanted a better life for me."

"And so, she left you?"

It was all Virginia could do to remain silent, but the words had to be worked through, all of them, including the words burning in her own heart.

"She was sick."

"You mean she was a drunk."

A shudder crept down Virginia's arms and moved through the fabric of her coat.

"She tried to take care of me, really," Joy began, "but without money, and being sick she..."

"She was *no good*, you need to know that."

"She was my mother."

"And I am your father."

The girl began to sob. She held Virginia's arm even more tightly.

The man walked closer. Virginia was cold and her feet burned. Richard finally spoke and it was just like him. He always waited to say just the right words at just the right time; and the time, evidently, had come.

"We plan on adopting Joy," he said. "Now that we know you're alive..."

The man coughed. "So that's it," he said. "You came all this way just to see me so that I could sign the papers. Well, I've been to *Safe Haven* and I've met the woman Jean." He smiled a sickly smile that made Virginia wince. "Of course, she didn't know it was me..." He looked down at Joy. "So, daughter, how about walking your good old dad to the car?"

"Where's the jewelry box?" Joy asked. Virginia hadn't looked at her cell phone in some time. What was it, 2 a.m.?

"You don't want that old thing."

"Give it to me and I'll go with you," she said.

"What? And leave these...fine people?"

"I need that box. Take me with you. Now."

"You sound just like your mother," he drawled. "Come, this way," he motioned, but Virginia's arm remained taut. "You are not going," she said.

"We will not let you go with that man," echoed Richard, taking her other arm. "You've got the diaries,

317

what could you possibly want with a broken-down jewelry box?"

"My mother's heart."

"Come on." Tom reached for her, and this time his fingertips brushed her coat.

Virginia drew the girl close. "You can't – go. We need you."

"Not as much as my father does. Look at him. I can take care of him and once he's sober he'll want to give me the box, and then everything will be okay. You'll see."

Richard turned the girl's chin upward. Even in the surrounding darkness, Virginia could see her small mouth trembling. "When will you come home?" he asked.

"I don't know," she replied, her breath stinging the air. "But...oh, I love you both!" Thin arms wrapped around them and then she was gone.

***

Days later the thought occurred to Virginia that the girl, Joy, now so very close to being a woman, might never return to them. She would get the box, Virginia was sure of that, but would she be able to leave her father?

She'd heard countless stories about children wanting to return to neglectful or abusive parents only to be neglected or abused again. It seemed a natural thing for children to be with a parent no matter how terrible the natural parent was. And so was the case with Joy.

The yellow journal, that's all she and Richard had.

It appeared to Virginia that life was never what she planned and no matter how she worked at it, the struggle was still the same. The stones - Listening, Trust, Optimism, Tenacity and Constancy - still sat as before on her mantel; and she looked at them every day. The stone of trust would occasionally turn black, just opposite of the stone of constancy which was as clear as a spring morning that was quickly turning into summer. Not surprisingly, she was constantly finding the black stone digging holes where holes shouldn't be, and the clear stone reminding her of her constancy with God.

And then she'd think of Joy.

Jean Rasmussen had been angry at the news. And she'd been angry at them. But the law was the law. If Joy was really with her father, there was nothing the shelter could do unless the father gave them just cause. The man named Tom Sorensen had never been seen after leaving his wife and child, but he had every right to her - at least until she turned eighteen. There was nothing any one of them could do.

KATHRYN ELIZABETH JONES

The Gift

It was nearing September. Almost a year had passed since the death of their little one. Beatrice was always on her mind, though most of her thoughts during the year had been about Joy. Oh, Joy, another girl lost, then found, then lost again.

The small lavender room was still empty, and maybe the space was as it should be. She was happy with Richard; happy with him and their small lives together. Perhaps they would never have children. Perhaps not having them was the way God wanted it.

She'd not quite resigned herself to the empty space; she wasn't angry anymore about what she didn't have. Rather, she was grateful for what she had. Richard. He was a blessing to her life. He loved her. And she loved him.

The leaves were just beginning to turn.

"Can you take me to Beatrice's grave?" she asked one Sunday after church, and Richard reached his warm arm around her.

It's about time, he could have said, but didn't. Instead, he walked her to the car and they drove to the same cemetery that Joy's mother had been buried in.

Funny, she hadn't even thought of the connection between the two, she hadn't seen the spot where the precious babe had been laid to rest, so it was no wonder.

Or was it a wonder? How could she have gone all of this time and not asked Richard the question? "So where is she?" she asked now, her heart beating quickly, her hands wetting, her mouth going dry. She couldn't do this.

"Funny you should ask, but I think I'll keep you guessing until we get there," he answered, turning on the ignition. And so they drove. At the cemetery entrance, Richard stopped the car. "Are you sure you're ready?" he asked.

"It's been a year," she answered quietly. "Don't you think it's time?"

He nodded, and as the car wove through the rows of orange and yellow trees along the cemetery path, Richard stopped. The car rested some ten feet from where Grace was buried!

"She's behind that tree," Richard said, pointing to a place just north of them. She looked and the view was breathtaking. Blue skies, little pinwheels perched on white sticks, flags blowing, tombstones standing as if at attention.

He took her hand. She wondered if he'd noticed the dampness that had accumulated there as well as on her face, but he said nothing. They walked through the crisp grass. As the sunlight streamed against her cheeks she thought she felt Beatrice near her. Such a little girl with such a big smile.

A small tear escaped her eye. She brushed it with her left hand and continued with Richard. A few yards later they had reached the tombstone. She looked down.

Beatrice Stone: Our Little Angel
Born: December 4.
Died: September 25.
She will always be in our hearts.

The little white headstone glittered in the sunlight. "It's beautiful," she said, placing the small daisies she'd found on the roadside near her daughter's name. The tears came freely now. "She was our beautiful little daughter."

"Still is and always will be," said Richard, squeezing her hand.

"I know. But it's not the same without her."

They stood for a long time after that, listening to the birds that had somehow found their way to the shade of the trees. The cars rushed by on the busy street to the east, and the other well-wishers, just a few, continued to journey to the cemetery on this already warming day.

Virginia adjusted her sweater, then decided at the last minute to tie it around her waist before asking her husband the question that hovered in her mind. "So," she said at last, "our little girl and Joy's neglectful mother are buried near each other."

"Don't call her that."

"What?"

"Neglectful. Grace Sorenson had...problems because she was sick."

Virginia shrugged. "I can't believe we allowed Joy to leave with her father."

"What else were we supposed to do? I didn't see you trying to stop her."

"I know." She shrugged again. "I wish we'd dragged her back to the shelter. Now we'll never see her again."

"We can't be sure of that. She came back once before."

Virginia thought about the moment and it was like yesterday. The way Joy looked - dirty and un-kept. A small lump entered her throat and tears welled in her eyes. "This stinks," she said. "Where is God now, now that we truly need him?"

Richard turned to her. "Do you really think God has abandoned us?"

She nodded, but in the nod, she knew she was lying. God would never abandon her.

"God is here, can't you feel him? Close your eyes. Can't you feel him?"

"Church is getting to you," she said, but she closed her eyes anyway and felt the warm breeze caress her face and cheeks. "It's just the sun," she said.

"Yes, it's the Son," he answered, still taking in the newness of the sky.

***

A week later the package arrived. A small box sat on the doorstep, just as she and Richard were leaving to go to church. She picked it up and looked down at the lid. Tears sprang to her eyes but she didn't open it. Not yet.

"Richard, come quick!" she yelled as she peered down at it. Oh, how the thing gave her hope!

"What is it?" Richard asked, peering over her shoulder. "Oh."

Inside was a key, Joy's key, and with it a little note. Virginia picked up the note written on the corner of something, it looked like an old envelope.

"This is just to help you to remember who you are. I think of you every day. Joy."

Virginia removed the key from the box. She held it up against the light. It was the first time she'd seen the key close up, and it appeared to be made of iron, plated with nickel; sections of the key had worn off so she could see the layers. The bow, or place of holding, was a sort of shamrock shape, and the barrel was short, the tooth at the end, small and simple.

Although the key was old the chain was quite new and was of basic design.

"Why don't you wear it?" Richard offered, taking it from her fingers and placing it around her neck. Virginia could feel the warmth of it almost instantly as it fell against her skin.

She looked out. It was cold, especially in the mornings, but Joy had been here regardless and she'd left this small gift. "How do you think she's doing with her father?" she hesitantly asked.

Her husband looked out and followed her eyes where they searched; there was only one faraway cloud clinging to the already blue sky. "I worry about her, but I try not to," he said, reaching an arm around her shoulders.

"Me, too. Are you ready?" she asked.

He turned, locked up the house, and together they walked to the car.

***

Near the end of October, the leaves gracing the roads and lawns had been covered by snow. And a month later, Virginia was dreading another Christmas without her little girl; without Joy. *Joy to the World.* It seemed a funny song, now that time was passing by without a child, without a teen to fill her heart.

But she had Richard, and with all of her heart she loved him. What wasn't there to love? He wasn't perfect by any means, but he was good to her - so good to her. The business was growing as well, and Virginia had begun her classes again. Most days, the lavender room was empty, but occasionally, like today, she'd find the cozy chair, a good book - sometimes even The *Good Book* - and read. Time would pass and Virginia would recall for a time the painful moments and what they had taught her: About life, about death, about continuing forward.

Listening to God was better than living life without him, she knew that now, although it wasn't often easy to take his advice. How well she remembered the last time. He'd stood in this very room and peered down at her as she'd read. She didn't see him, but she knew he was there, watching and helping her as he had always done.

And then Richard had entered. "Good book?" he'd asked. He was still wearing the apron that he'd purchased for her and was holding a silver bowl.

"What have you got in there?" she asked.

"Chocolate. God told me it was time to give you some chocolate."

She laughed.

"I'm serious. I almost heard him, too. 'Virginia is feeling sad,' he said. 'Make her something sweet.' And so, wa-la! Here I am."

"Here you are," said Virginia. "The book is good," she added, realizing she hadn't answered his question.

"What is it?"

"Raising a Teenager." She held up the book.

Now it was his turn to laugh. And then he grew solemn. "So, you expect her back soon?"

"Oh, I don't know about soon," said Virginia, waving him over so that she could lick the bowl. There was a wooden spoon in it, which Virginia pulled out. "But I think..." She took another taste, "I think it will be soon. And if not..."

"If not?"

She peered up into Richard's eyes. A fine line of chocolate was just under his chin. So, he'd snuck a bit before coming into the room. She smiled, tears forming in her blue eyes. "I have been filled with such a deep peace these last few days," she said.

Richard squatted next to the chair, the same chair that had rocked the new little one that had left them like a breeze. He placed the bowl on the carpet next to him. "I have been feeling pretty good, myself," he said, "but I figured it had to do with us going to church together."

"And reading the Bible," said Virginia. "And praying."

"It isn't as if we have just been sitting around waiting for God to answer us," said Richard, touching her lightly on the arm.

"We've been busy," added Virginia. "And besides..." She took her husband's arm and pulled him closer to her. "...Joy is a strong girl. She will take care of her father, and one day she will return home to us."

"Are you really that sure?"

"If not..." Virginia smiled again and Richard leaned in. The smell of his aftershave wafted to her nostrils and reminded her once again of the mountains where they'd been married, and where, on another early spring day he'd proposed to her once again.

***

The announcement arrived that morning, almost two weeks before Christmas. John was dead.

She and Richard had visited him only occasionally since Joy's departure from their lives, but even in those times John would blink and then he'd remember who they both were, though sometimes it took some doing to get him to that point.

How well she remembered their last visit.

"So you've come to sell me pots and pans," he'd muttered under his breath. "I don't need none." They stood on the porch, she, her husband, and the man who was always forgetting things. Once he remembered, he would ask them about Joy and about her mother; where was she anyway?

They would tell him she was dead and he would remember. A small tear would crease his left eye, or his right, and his hands would fumble for something to wipe his eyes.

It was always and forever the same.

Except for today. The funeral was Saturday, their busiest day at *Just Desserts*, but they had to go; both of them. At the back of her mind Virginia wondered if Joy would somehow make it, and if so, if they'd have a moment or two to visit. She didn't say anything to Richard.

But by the time Saturday had come and gone, including the funeral, with a *no appearance* by Joy or her father, Virginia knew the truth, or at least, she thought she knew it. Joy was merely wrapped up in caring for her father.

Whenever she was around the park, the freeway or *Safe Haven*, she would take a second or a third look, just to be sure. She'd talked to Jean only twice since Joy had gone back to live with her father, and Jean hadn't seen the girl, which, she said *made her sad to even think about*.

As for Virginia, she tried not to dwell on the sadness, but what God had given them both. She was deep in thought about this very thing when she heard a knock at the door. It was just two days before Christmas.

Virginia blinked. "So, you've come to the door this time," she said.

"I have a message."

Virginia ushered God in. Richard peered from the couch, stood, and met them at the front door.

"So how are you doing today?" God asked, extending his hand.

"Fine, fine."

"And you, Virginia? How are you doing?"

"Good. And you, God?"

God smiled, and the brightness of his smile filled the room and added to the glow of the Christmas tree. "Well, I'll be. What a beautiful tree." He left them and walked closer to it.

Virginia and Richard had decorated the tree extra special this year. The homemade ornaments had been saved from their childhoods, and now graced the green tree along with glittering white lights. An uneven star topped the tree - a star Richard had made when he was only six. It was made of cardboard and glitter, most of which had already rubbed itself off.

"I remember the year you made that," said God. "You had just lost your mother."

Richard blinked.

"How...I mean, yes, that was a hard year."

God turned and all Virginia could think about was the little Richard had spoken about his mother. She didn't know much - only that his mother had gotten sick, after which his father had followed close behind. Within weeks he was buried alongside her. It was sometimes like that when the grief was too great.

Like herself, Richard had spent much time with his grandmother; in fact, she had raised him after that. What she knew of the star wasn't much, only that he'd made it that year; and his grandmother had made such a fuss over it that she'd put the new star she'd recently purchased back in its box, and it had remained there until she died.

"And you, Virginia..." God looked to the center of the tree where she had hung the Santa Claus ornament made of clay that she had also painted in school. Most, but not all of the paint had worn off.

"I can't believe it," God said, reaching for the memory and holding it up in his palm. "The day you painted this, do you remember what happened?"

Virginia shrugged. "I was in school."

"Yes, and the teacher, a Ms. Graham, as I remember, complimented you on such fine craftsmanship."

Virginia might have blushed, but her heart had quickened. Why would such a simple, long ago memory make her heart race?

Still holding the ornament, God caressed it lightly. "The colors have faded, but I can still see the beauty."

Virginia reached for it. "It's pretty ugly now," she said, taking the gem in her hand. Tears filled her eyes though she did not know why.

"Not ugly, just growing to perfection," God said. "Like the stones, this symbol of life can teach you many things. I've been to see Joy," he said.

Virginia was still holding the Santa Claus ornament. She released it now and watched the little man swing back and forth, back and forth, on the extended branch. When the ornament had stopped swaying, she finally had the courage to look up at God.

She wasn't sure why she suddenly felt like she'd need courage to look up just then, but as their eyes met she somehow knew that the news God had for her was not good.

"Joy. She's dead," Virginia said.

God reached for her. Holding her within his arms he began to whisper. His voice was like the stillness of a lake in spring. "She is alive," he said. "But she has been hurt." Still in God's arms she felt his hands caress her hair. "She was in a fire."

"What?" Richard's voice was a flame as it passed by her ears. "A fire? When?"

"Just yesterday."

331

Virginia looked up at God. Tears streamed down his own cheeks. "She needs you," he said.

***

Virginia tried not to think about the last time she'd been in this hospital with her friend, Paul, but the memories of that time in her life came flooding back the moment she stepped through the door. She remembered another time, when, anxious to get the new babe that had just been born, she'd raced up the hallway only to find that the little one had already left this earth.

Nurses surrounded them, and the smell of antiseptic filled her nostrils as she thought about Joy and all that God had told them. It was unbelievable really. Why would a man start an old abandoned house on fire with his daughter inside?

But he was drunk, and *people do things they might not usually do, when they have been drinking,* God had told them; Virginia and Richard raced through their house for coats and shoes and the keys to the car. Only when the front door had been safely locked behind them had Virginia noticed the tree in the window.

It was still lit.

Richard held her hand. They did not speak, they ran, and once the room was found they didn't knock, they went inside. Joy's father was by the bed. They couldn't see his face, only his greasy hair, his clothing hanging limp and dirty around his arms. They did not speak to him.

Joy's face was covered in white bandages, as also, sections of her arms. Her legs, probably covered with the same white material lay hidden underneath the blanket. Only her eyes showed. She appeared to be asleep.

The man was sobbing.

Virginia's heart pounded. She was angry, but she could not speak. *Joy!*

Walking to the other side of the bed she peered at her daughter, for surely, this was the daughter that had always been meant for them. This...this...man didn't deserve her!

Virginia almost spoke then, as the stillness filled her mind and heart; it was almost like death had surrounded her, taken in her very soul and had come back for more.

She remembered God's words. "She needs you," he had said. And she had felt those words even as they had pierced her soul. She'd known then what she must do.

"How long?" she asked the man on the other side of the bed.

"Since she arrived. I'm sorry," he added, pressing his face against the sheets.

"How much of her body?"

The man didn't look at her. "They say almost half."

"Will she see?"

The man looked up from his weeping. "Who are you?" he asked. His face was streaked with dirty tears, the same sort of tears Virginia had seen only months ago when Joy had returned to them only to be taken away again.

"We're her parents," she answered, and the man blinked, once, and then buried his head again in the sheets. "I'm sorry," he said again.

Richard reached for her hand. She held it tightly, even as she wept.

A day later, even before Joy awoke from the deep sleep the fire had brought upon her, Richard had discovered the jewelry box. It sat, mended somehow, on the silver tray that served as Joy's end table. For the first time Virginia was able to trace the engravings on the box.

On the front she could see small houses, a couple of engraved trees and swans in the forefront, taking a leisurely swim on the lake. Turning the box in her hands, Virginia could see that on the right side of the box, it appeared the same swan was standing as if waiting for a swim. At the back of the box a couple held each other in a loving embrace, their home and trees in the distance; the left side showed the same swan, now swimming next to the reeds within the lake called home.

The hole where the key entered was cracked, though some gluing had again put the box in order. She didn't look inside.

They'd spent hours in the hospital before Joy finally regained consciousness and during that time Virginia and Richard had learned some frightening things. Though Joy's heart had been monitored as well as her breathing, and even though she'd been hooked up to an IV and her pain had been treated with morphine, the biggest shock came in the form of what had become of her belt and her shoes. Not only had the fire melted them off of her, she'd had to have dead skin washed from her wounds so that the extent of her injuries could be determined. Joy's face had received superficial burns, but those on her arms and legs had been third degree.

Virginia hadn't spoken with Joy's father. As she watched him, still in his pitiful state, she decided that, at least for the time being, she would remain silent. As Richard sat next to her, his arm around her shoulders, waist, and taking her hand upon occasion, Virginia couldn't help but be grateful.

How could she do any of this without Him? Without God?

Even now, as she continued to watch her daughter in the bed (she'd gone to sleep again) she couldn't help but remember her beautiful green eyes upon awakening.

"Mom, is that you?"

The girl's eyes blinked open, a tiny mouth revealed through the white cloth. The doctor had told them that because she was young and hadn't inhaled too much smoke, which might have damaged her airways, she could speak.

Virginia blinked back the tears, but that did not stop them from falling down her cheeks. Joy had never called her Mom before. She reached for a bandaged hand, and then thought better of it. Instead, she peered closer at the green eyes that lay blinking before her.

"What happened?" Joy asked. "I feel so strange."

"You're in the hospital. A fire began in the house; you were asleep..."

Joy's eyes tightened shut. A small tear was released. "My father, is he here?" she asked, her eyes still closed, the small tear wetting the white fabric.

"Yes."

"I want him out...out..." she said, not turning.

"Joy..." The man's voice was like a hollow tube. "You can't mean that. I..."

335

"I can. Out," she said again.

***

"He's gone."

Virginia looked down the hall as if Joy's father might still turn the corner at any minute. She didn't know if she could hold her anger in any longer. She didn't know how much longer she could hold the pain that was filling her soul for Joy.

What would Joy's life be like, now that she'd experienced the mental and physical pain of fire searing through her body? How could she live, knowing her father had caused her pain?

She swallowed. "Where is he?" she asked.

Richard took her hand. They were in the hospital waiting room. It was late. Other than a few couples at the other end of the room, they were alone.

"He has gone to a hotel. I gave him some money."

"You what?"

"He had nowhere to go!"

"After what he did to Joy?"

"He's a human being who has made a terrible mistake. He needed a place to sleep."

"So he was drunk," she said, not daring to look into his eyes for fear of what she might find there - sympathy, some sort of love for a man who had scarred their daughter for life.

"He was cooking in the abandoned house. A grease fire. He says he must have passed out. When he woke up Joy was screaming in the room just off the kitchen. He went to her and somehow managed to douse the fire. She'd been sleeping on the couch."

"He should be in jail."

"Probably. But right now we need to think of Joy."

The lump rose in Virginia's throat. "I'm sorry," she said, "I'm just so angry...at him. I'm just so worried about Joy."

"I know."

***

Weeks later, Joy's wounds were healing and closing. She'd also been through some rehabilitation. Reconstructive surgery would come next, followed by counseling, and integrating Joy into her new life.

Joy's father was in jail. It happened within the week as more was learned about the fire that had completely gutted the old shack. His drinking was completely out of hand; an understatement according to Virginia, and much therapy was needed before he would be able to step back into civilized society.

Joy was constantly in pain; she writhed at times on the hospital bed, even though she had been given drugs to keep the pain at bay. More medication was given before a dressing change or when she went in for physical therapy, but the pain was still there. Virginia could see it in the girl's eyes, even when she wasn't moaning or crying out because of it.

The tub room was the worst, and the tweezers used to pull off dead skin ran a close second.

Virginia, when she was not in the room with Joy, sat alone or with Richard in the hospital chapel. It was quiet there, and much too neglected in her opinion. She prayed there and thought about God and all he'd done for her. How would he help Joy now?

She could feel him, although his presence since leaving their home, had escaped her. But she knew that he was there, watching over her as well as Joy. She didn't have to see God to know that.

Just five days after the accident, doctors took care of the burns on Joy's left arm and began grafting the skin from her thighs. More grafts continued, and for Virginia, more visits to the chapel were necessary. She'd never felt as close to God as she did in those long weeks following the accident.

Bible reading had become a necessity along with prayer and speaking to Joy whenever she could, encouraging her to keep moving forward with hope and faith. Three weeks later, it was time for Joy to take her first short walk in the hospital hallway.

But Joy was afraid.

She sat on the edge of her bed, her legs draped over the side like limp towels. "Blood is coming out through my skin, blood is coming out!" she screamed. "What if I can't stand? What if my legs break?"

"Just hold onto the walker," the nurse counseled her, "and push up. Your arms will support you when you begin to push forward. I will be here if you need me."

Richard placed a firm hand against Virginia's back. She tried to breathe.

"You can do it, Joy," she echoed.

Richard smiled at her. "You're tough," he said, and Virginia wondered, in that moment, if Richard was speaking of her or of their daughter, but it didn't matter. All of them would have to be tough the next few months to get through this.

Joy looked at him and Virginia thought she smiled. "Okay, but you'll be here to catch me if I fall?"

When the nurse nodded, Joy gripped the walker and slowly, as if her legs were truly made of Jell-O, stood. For a few moments she wobbled, but still held tight to the walker.

"Now, take your first step," said the nurse.

A short step followed, and then another. When Joy had managed five, she began to cry.

"I can't believe it. I did it!"

"And you'll do many more things," said the nurse, as they returned her to her bed.

***

The day Joy asked for a mirror, Virginia wondered what she should say to her. She'd already brought over the old jewelry box which the girl had promptly opened using the key Virginia still wore around her neck.

Inside were the two diaries - one was Joy's mother's, the other, her grandmother's, and something else. She reached in to retrieve it.

Joy held up a framed picture. She turned it. It was a picture of her mother and someone else, older surely, but still beautiful.

Joy caressed the picture's face. "Grandmother was just as beautiful as mother was," she began. "Will I be beautiful, too?"

A large lump grew in Virginia's throat. Her eyes filled with tears. "You will always be beautiful," she said.

"The doctors, they said the fire got to my legs and arms pretty good, but my face was looking better. I don't see what they mean," she added, tears forming in her eyes. "What's all this red stuff? Will it go away? Will I have...scars?"

Virginia blinked. Though some redness and scabs remained, Joy's face was healing nicely. They had been in the hospital all of three weeks, and the doctors were already talking about a release.

Joy placed the mirror on the bed. "I think I'm ready to go," she said. "Can you feel it? It's almost like my mother and grandmother are here, you know? It's almost as if they're saying, 'You can do it. Just remember who you are.' You know what that means, don't you?"

"That you should always think highly of yourself," said Virginia.

"That you shouldn't give up," added Richard.

"Yeah, sure. But that's not the most important part." Taking the jewelry box again into her hands and stroking the sides just like the old man had done, she looked inside. "I am God's child. That's who I am."

The Gift: A Parable of the Key

Afterword

The tree was still lit, although Christmas had ended almost four weeks prior. The gifts were still gathered around the tree and the spirit within the room was as real as if it was still Christmas day.

And perhaps it was, at least for Virginia, Richard, and Joy.

One gift in particular sat near the back of the tree until the very end. It was dressed in white with a red bow. The key hung where the tag might have been.

"This is for you," Virginia said.

The girl's face glowed. She was healing well and the short few days the family had spent at home would be remembered. Her face, though a splotchy red, was looking better. It would be some time before she healed completely, both emotionally and physically, but she was making good progress. Virginia, looking at their daughter now, knew she could do it. Richard was smiling, eager for the red bow to be removed along with the white paper. Virginia was just as eager.

What would Joy think?

"You guys, you've bought me too much already," she said, taking the ribbon in her delicate hands and pulling at the strands. "I love this paper," she said suddenly. "It's white, like God's flowing robe."

Virginia touched her lips and tried to hold in the tears, a lump forming in her throat.

"Tear the paper," Richard coaxed, but the girl placed her delicate forefinger under every piece of tape and lifted each flap with her charred hands. She had regained much movement in her fingers as well as her legs; but there was a long way to go. There were still dressing changes, rehabilitation and a topographical suit she'd need to wear day and night to flatten out the scars on various places on her chest, arms, and legs. She couldn't use the stairs, either, but was walking more every day. The coming year still held many challenges.

The paper removed, she sat it beside her. "I have no idea what this is," she said, smiling at them both. "But whatever it is, I will love it," she said, "just as I love you."

Virginia begin to sob then, and Richard, for the first time since she'd first met him, had fresh tears rolling down his own cheeks.

Joy opened the lid. Inside was a piece of paper. She lifted it out and began to read:

KATHRYN ELIZABETH JONES

Certificate of Adoption
This is to certify that
Joy Sorenson
Has been formally adopted
into the *Stone* family

signed by *Jean Rasmussen*
On this 24th Day of
December 2015

Safe Haven Community

Dear Reader,

Thank you so much for purchasing *The Gift: A Parable of the Key*. In case you're unaware, this is the final book in the Parable series, and the last book I will be writing about Virginia Bean.

This saddens me. As an author, you want your characters to live on, but the time comes when new projects are in the making in which you're drawn to. And there is one drawing my attention now. The good news is that you can begin the series again with *Conquering Your Goliaths: A Parable of the Five Stones*, and then travel to *The Feast: A Parable of the Ring* without even leaving your home.

I hope you do.

When I wrote *Conquering Your Goliaths*, I had no idea that the book would turn into a series. But when you have a husband like I do, who gently nudges you on to the next book, it's all you can do but move forward to the next.

Virginia is a lot like me, and an awful lot unlike me. I appreciate what she's taught me about God and about not only conquering my own goliaths, but reaching for that joy that only comes through service to others.

I appreciate all of the reviews I've received on my books thus far. As many of you know, I also write mystery, Christian nonfiction, and science fantasy. Every review is priceless to me, even if it isn't as positive as I would like. As an author, I am also on a journey; a journey of self-discovery and creativity. I learn as I write and I get better as I write.

Will you review *The Gift*? And if you haven't done so already, will you review *Conquering Your Goliaths* and *The Feast*?

Thank you so much.

I am always open to emails from readers, so feel free to write and share your thoughts about God, about my books, or anything else the books have brought to your mind and heart.

With Love,

Kathryn

kathy@ariverofstones.com

Amazon Page:
http://www.amazon.com/author/joneskathryn

Twitter handle: @kakido

Facebook page:
http://www.facebook.com/kathrynelizabethjones.author

Blog:
http://www.ariverofstones.com

Notes

Notes

About Kathryn

Kathryn is a lover of words and a bearer of mood swings. When she is feeling the need to inspire, she writes a Christian fiction book. If a mystery is waiting to be uncovered, she finds it. If something otherworldly is finding its way through her fingertips, she travels to it.

Kathryn has been a reader since she was a young child. Although she took classes in writing as a teen, it wasn't something she really thought would become her career until she was married. And even then, it took a few more years for something worthy enough to publish to manifest itself.

Kathryn's first book was published in 2002. Since then, many other books have found their way out of her head depending on the sort of day she is having. Kathryn is a journalist, a teacher, a mentor, an editor, a publisher, and a marketer.

Her greatest joy, other than writing her next book, is meeting with readers and authors who enjoy the craft of writing as much as she does.

KATHRYN ELIZABETH JONES RESOURCES

Read my daily blog, follow me on Twitter:
twitter.com/kakido

Get a signed copy of "A River of Stones"
Additional signed copies of "Conquering your Goliaths"
-Or-
Purchase the WORKBOOK to "Conquering your Goliaths—
A Parable of the Five Stones" by visiting
http://www.ariverofstones.com/books.html

Live in or near Salt Lake or Davis County, Utah? Sign up
for a mentoring class!
www.ariverofstones.com/contact.html

Book Kathryn to speak at your next event!

A speaker that is fun, exciting and motivating.
Kathryn will get you on the road to changing your
life. Topics include:

❖ Conquering your Goliaths – an hour speaking
  event that will change your life.

❖ Conquering your Goliaths – a Spiritual Journey. I will discuss my book and workbook and hands-on writing experiences will be provided, 2-hour in-depth class.

❖ Writing is Exciting! – An hour speaking event that will get you writing!

❖ Writing your Book – Each of us has a book within us, a hands-on workshop that takes you through idea, plot, setting, and characterization and gets you started on your first winning paragraph. An hour and a half workshop.

The ultimate "Conquering your Goliaths Using the Five Stones" CLASS! Sign up for a TWO-DAY Idea Creation Workshop with Kathryn. Learn more at: www.ariverofstones.com/coaching.html.

For more information, Contact:

Kathryn Elizabeth Jones
4948 Royal Ann Drive
West Valley City, UT 84120
801-969-9351
www.ariverofstones.com www.kathrynelizabethjones.com
kathy@ariverofstones.com

Also, be sure to ***Read my daily blog, follow me on Twitter:*** *twitter.com/kakido*

Notes

Notes

Notes

Notes